I0660081

# HER Cry HER Prayer HER Praise

## LOOKING THROUGH HER WINDOW OF LIFE

### ◆§ SECOND EDITION §◆

# Kimberly Robinson Green

C.L.J.P.
Creative Unity Publishing

This book is a work of fiction. Names, characters, places, and incidents either are products of the author's imagination or are used fictitiously. Any resemblance to actual event or locales or persons, living or dead, is entirely coincidental.

Her Cry ~ Her Prayer ~ Her Praise

Looking Through Her Window of Life

Copyright © 2014 by Kimberly Robinson Green

All rights reserved. Printed in the United States of America. No part of this publication may be reproduced, stored in a retrieval system, or transmitted, in any form or by any means electronic, mechanical, photocopying, recording, or otherwise, without the prior written permission of the author except in the case of brief quotations embodied in critical articles and reviews.

ISBN 978-1-949402-00-1

Cover Design: Donna Osborn Clark at CreationsByDonna@gmail.com

Layout and Interior Design: www.CreationByDonna.com

Editing: Shell Vera at eyesstraightahead@gmail.com

Author Photo: Trenelle Doyle - Trenelle V. Photography
          at www.trenellevphotography.com

Makeup Artist: Isabela Rega - Iruemakeup
          at Isabelarega@gmail.com

Published by: Creative Unity Publishing
www.CreativeUnityPublishing.net

Manufactured in the United States of America

Second Edition

This book is dedicated to the man who taught me how to be a woman of standard. He raised me to love others despite the return and has shown me how to smile even when the pain of life compels me to cry. This book is dedicated to my father, Elder Lee E. Robinson Sr., who was called home to be with God.

Daddy, words cannot explain the pain that I feel when I think of you not physically being here. It has been hard but I'm still standing. Your love and support as a father really demonstrated God's love in your life. Now that you're gone, I understand a lot more and see why you made the sacrifices you did. Thank you, Daddy, for everything. This book is for you. Although you didn't get to see it, you knew about it and that gives me peace! I know you're resting now and I'm happy for you. I will continue to make you proud of me; I know I will see you again one day. I love you!

Elder Lee. Robinson Sr.
August 18, 1936 – December 11, 2011

# Acknowledgments

First, I would like to thank my heavenly Father above, God has been so faithful to me on this journey, and I'm so grateful. To my Husband David Green Sr., the one who's always there to support me in all I do, thank you for everything I love you. My sons David Jr, Dezmond and Daniel Green, you guys are a gift from God and my life is better because of you. Thank you to my Mother Mrs. Christine Robinson, words cannot explain how much your support means to me, you have taught me everything I know, and I love you for it all. My Publisher Donna Osborn Clark, you know how much I appreciate you, you're incredible. To my editor Shell Vera, you are simply Amazing, and a God send, I thank you from the bottom of my heart.

And to the countless others who have supported me, encouraged me, and helped this second edition become possible: THANK YOU, I appreciate you all.

To God Be The Glory!

# Chapter 1

# From Thelma's Heart

It has been said that there is a rainbow at the end of every road. Well, here I am–and I'm still waiting for my rainbow. It seems like things will never get any better for me. It feels like the weight of the world is on me. Yes, I know that God loves me. I know that trials and storms come to make you stronger. But I'm tired. I take great pride in all I do, but trying to be close to perfect has become a nightmare. I try to make my parents proud of me but it seems my best is never good enough when dealing with Momma. My friends often make remarks like, "Thelma, when you gonna start living for yourself?" I tell them that I already am, and that they should mind their own business but deep down inside I know they're right.

Listen, I love going to church. Before my daddy preaches on Sunday mornings, I sing his favorite song, "I Surrender All", and I feel some kind way as I give my gift back to the Lord and let Him use me in front of all those people. But there are times I just want to sit in service and not do anything. I don't wanna sing. I don't wanna praise. I don't wanna do anything but sit there and take it in. But Daddy works so hard for the Kingdom, I never want to hinder that in any way. Momma is another story; that woman is something else. Sometimes she is extremely demanding of me. She acts like she resents me; it seems I can never do anything right in her eyes. She constantly reminds me how hard my daddy has worked to gain the respect and prestige that he has. She tells us too often that as his children we must dot every "I" and cross every "T". It gets on my last nerve! Lately it has gotten really bad. I can hardly stand to be in the same room with her, so when she walks into a room I often walk out. Daddy says he's noticed the separation between the two of us, and he is praying it will get better; but I'm sorry, Daddy — don't hold your breath. I'm not seeing it anytime soon! All of this pressure — being a role model for my siblings, dealing with school, and more — I could just run down the street and scream! "LORD, JESUS, HELP ME, PLEASE!"

I was called up front in a prayer meeting one night by Evangelist Smith from Kansas City. I'll never forget it. He said, "the hand of God is upon you, and you are to sing the gospel of Jesus Christ and bring many to Christ through song." I'll never forget that experience as he laid his hands upon my head and begin to sing this song, "Yes Lord." It sent chills up and down my spine. He began to pray over me, speaking that I had a spiritual birth inside of me. I began to weep. I was only seven years old. He was from the Church of God in Christ and was brought in because Daddy said he wanted to start reaching outside of our Baptist tradition. I will never forget that song as long as I live. It was as if my soul connected with it! Momma tried to sing it during our service, but it never felt the same. This Evangelist was what they called a prophet. He also told me, "You will hear the voice of the Lord when the time comes. You will endure a lot of heartache, but God will use you in a mighty way."

I wasn't ready for all of that, I mean, after all, I was young and needed to do me first. Those evangelists are always trying to speak something over you. I have to admit that it scares me a little. I hate when they are speaking to the audience, but their eyes target you. Us kids would try and sneak out the backside of the church when my daddy would have those church evangelists come, but Mother Gertrude would always be the one to make us come back inside. Not only that, but sit us on the front pew. Man, we couldn't stand her, and then she would sit across from us looking all mad with them cocked eyes. We never knew who she was looking at when she looked at us. Lord, forgive me for saying that; I know it is wrong, but so true.

Back to the evangelist. Now, don't get me wrong, I totally respect the voice of God when he speaks, and I believe everything that was spoken over me back then, but I also have a lot to do even now before I can really apply what he said to me. With all that being said, it's funny because I have never felt complete. I know I have a marvelous family, great parents and siblings...but for some reason, I know in my heart that something is missing. Something isn't right. When I lay down at night, I pray "God, please help me."

I cry myself to sleep a lot of nights. The tears fall and I don't know why. I keep rebuking the devil telling him to flee, to stop confusing my mind, but that doesn't work. Am I crazy? Is something wrong with me? And I keep having these really strange dreams. In these dreams, Daddy is on one side of a road and I'm on the other. I keep reaching for him, but he keeps telling me to go on without him. Even the thought of this dream makes me weary. It's the same dream every time; I don't even like to talk about it. At this point in my life, I'm very fearful and I'm not sure why. Others may say I'm making something out of nothing, but deep down in my heart I feel I'm not! I will continue to pray and ask God to guide me and, most importantly, try not to let my feelings consume me. I know God has something great awaiting me. I haven't heard the voice from God for myself so I'm going to live my life my way.

It's hard being a young Black girl and feeling as if your life has been set up for you to fail, because what people see on the outside of you is not always at all what you feel on the inside. You put on this facade so people can't see the true you. So they won't know that you're hurting inside. You smile so you won't cry. Well, I've made up my mind that this year I want to be delivered from people and their judgment calls concerning me. My daddy preaches about accepting who God has made us to be. Well, how can you accept who he says you are, when you don't even know yourself? Lord, if you will help me get through this feeling that I have, I will forever be grateful, I'm trying so very hard to move past it. Furthermore, Lord, how can you call someone like me, especially knowing how I feel? Well, for now I'll just have to, as they say, "Trust the process."

# Chapter 2

## Family First

## ~TiTi~

Her name is Thelma McKinney. She was born and raised in Arkansas in a little town called Pine Bluff. Raised in a God-fearing home where her father is the honorable Reverend Greg McKinney; the pastor of The Holy Rock First Baptist Church, with a congregation of about sixty people. Moving in the power of the Lord, healing, delivering, and setting the captives free. We had a powerful church, although it was smaller than the others, but that didn't matter because Daddy always said, "It's not the size of the church, or how many members you have, it only matters that the spirit of God would move upon us!"

Oh, by the way, my name is Tonya McKinney, but my family and friends call me TiTi. Thelma is my very best friend and my big sister, we share so much together. Even though Thelma is older, we are always there for each other. Kind of like twins, only not the same age. We also looked quite different, too. I always thought she was the prettier sister. I used to tell her that she looked like Lena Horn; she was so beautiful to me. Thelma's eyes were light green, mine were dark brown. Her hair was a sandy-brown color, and the roots of her hair were almost blonde. My hair was jet black. And the most noticeable thing is her skin complexion. It is very fair and I am the dark-skinned sister. Thelma tells me that beauty is only skin deep and that I am her 'pretty little chocolate baby doll'! She had always told me that. It's like she knew something that I didn't. But no matter how mad we got at each other or how different we were, we would always come back and say to each other that, "I'm okay, as long as you're with me." I always felt that we shared that special bond as sisters!

I remember when we first moved into our neighborhood. It was in the summer of 1970 on a hot Wednesday, I remember this like it was yesterday. The first people we met when we moved there were the Williams family. Gloria Williams and my sister, Thelma, became the greatest friends, and at times, I felt left out. But it was cool because she had become like our very own family. And Gloria's brother, TJ, was so cute. Thelma said he was much older than me, but that never stopped me from looking!

Pastor Graves had passed away. He was the previous pastor, and they needed another pastor to take over the church, and Momma said, "God sent your Daddy to this dying church to bring life into it again." My mother's name is Mary McKinney. She was a Missionary, First Lady, and church Choir President. She was very firm, but sweet, and very dedicated to the ministry. Now, when I say that Momma was firm, I mean no staying out late, no music unless it was gospel, and no—and I mean absolutely none at all— boys allowed…not even on the phone. Thelma always found a way around that rule. She loved to say, "Just because Daddy and Momma says we will go to hell if we see boys, don't mean we will."

I was the baby of the family. Thelma was our older sister, and we had two brothers, Tim – who we called Word because he constantly went around quoting scriptures, and he always had a biblical Word for us – and Mickey, he was the oldest between the two, but Thelma was the oldest of us all. My two brothers really got on my nerves, but when Mickey left for the military, I really missed him. I loved my life and my family. As the years passed, my siblings and I learned that people like to dictate your life, but not their own. Basically, since we were PKs (Preacher's Kids), we couldn't do anything wrong, or it would be made out to be a really big deal, but other kids could do the same as us and nothing was said. Man, I hated that. Momma always told us, "Now, children, your father is a very important man of God. He has worked very hard for what we have, so don't you go out there making a muck of yourself and bring shame to your daddy's name." If we got a dime every time we heard that speech, we would be rich today.

Momma was always worrying about what people thought, but not my daddy. He always taught us to just be ourselves. Although we had our ups and downs, we are a close-knit family and did everything together; mostly on Friday nights because we had no church. On Saturday nights, my parents loved to host a dinner for the church members and whoever else wanted to come. Momma would cook soul food like black-eyed peas, fried chicken, candied yams, cornbread, and more. Thelma would want to help Momma cook, and I would, too. Every now and then, Momma would let Thelma cook with her, but not often. It was really weird to me, and I didn't like it at all. Momma would always let me. She would sometimes go as far as ask me right in front of Thelma. I would say, "Momma, it's alright. Thelma can do it." But Momma would always make such a big deal out of everything when it came to Thelma, until Thelma would be like, "Forget it." It was weird. I would always say to myself, "If I had two daughters, I would never treat them differently." How can a mother choose to love one more than the other? I know Momma loves her, but sometimes, it doesn't feel much like it. I would feel sorry for Thelma, because she would look so hurt when Momma acted like this towards her. I would watch how Momma treated Thelma, but then would go to church and be so sweet and loving to all of the other girls there, hugging them, and smiling at them. I never understood that. Now, Daddy, on the other hand, was like a

Prince out of a fairy tale book. I love Daddy because he is fair. He gives us security and plenty of love. I admired my daddy, because no matter how bad things would get — or how much we cut up — he always made sure we knew at the end of the day, how much he loved us. No matter what. He never treated any of us differently, but in some strange way, he made us feel like we were all his favorite child. He loved us all. I look up to my father, and I would do anything for him.

Daddy has a great supportive staff at the church. There is Elder Martin, who helps Daddy out with the finances of the church, and Deacon Mack, who Momma always says if it wasn't for him, Daddy wouldn't know his hand from his foot. Mother Tassel, who is over the Mother's Board, and then there is Sister Knowles, she happens to be the church secretary. Her job is to oversee all of Daddy's appointments. She is also responsible for scheduling guests, keeping up with who is sick and shut ins, and anything else she can think of, just to get close to him. I never liked Sister Knowles, she is always trying to come over to our house for something. I asked Momma not to invite her over for Saturday night dinner, but Momma said, "We must treat and love everybody the way God loves us."

The summer nights are so fun, we all love to go down to a place called The Nich in front of the Piedmont store and sit, and watch the different old people come by. Our favorite game we love to play is called "What my name is". The title may sound incorrect, but that's how we called it. Let me see, it was me, my sister Thelma, my brother Word, TJ, Lil John, Gloria, and big mouth Lisa. The rules of the game were to watch the elderly people walk past the store and then guess their names, or say what they looked like their names were; then my crazy little brother Word would be the only one bold enough to go and ask them. I mean, it sounds corny, but there isn't much to do in our town. But the love we all have for each other is pretty cool. I have to say that the game got old, because after a while, we would see the same old people, in the same area. I learned at a young age that family isn't always your blood, but it's the people that your heart would connect with.

The kids that we play with all of the time became our play cousins. Granny and Pop Pop Ridge at the church are like our grandparents. Whenever Daddy would leave out of town for speaking engagements, and Momma would sometimes want to go with him, we stayed with Granny and Pop Pop from the church. There's nothing like family. Thelma and I had been helping set up the new children's ministry at Daddy's church. I always told Thelma that I didn't like it that Daddy worked down at the church because sometimes that ole Sister Knowles would try and go down there too. I don't know why I'm the only one that can see straight through her little crush for my daddy. But I'm watching her. Being at the church is also good because the Williams family moved away to New York City, and that took Gloria from Thelma. Daddy says the light went out of Thelma's eyes when Gloria moved away. Gloria was like a sister to her, but Mr. Williams always wanted to move to New York. He left for a better job offer. I miss Gloria, too! I hate to admit this, but sometimes, I was a little jealous of Thelma and Gloria's relationship, and it's weird.

I felt that my sister and I would grow closer after she moved. Don't get me wrong, we are very close, but I think they shared more because of their age. Thelma began to act very different in the years after Gloria moved. She and momma seemed to always argue. Momma says she feels Thelma is trying to isolate herself more and more. I don't know what's going on. I keep asking Thelma to talk to me, but she just keeps saying that she's fine. But maybe you should be the judge.

Here's our story...

# Chapter 3

# Graduation Day

"TiTi, wake up, we're going to be late for school." Thelma is standing in the arch of TiTi's bedroom door, smiling at her little sister and happy to irritate her this early in the morning.

"I'm not ready to get up, Thelma. I didn't go to sleep until midnight last night." TiTi yawns and wipes her eyes. Thelma knows it's not time for school, she just needs her little sister's advice on what to wear for her graduation.

"Girl, if you don't get up. And besides, I want you to see my dress for my graduation tonight. I need you to tell me which one I should wear, so wake up." Thelma walks over to TiTi and hits her in the head with a pillow. Thelma had a lot to be excited about. They attended Gregory Palmer High School, which was a predominantly Black school, but with a few whites and maybe two Latinos there. Thelma is a senior, a straight "A" student and the head of the council for her senior class. She was excited to be graduating later that evening.

"Thelma, what time is it anyway?"

"It's 5 o'clock in the morning."

TiTi, squinting her eyes, glanced over at the clock on her wall. "It's not time to get up for school. Thelma, you play too much.

Good night!" TiTi rolled back over and placed a pillow over her head.

"Come on, TiTi. I need your help," Thelma said, pulling the blanket from underneath her sister. "Oh no, I'm going back to sleep, and it's a late start, too."

"TiTi, please get up and tell me what you think," Thelma insisted.

"Ok, hurry up then." TiTi sat up and leaned back against the headboard with her eyes closed.

"Ok, I'll be back." Thelma rushed out of the room.

TiTi blows out a deep breath, folding her arms across her chest. "What, are we having a fashion show? Can't you just bring the dresses out and I'll help you choose?" TiTi lays back down, covering her head!

"Relax, TiTi, it will only take a minute." Thelma is outside of the room door, changing in their mother's powder room in the hallway. Once changed, she walks back into TiTi's bedroom. "Okay, look, what do you think?"

TiTi frowns at Thelma's choices of dresses. "I don't like it, it makes you look wide with all of those zig zags. Wear that black dress that you wore at Daddy's church banquet, now that's classy."

Thelma reaches for the black dress hanging from the door. "Yea, that was going to be my next choice."

"No! Let that be your first choice."

Thelma puts her hands on her hips and smacks her lips. "Ok, TiTi, I got your message. Can I try it on for you?"

"I already know what you look like in it."

"Just humor me, please? Geeze!"

TiTi yawns and lays back across her bed, covering her head with her blanket. "I'm waiting," she calls, covering her mouth as she stifles a yawn. TiTi sits up as Thelma walks into the room with the black dress on.

"Ok, what do you think?" Thelma asked anxiously.

TiTi smiles, putting her hand in front of her mouth, with a surprised look. "Oh, Thelma, you look so pretty. I love that dress on you."

"Really, TiTi?"

"Yes, chile, you look elegant and beautiful. I want you to know how proud of you I am, Sis. You are the best. You set a great example for me to follow."

"Aww, TiTi, you mean it?" Thelma walks over to give TiTi a hug and a kiss on the cheek.

"Yes, and stop being corny." TiTi flops back on the bed. "Now can I go back to sleep?"

Thelma grabs the pillow that is tucked under TiTi's head and hits her with it.

"It's time to get up now." Thelma laughs and then pauses for a moment. "No, I'll wake you up in about an hour, okay?"

"I was going back to sleep anyway, now turn the light off, please!"

"Yes, girl, now go back to sleep." Thelma heads back to her room.

Thelma is too excited to sleep. There is a knock on her door. "Come in," she answers as her father walks through the door.

"Hey, baby."

"Good morning, Daddy. Why are you up this early?" Her dad walks over and sits on the edge of Thelma's bed beside her.

"Oh, I couldn't sleep," he said, taking her hand.

"What's wrong, Daddy? Why couldn't you sleep, did I wake you?"

"No, sweet cakes, you didn't. I'm just up thinking about you, and how proud I am of you. You're a special little lady, you know that?"

Thelma dabs the corner of her eyes with her finger, to keep from crying. "Thank you, Daddy, but I'm always going to be special to you. But will the rest of the world see me the way you do?" she said, looking up at her dad as if she was five years old again.

"Oh, in time they will, but right now, as long as you know how much your family adores you, that's all that matters," he replied, shedding a few tears.

"Oh Daddy, you're such a cry baby. Now stop it, you're going to make me cry." She gently wiped her dad's face.

14

"I really can't help myself. I want to give you something." He pulls out a box, and looks down at his hands.

"What is it, Daddy?" Thelma reaches towards her dad's hands, touching the box softly.

"These are your great grandma Whitney's pearl earrings and necklace set, and I want you to have them."

Thelma gasps and wipes her eyes. "Daddy, are you sure? They are beautiful!" Thelma begins to cry.

"I couldn't be more sure, baby. I've been waiting for this day. I thought I would give them to you on your wedding day, but I figured now is the time."

"Daddy, I'm so honored to wear them tonight!" Thelma replied excitedly. She had always admired her grandmother's jewels, and knew how important it was for her dad to give them to her.

"And I'm honored that you're my baby girl, and you will always be." They both embrace each other, and shed a few tears.

# Chapter 4

# The Big Day

"Hey, lady," TiTi bounces into Thelma's room. "It's Tuesday and someone is graduating. How are you feeling, sis?"

Thelma wipes her eyes before TiTi sees the tears in her eyes.

"Thelma, what's wrong, why are you crying?"

"I'll be okay, TiTi. You know…it's funny, but it just seems that no matter what I do, or how hard I work, it's never good enough for her," Thelma said in a quiet, shaky voice, looking toward the hallway.

"Who, Mom?" TiTi looks towards the hallway with Thelma.

"Yes, Momma hasn't said much to me at all, but... maybe she will later," she whispers, dropping her head to look down at her hands.

"Yes, sis. It's your day, try and not worry about Momma, ok? She will come around."

"Yea, let's just excuse her for her action, whether she's wrong or right." Thelma stands up and walks towards her window, folding her arms."

"No, T, that's not what I meant at all. I'm just simply saying that it's your day, and not to let anyone take away your feeling of accomplishment, not even Mom!" TiTi responded, rubbing Thelma's shoulder.

"Yes, you're right," Thelma said, taking a deep breath and sitting up straighter. "Let me get myself together."

TiTi could see the determination return to her sister's eyes.

"I don't have to go to school today. I just have to be there at 3 o'clock for rehearsal, so I have to be ready to leave in approximately one hour. I sure miss Gloria…you know, TiTi, if Glo was here, we would both be getting dressed at the same time?"

"Yes, I know y'all would. Well, let me go so you can finish getting ready, sis." TiTi walks out of Thelma's room slowly."

"Thanks, TiTi." Thelma looks back at TiTi as she leaves her room.

There is a knock on the door. "The door is still open, TiTi."

"No, it's Word." "Oh, come on in, Word. Now what did I do to deserve this honor?" She smiles at her brother.

"Hey, T, so it's the big day, huh?"

"Yes, it is, and I'm glad and scared at the same time."

"Are you going to consider the scholarship for Spelman University for that environmental Science Program?"

"You know what, Word? I'm not sure what I want to do. I have some other offers out there as well."

"Thelma, I don't want you to worry about us. If you leave, we will be okay. You are a big part of us, and yes, at times we depend on you for a lot, we all do. But it's your time, Sis. Time for you to live!"

"Let's not focus on that right now, okay?"

"Yep, you're right." Word looks down at the ground, seeming sad.

"Word, what's wrong? You seem upset or worried about something. What's going on?"

"I'll be just fine. Thelma, I have something to tell you, but I don't want to upset you on your graduation day." Word still wouldn't make eye contact with Thelma.

"What is it, Word? Look at me, you're scaring me."

"No, sis, it's nothing to be scared about. It's just..." Word pauses before speaking. "Thelma, earlier, I overheard Momma and Dad arguing. Dad was telling Momma that she should act like she is proud of you. He was telling her that he doesn't see her participating in anything concerning you and your graduation. Man, I'm sorry, Thelma. I shouldn't have even brought it up to you."

"No, Word. I'm glad you did. I know that's upsetting to you, and it bothers me, too, but I'm not going to let anything spoil my day, especially not Momma. I love Momma, but she has always treated me different than the rest of you. It's cool, don't sweat it, okay?" Thelma reassures her little brother that all was well and nothing could spoil her special day.

"Well, Momma wants to see you in her room, she sent me in here to tell you."

"What? I really don't want to go in there with her right now. Nothing that's going to come out her mouth will be sincere!"

"Thelma, I'm sorry about all of this. I love you, sis."
"I love you, too."

"Thelma, always remember that Romans 8:28 says 'Things will work out, for the good of them who loves the Lord.'"

"Thanks, Word," Thelma couldn't help but smile. "I love you and I'm proud of you, too, my little preacher."

"Thank you, sis."

"Your encouragement always means so much to me."

"No problem, after all, that's what big little brothers are for, right?" Word smiled before closing the door behind him.

After a few minutes, Thelma walks down the hall to her mother's room and knocks on the bedroom door. "Can I come in?" Thelma's hand is on her mother's doorknob.

"You sure can, my graduate."

Thelma looks as if she's speaking to a total stranger, not being used to her mother ever talking nice to her. As Thelma walks in her mother's room, her mother turns to look at her as she walks through the door. Mary McKinney gives Thelma a slight smile. "Look at you… how do you feel, Thelma?"

"About?" Thelma looks at her mother with a raised eyebrow.

"About you being a graduate. Not only that, but at the top of your class."

"Oh, I'm okay, Momma."

"You certainly don't seem excited about it." Thelma's mother looks at Thelma, trying to make conversation.

"I am, Momma, I just have some other things on my mind at the moment."

"Well, Thelma, I just want you to know that I always knew you would make us proud, and you have done a wonderful job. Have you decided about what school you will attend next? I think Spelman would be a great choice, you haven't said much about that."

Thelma looks at her mom wishing she would stop talking as much.

"I've heard you talk more about other things that really don't matter, what's wrong with Spelman?"

"MOMMA! Not right now, it's a little much. No disrespect, I just want to get through the night and maybe we can talk about this later."

"I understand. I know if it was your father, you would probably want to talk to him, but it's me. But it's okay!"

"Momma, don't do this."

"Do what, Thelma?"

"Pick a fight and make this about you, on my graduation day. Please don't."

"Is that what you think I'm doing?" she asked with raised eyebrows. "I was trying to do like most mothers do, and congratulate my daughter for graduating. But that's not even good enough for you!"

"Mom, I think it's best that I leave the room. Please excuse me," Thelma said, heading for the door.

"Go ahead and leave, Thelma. It doesn't even matter," she called after her.

Thelma stopped before she reached the door and turned to face her mother. "I know it doesn't matter, Momma. Nothing I do ever matters to you," Thelma said sadly.

Her dad walks into the room. "Is everything okay in here?"

"Yeah, Daddy. Everything is fine."

"Well, if it is, why do you seem upset, baby girl?"

Her mom snaps, "Is that all you care about, what Thelma is feeling, Greg? What about me?"

"What are you talking about, Mary?"

"I'm talking about Thelma coming in here and being very disrespectful. It just hurts me to know that my own daughter despises me!"

"Daddy, I didn't do anything."

Thelma's dad walks over to Thelma and places his hand under her chin and lifts it up. "Thelma, you have a graduation to attend, and this is supposed to be your happy day, so you go and get ready for it, okay, baby girl?"

"Yes, Daddy," Thelma replied. She looks at her mom once more before walking out. "Daddy."

"Yes, baby."

"It's time for me to head over to the school. I'll see you over there." Thelma walks towards the door, saddened that she and her mother argued before her graduation.

"Alright, baby. You head over there, and will see you in a little bit. My girl, getting her diploma." He watches Thelma walk away.

"Goodbye, Daddy, see you later, Mom." Thelma closes the door.

"Greg, I don't like how you just handled that, it seems like you always go against me. Especially when it comes to her!"

"Do you mean, Thelma? Why do you always refer to Thelma as her? Mary, I don't know what's going on with you lately, but..." Pastor Greg walks over to the door and opens it, making sure they're not being heard by their other two children.

"Greg, I feel that you don't try and understand me. It's always about Thelma and her needs."

"Look, Mary," Pastor Greg holds up his hand. "Not now! I'm going to my study!"

The time has finally arrived to head to the graduation ceremony.

"Is everyone ready? It's time to head out for Thelma's graduation and I don't want to be late," Pastor Greg says, walking into the living room, looking up the stairway.

TiTi and Word are coming down the stairs towards their dad, excited about their sister's big day. "Yes, Daddy, we're ready," TiTi says smiling.

"Well, don't you look pretty, Tonya. Wow! Where is Timothy?"

"Here he comes we his big ole head."

"Yes, here I come. And I might have a big head, but I'm looking sharp as a tack tho!"

Word walks over to the full-length mirror admiring himself, "Boy, am I clean. If you're going to dress up, this is how you do it." He looks over at his sister TiTi, teasing her.

"Whatever, boy, move." TiTi goes over to the mirror.

"No, you move," he replied firmly, gently shoving TiTi away.

"Now both of you stop it! You both look very nice!"

"Thanks, Daddy," they both replied.

"Where's Mom, Dad?" TiTi asked, walking over to look outside in the car.

"I don't know, Tonya, she was up in the room. Tell you what, Timothy, take the car keys and you and your sister go and get in the car."

"Yes, Dad." Word, takes the keys out of his dad's hands.

Pastor Greg goes upstairs to check on his wife. "Mary?"

Mary McKinney is sitting on the edge of her bed, not dressed for the graduation.

"Mary, why aren't you fully dressed? We are supposed to arrive by 6:30, what's wrong?"

"I don't know if I'm wanted at her graduation, I don't feel a part of this celebration."

"Mary, we are the parents, and as parents, we should lead by example. Now I don't know what this is about, but this has to change. Can't you at least be happy for your own daughter? Look, Mary, I don't want to be like this, but if you aren't ready in ten minutes the children and I will be leaving!"

"Of course you're going to choose her over me."

"WHAT ARE YOU TALKING ABOUT, MARY? I'm not going to do this," Pastor Greg replied sternly. "Ten minutes! I'll be in the car!" He leaves and goes to the car where the other two children are waiting.

"Daddy, is Momma coming?"

"Word, please, just say a prayer tonight for us all, OK?"

"Yea, sure, Dad."
About ten minutes later, Mary McKinney comes outside to the car.

"Here comes Mom."
"You look lovely, honey." Pastor tries to cheer up Mary McKinney. Mary fastens her seatbelt and sits there without speaking.

<><><>

A few hours pass and Thelma is a now a graduate. The family is meeting her outside to see her and to take pictures. "Do you see her, Word?" Pastor says, looking around the crowd.

"No, Daddy, I don't."

At that moment, Thelma walks through the crowd.

"Here she comes. THELMA, over here!"

Pastor, Mary, Word and TiTi wait for her to walk over. "Hey… there she is, Daddy's beautiful straight A student! Congratulations, baby."

"Thanks, Daddy. Hey, Momma." Thelma walks over to her mom and gives her a kiss on the cheek.

"Well, look at you, Thelma. I am proud of you!"

"Thanks, Momma."

"Thelma, we are so proud of you," Word replied.

"Yea, Thelma, we all are. Wow, I pray I can one day do as well as you." TiTi says, handing a bouquet of balloons to Thelma.

"Oh, TiTi, not only that, but you will do better than me!"

# Chapter 5

## Sunday Morning

Every Sunday morning the family attends testimony service, a place where people of God can come and share what the Lord is doing in their lives. During this service folks essentially tell one another, "What God is doing for me, He can do for you. Hang on."

Sister Cristy walks towards the microphone to sing "Yes Lord". Thelma loved to hear sister Cristy sing that song. When she belted out that first word 'Yes' Thelma always got chills up her spine, and the hairs on her arms would raise up. "Yes Lord" is a song that all church folks sing in this area; it is that song that no matter where you are when you hear it, you either cry or lift your hands. Even when Thelma was a little girl and she heard it, she got that same feeling. She used to ask her dad why that song effected everyone who heard it, and he would say, "Well, baby, it's because the words 'Yes Lord' is a total surrendering to God, unveiling the very heart and soul of all of the hidden secrets, lies, hurts, and more. It causes you to want to release them all, and your soul connects with the one who made you!"

When the song is done, Pastor McKinney heads to the front to deliver a few words to the congregation. "Praise the Lord, everybody. I was glad when they said unto me, 'Let us go into the house of the Lord.' Today is a special day for me…well…for my entire family. My daughter Thelma is a high school graduate! She graduated on Friday night, and at the top of her class. I can't tell you how proud I am of her and how good God is! So turn to your neighbor and say, 'Neighbor, I don't know about you, but God has been good to me.' Amen! Before I preach, I would like it if my daughter Thelma could come up and sing a solo for me this morning."

Thelma goes up to the front of the church to sing for her dad, as the church welcomes her with the clapping of their hands. She is exhausted from all of the excitement of her big weekend, but she wants to make her dad happy, so she sings his favorite song. "I Surrender All," and as usual, the anointing on Thelma through song touches everyone who is listening.

Pastor McKinney provides the altar call, at the leading of the Holy Spirit. "Saints, God is leading me in another direction. While the Spirit is moving, the doors of the church are open. If there is anyone that wants to surrender your life to the Lord today, God is waiting. Tomorrow is not promised to you, so while the breath is in your body, come to Jesus right now," he spoke reverently, extending his outstretched arms to the congregation. "Thelma, can you come back and sing that song again?"

People come up for prayer with their hands lifted high towards heaven, and Pastor McKinney works in his gift, laying hands and praying for those who are lost. Word heads up to the altar to help in the prayer lines, anointing folks' heads with blessed oil before Pastor McKinney prays for them.

Thelma loves seeing her dad flow under the anointing and thinks of how this visual is always a sight to see. She admires the work of the Lord as she continues to flow in her own anointing through song.

# Chapter 6

## Breaking Bread

A few months later, the family is gathering together for dinner. "Y'all come and sit down and eat. I made all this food and my feet hurt now."

"Oh, honey, you always do such a great job bringing us all together every Saturday night; whether you're sick or well."

"Thanks, honey. Honey, can you go ahead and bless the food?"

"Yes, of course. Father God, in the name of Jesus, we just thank you for the food that we are about to receive, bless the hands that has prepared it… and all that are present. You are the Almighty and we give you thanks, in Jesus' name, Amen!"

"Beautiful prayer, honey."

"As your pastor, I just want to thank you all for coming over for the last few years to our home, sharing these wonderful fellowship dinners. Our social hall is almost finished, and I would like to carry the dinners over there, just so more can come and have supper with us."

The entire time, Sister Knowles keeps eyeing Thelma. "Miss Thelma."

"Yes, Sister Knowles?"

"First, I wanted to congratulate you on your success in graduating. We all are so proud of you. I've known you before you could walk, and you have always been a bright young lady."

"Thank you, Sister Knowles."

"You're welcome, honey. Now, with that being said, I thought I saw you over by Deacon Ramsey's house the other day, talking outside to Deacon's son Johnny. Was that you?"

Thelma drops her head.

"Well, Thelma? Hmm? Well, I sure hope not because I heard that boy just got out of jail. On top of that, rumor says he done went and got some girl pregnant and — "

Pastor interrupts. "Well, seems we need to pray for that young man. Everyone needs some encouragement."

"ENCOURAGEMENT? That boy is just bad news...on Monday through Friday."

"Well, like I said, Sister Knowles, prayer is the answer," Pastor Greg said plainly.

"You're right, Pastor!" Thelma sighs. "My stomach hurts, I'm not hungry."

"Thelma, Sister Knowles is asking you a question."

"I don't know what you are talking about, Sister Knowles. That wasn't me."

"Wait a minute, Thelma, that is no way to speak to our guest."

"Momma, I wasn't being disrespectful, though."

"I apologize for Thelma's behavior, Sister Knowles."

"It's okay. Thelma, are you still missing Gloria, honey?"

Thelma gets emotional and turns towards her father. "Daddy, I just don't feel too well, can I go upstairs?"

"Wait, baby. Just try and eat something, honey."

"The way I'm feeling, I think I may throw up, Daddy."

"Thelma, I'm not going to baby you like your father does, SIT DOWN!" her mother demanded.

Thelma sits down at the table. Taking a deep breath, she said, "Again, no disrespect, Momma, but I will be eighteen years old and I've already graduated school, so you yelling at me like this, ain't going to happen!"

"Let me tell you this… I don't care if you're going to be twenty-eight years old, you won't get away with talking to me any and every kind of way. Thelma, why is it every time we have company you come up with a way to ruin everything?"

Thelma could tell her mother was angry, but she was so tired of sitting back and letting her mother walk over her. At some point, she had to stand up for herself, and that time was now. "I'M NOT TRYING TO RUIN ANYTHING, MAN!!!"

"Thelma, have you lost your mind? I will not allow you to use that tone with your mom. Furthermore, you will not show any disrespect to the woman who gave you life!" Pastor said sternly.

# Kimberly Robinson Green

"The one who gave me life, huh?" Thelma smirked.

"Excuse me, young lady?"

Thelma looks at her father. She could see the disappointment etched in his face. "I'm sorry, Daddy. I just don't feel well."

"I hear you, but what you're not going to do is yell at your mother. Now apologize and excuse yourself from the room, please!"

"Daddy, you didn't hear how she was talking to me?"

Her father raised his hand to halt any further discussion. "That's your mother, and that's all I'm going to say!"

"I apologize, Momma," Thelma said, standing and looking at everyone else seated at the table. "Please forgive me, everybody!" she said before walking out of the room.

"Wait, Thelma. I'll come with you," TiTi calls after her.

"Oh no, you won't, TiTi, she will be just fine."

"Yes, Daddy."

"Where is Word?" Mrs. McKinney asks. "Tim, Timothy Andrew McKinney, where are you?"

"Oh, he's right outside, Momma," TiTi answers.

"Well, go outside and tell your brother that I said to come and eat his supper, it's getting cold."

"Oh, okay, Mom." TiTi walks out of the door.

"Man, it's cold out here," she said, trying to stop her teeth from chattering. TiTi walks towards the garage not knowing that Word is in there with a girl. "Word… Word, where are you?"

"Oh my God, that's my little sister."

"So what!"

"What do you mean so what? If we are caught out here together, my momma and daddy will kill me."

"That's why I should have listened to my friends. They told me not to mess around with church boys, after all, we're just kissing. You would think that Jesus himself was coming the way you're acting."

"I will be meeting 'Jesus' real soon, if my big mouth sister finds us out here. I think you'd better go, and now!"

"You sound just like a little choir girl crying, but out of tune."

"Whatever, Lisa, just go!"

"Fine, and if I leave, don't bother calling me again!"

"Yea, yea, hurry up go."

"Shhhh, what's that noise?"

"What noise?"

"That bump." Tonya walks into the garage.

"Oooooooh, I'm telling on you, Tim. I'm telling Momma and Daddy that you're out here with a girl."

"Come here, Tonya."

"NO! I'm telling on you."
"No, you come here, Tonya. Let me talk to you, please."

"Alright, but first, you better tell your little girlfriend to leave."

"Please, Lisa, can you just go?"

"Yea, whatever!" Lisa walks away, rolling her eyes at Tonya.

"Hey, little sis. Let's rap."

"Rap about what? About you having your little girlfriend out in the garage doing stuff you're not supposed to?"

"Tonya, first of all, we were just talking?"

"Hahaha, talking? Nice try, big bro. Yea right. If you were just talking to her, then why do you have all that lipstick on your face?"

"Okay, I kissed her. But that's all I did, so please don't tell on me. Please?"

"I won't tell if you can do my chores for the next week."

"What? Man, Tonya, you always tryna get something out of nothing."

"Yes or no? I can go and…"

"Okay, okay, you have a deal. Man, you make me sick sometimes, I'll do it."

"You pinky swear?"

"Yea, Pinky swear!"
"Hey, Word."

"Yea?"

"You know that Sister Knowles is at the table, making googly eyes at Daddy."

"There you go again with that mess. I like Sister Knowles, she's cool."

"NO, she isn't! She has everybody fooled, but not me. I can see straight through all of that mascara and makeup on her face."

"Wow, that's cold, little sis... OK, when we go in for dinner —"

Momma calls out, "Tim, TiTi?"

"Yes, Momma?" they reply in unison.

"Yawl get in here, the food is already cold, come and eat."

"We're coming. Like I was going to say, watch how much she talks to Daddy and how less she talks to Momma."

"Oh TiTi, ain't nobody thinking about Daddy, but Momma."

"That woman is after Daddy, and it seems that I'm the only one who notices. Word, will you promise me that you will help me get rid of her?"

"Now how will we do that, little sister?"

"Let out Cecil and place him under the table right by her feet, and watch her scream and then run out of the house."

"How do you know, she may like tarantulas."

Tonya laughs. "Hahaha, you're right, besides, she probably would use that as a way to scream and run into Daddy's arms and cry, 'Help help, save me, save me.'"

"You are so crazy. Come on in the house before we both get in trouble with Momma."

"Oh yeah, you missed it."

"Missed what?"

"Well, when you were out here playing house…"

"Shut up, ok?"

Tonya giggles. "Thelma was going off in there."

"What?"

"Yeah, she started yelling at Momma, and Daddy was not happy."

"Man, that's not the first time she's done that, something is going on with her; she's been acting really strange. Maybe I'll get to talk to her later."

"No, Tim, don't say anything, then she will think that I'm running to you telling her business."

"Like Daddy always says 'yawl ain't got no business.'"

"What are you talking about we ain't got none?"

"Oh yea, that's right, you do have some business, Word, with that girl! Anyway Word, I'm really worried about Thelma. We have always been close enough to share and talk about everything, you know that... it's the same with you two also, but lately, Thelma's been so different. I know she's been waking up and crying at night. She says she's having this dream that keeps repeating itself."

"Dream? What dream?"

"You talk to her, Word. You're good with the Bible stuff, maybe you can interpret the dream to her."

"I'll talk with her, but I ain't telling her that I know anything. I'm not having Thelma kill me."

<><><>

At the dinner table, Word walks in the room, greeting everyone. "Hi, Daddy. Hi, Momma, everyone…"

"Hello, Timothy."

"Come and join us, son." Pastor McKinney smiles and pats his son on the back.

"Sorry I'm late for dinner, Mom. I got caught up in working out, getting ready for football camp."

"Yea, working out alright," TiTi says, laughing and clearing her throat.

"What did you say, TiTi?" Mary McKinney asks.

"Nothing, Momma. She's talking about nothing, as usual." Word looks at TiTi and with his eyes, begging her to be quiet.

Sister Knowles interrupts. "Well, Pastor, this is a wonderful dinner you all put together tonight."

"Thank you, Sister, but I can't take all of the credit; my wife cooked all of this delicious food," Pastor replies.

"Yeah, that's right. My momma did this, Sister Knowles, and you know she did." TiTi looks at Sister Knowles with an attitude, and rolls her eyes.

"TiTi, I did not raise you to be so disrespectful like that, apologize and I mean now RIGHT NOW!" Mary McKinney, raises her voice and hits the table with her right hand.

"Yes, Momma. I am sorry, Sister Knowles." TiTi apologizes, looking down at her hands, not making eye contact as she keeps her attitude.

"Well, I was going to see if something was going to be said to you, young lady. Seems to me it's much disrespect going on around here," Sister Knowles replies.

"Now I had my daughter apologize to you, Sister, but for your information, my husband and I work very hard around here training and raising our children right, so I don't appreciate your snide remarks." Mary begins to fidget around with her table napkin, trying to stay calm.

"Now, everyone just calm down. We are a church family and God don't like any confusion," Pastor McKinney says, as he's stands at the head of the table, rubbing his wife's shoulders.

"Amen Pastor," Deacon replies. "After all, we all know that you both have done a marvelous job with your children." Turning his head looking at Sister Knowles.

"Well, thank you, Deacon," Mary replies, moving the sweet potatoes to the center of the table.

"You're welcome, First Lady, and I might add, dinner was wonderful. I would love if I could take some cobbler home to the wife."

"Of course you can, actually, you can do better than that. I made her a small pan of her own. I knew she couldn't come out because of her surgery. I'll be right back." Mary walks over to the kitchen table and brings out a long pan of peach cobbler for deacon and his wife.

"Thank you, sister. You all are just like family to us and I thank God every day for adding you to our lives," Deacon replies, shaking Sister Mary's hand.

"We feel the same way, about all of you! We thank you all for coming over to visit us. We will see you all tomorrow at Sunday school," Pastors replies, while everyone is starting to leave.

"Yes, sir, be there with bells on. And I'll have to place that order for those Sunday school books in the morning. Sorry, Pastor, I'm running behind," Deacon says.

"No worries, Deacon, you always come through," Pastor says, holding the door as Deacon and others leave.

Pastor McKinney and Mary, sit at the table after everyone leaves. They catch their breath from all of the excitement at dinner.

"Honey, we really need to have a talk with Thelma about her behavior."

"Yes, I know, dear. I really feel she's under a lot of pressure lately."

"Yes, I know, but that's all part of life and your little girl is out of high school and definitely knows right from wrong by now. Covering up for her every time she does wrong is not the answer."

"And I fully agree, dear, but at the same time, as her parents, we must show her that our love is unconditional."

"Thelma, can you come downstairs, please? Your father and I would like to speak with you." Mary gets up from the table and walks over to the kitchen window.

Thelma comes downstairs with her arms folded. "Yes, Daddy?"

"Umm, excuse me, Thelma, but I believe that your father and I both called you," Mary replies to Thelma.

Thelma never acknowledges her mom. "Thelma, did you hear me? I am speaking to you."

"Yea," Thelma says with an attitude.

"Yea, what, Thelma?" Mary looks at Thelma with disbelief of her lack of respect.

"Yes, Momma, I heard you." Mary turns and looks at Pastor McKinney.

Thelma's still doesn't acknowledge her mom.

"You know what? I'm going to let you deal with her, Greg. I am tired and I'm not going to deal with any disrespect right now!" Mary turns and walks away from the window.

"Dang, I ain't even done nothing and I'm already getting blamed. But I bet if it was TiTi or Tim it would go differently," Thelma said, standing in the doorway with her arms folded.

"It would go differently because they are not mouthy like you are," Mary replies.

"Wait a minute, both of you."

"Both of us? I am the adult here and Thelma is the child, Greg. She is the only one who needs correcting!" Mary, visibly annoyed, walks towards the steps.

"Mary, we cannot do this right now. How can we teach our children anything or anyone else for that matter, when we're not in agreement," Pastor says.

"I usually agree with you about almost everything, but not this disrespect. And Thelma popping her neck and rolling her eyes at me, I WILL NOT TOLERATE IT, from her and no one else."

Pastor walks over to his wife and holds her hand, trying to guide her toward the table. "Let's all just sit down and talk things over, ok, honey?" Mary pulls her hands away from him.

"Honey, please, we have to get to the bottom of things," Pastor says, holding Mary's hand and rubbing it.

"Yes, you're right," Mary replies.

"Thelma?"

"Yes, Daddy!"

"Now, first off, Thelma, speaking and showing your mother disrespect the way you have will not be allowed. The way you showed out earlier, when our church members were here, should not have happened."

"I apologized, Daddy, and I'm not trying to be disrespectful, but doesn't the Bible say 'Parents should not provoke their children?'"

"Now I know you're not trying to use the Bible to justify anything, child," Mary replies.

"Well, I do feel that you pick on me all of the time for no reason, and it's not fair, Momma. You act as if sometimes you don't even like me." Thelma's voice cracks as she holds back her tears.

"Thelma, you know that I love you, with all of my heart and soul. You're my little girl that is turning into a beautiful young woman and I am very proud of you, but...you have to show me more respect than you do!"

Thelma goes and lies under her dad's arms and looks at her mother.

"We have to really come to some conclusion on what's really going on here. I can't be preaching in the pulpit to others and my own house is falling apart. We will finish this discussion tomorrow, I'm just worn out," Pastor replies, rubbing his hands across the top of his head.

"I think we should finish this discussion now, not later," Mary says, turning to face her husband.

Thelma goes upstairs to her room, looking back at her mother and father as she leaves.

"You know, dear, sometimes is good to let the fire go down a little before adding more wood. Mary, I know you love Thelma and I know you're trying to do your best with her. And I love you for being such a great mother to all of our children." Pastor kisses Mary on the cheek. "Now, I'm going down to the church and study for a little while. I'll be back for our nightly family prayer. Ok, honey?"

"Yes, honey, and you be careful driving down to that church."

"Oh, I will," he replies, standing at the door putting his hat on. He takes a deep breath. "I love you, Mary."

"I love you, too, Pastor McKinney," Mary says smiling.

Thelma is in her room, lying across her bed crying, and saying a prayer. "Lord, I'm not happy anymore, it seems like everything is going wrong. It's killing me to pretend that I don't know the truth, I just want to be left alone. I wish I could go away or just disappear. Lord, can you please help me? I can never do anything right at home, Momma hates me and I feel like Daddy is giving up on me... No one understands me. God, please!"

There's a knock on the door. "Thelma, it's TiTi, can I come in?"

"No, go away please."

"Please, can I come in?" Tonya opens the door. "Thelma, what's the matter, why are you crying?"

Thelma looks up at TiTi, with tears rolling down her face. "TiTi, I told you not to come in my room, now can you just go."

45

"I know you did, Thelma, but you're my sister and I'm worried about you."

"I'm alright," Thelma replies, wiping her face.

"No you're not, T. You've been acting very strange lately and Tim was saying that he was going to talk to you."

Thelma gets angry. "Tim? Oh, now you all are talking about me?"

"No, Thelma, we're just concerned about you."

"Well, what do you mean?" Thelma asks.

"I told him that you got into it with Momma at dinner, that's all," TiTi responds to Thelma with concern.

"Don't nobody need to worry about me, I'M FINE!" Thelma starts to cry again.

TiTi walks over to Thelma. "Thelma? What's wrong, I mean, what's really going on?" TiTi kneels down in front of Thelma.

"I can't explain it, TiTi, you're much too young to understand."

"Young? You only got me by four years, Thelma." TiTi starts laughing.

"Well, I guess you're right, but you have to swear on the Holy Bible that you won't ever repeat what is said to you today, you swear?" Thelma says to TiTi.

"Where is the Bible?"

"Right here." Thelma says, holding out her Bible. "Place your hand right here, TiTi…and say, 'I, TiTi.'"

TiTi looks at Thelma, like she's crazy.

"I'm very serious, girl. Put your hand on this Bible and repeat after me! Say it. Say 'I, Tonya Nicole McKinney,'"

Tonya repeats after Thelma and promises her sister to never tell.

"Sit next to me, TiTi." Thelma is preparing her sister for some news. "You know I love you, right?"

"Yes, Sis, I know you do."

"And I never wanted to let you down." Tonya starts to cry.

"Thelma, you're scaring me." TiTi looks real worried for her sister.

"I have something to share with you and you're the only…"

"THELMA!" Tonya yells. "Tell me, Thelma."

Thelma looks at Tonya with tears in her eyes. "I'm pregnant."

The room goes silent.

"Pregnant?" TiTi looks down at Thelma's stomach, and reaches to touch her stomach.

"Yes, TiTi. I am."

"What? Who?" Tonya starts to cry. "Oh, Thelma, what are you going to do, and who is the father?"

"It's Johnny Ramsey."

"You mean, Deacon Ramsey's son?"

"Yes, TiTi." Thelma walks over to a laundry basket and brings it back to her bed, and begins to fold clothes.

"Thelma, are you going to keep your baby?" TiTi asks.

Mary walks into the room as TiTi is talking. "Baby, what baby?"

"Momma, umm we were talking about…" TiTi tries to cover for Thelma.

She interrupts them both. "You were talking about what, Thelma? I heard everything you said."

"Momma," Thelma gets frustrated and begins to cry a little. "Momma, what? Thelma, I don't know what we're going to do with you. Your father is a very well-known, prestigious pastor in this town and you're trying to destroy his image."

"Momma, I would never try and mess anything up for Daddy. I love my Daddy."

"Well, you sure aren't acting like it. If you love him, then you wouldn't have done this to him." Mary McKinney begins to cry.

"Done this to him or you? Momma, that's not fair."

"Thelma, you have one more time to be disrespectful to me!" Mrs. McKinney yells, pointing her finger at Thelma.

"MOMMA!" TiTi stands in front of her mom, blocking her from yelling at her sister.

"YOU STAY OUT OF THIS, TONYA! In fact, you can leave the room, and I mean now!"

"NO!"

"What did you say, Tonya?"

Thelma walks over to TiTi and grabs her hands. "TiTi, it's okay." Reassuring TiTi, she will be fine.

"Thelma, just let me stay."

"No, TiTi, just do what she says. It's already too much going on around here. I don't want you involved."

"No, I will not leave you in here with her."

Mary walks over to TiTi and slaps her across her face.

"Have you lost, your mind, hitting my little sister in her face?" Thelma says, feeling very upset.

Tonya runs out of the room crying. "Naw, I haven't lost mine, but you must have lost yours. All you do is cause confusion in this house, are you happy now, Thelma? You've now turned your little sister against me, you're nothing but the Devil. I told your father that something was going on with you."

"Okay, Momma, why don't you come clean about some things yourself." Thelma leans towards her mother, with anger.

"What are you talking about, girl?" Mary looks over at Thelma.

"Momma, I know, I know everything...I found the letter." Mary McKinney, stands looking at Thelma, as if the cat had swallowed the canary.

"What letter, Thelma?"

"Momma, you can stop pretending now. I know now why you never really liked me. I know now why you treated me different than my brothers and TiTi. And finally, it makes sense why my eyes are green and my hair color is different than everyone else. My real mother's name is Estell Markinson. She gave me up for adoption, but Granny took me instead, until Daddy married you. Right, Momma? I was just a baby!" Thelma is standing in the middle of the floor, with her hand on her chest, crying!

"Oh my God...Where did you get this letter?"

"Daddy must have kept it, I don't know, but what I do know is my real momma left me this letter so I would know the truth one day."

Mary gets upset again at Thelma. "Your real mom? I am your real mom, Thelma. I've done everything that I could to love you. Blood doesn't make a family real, Thelma. Your father promised me that he would destroy that letter, where is it?" Mary feels like she has lost control of control of the situation, and has tears forming in her eyes.

"I'm keeping it, because it's the only thing that has not lied to me around here!" Thelma runs out of the room crying.

"Honey, come back please!"

&lt;&gt;&lt;&gt;&lt;&gt;

It's Saturday night and it's been a few hours since Thelma has left home. Mary McKinney is starting to get worried because there is no sign of Thelma and she knows Pastor will be home shortly from studying at the church. He is not aware what has taken place while he was gone from home. Tonya and Timothy are coming downstairs to check on everyone after the big argument.

"Momma, are you okay?"

"Yes, Tim. I am."

"Is Thelma going to be okay?" Word says.

Mary is sitting at the table with her Bible. She looks down at it, acting as if she didn't hear Word ask about Thelma. TiTi walks over to the window and breaks out in tears. Word pulls his little sister close to him.

"No need to worry, God will take care of your sister and she will be home very soon."

"Well, Momma, is it true?"

"Is what true, Timothy?"

"That Thelma is not really your daughter?"

"Boy…No, that's not true!" Tears flow down her face. "She is mine, just like you're mine."

"But, Mom, I overheard…"

Mrs. McKinney cuts Tim off. "You overheard a mother and daughter having a disagreement and that's all you heard. Do I make myself clear?"

"Yes, ma'am," Word replies respectfully.

Tonya is still angry with her mother.

"Tonya, is that clear to you?" Mrs. McKinney asks, glaring at her youngest daughter.

"Yes, ma'am," TiTi replies quietly. Although wishing to remain respectful, she is concerned about her sister being somewhere out there all alone. "Mom, if it's ok, I want to go and look for Thelma."

"I already told you she is fine! She's probably over to Janet's house or something, and besides, it doesn't make any sense for both of you to be gone. I already have to try to explain all of this to your father as it is!"

# Chapter 7

## The Truth

A sound of a car door is slamming outside. Tonya gasps with excitement. "It's Daddy."

Tim pulls Tonya by the arm. "Come on, TiTi let's go upstairs."

Pastor walks through the door, calling for his wife. "Mary."

"Here I am, honey, in the kitchen."

Pastor walks up behind her and kisses her on the cheek. "Thank you, dear. You're making me coffee this late at night?"

"Yes."

"Well, it sure smells good, I think I will have a small cup."

"It's already poured, so come here and sit down so you can relax, honey."

"Well, baby, I felt awful about how I left earlier without resolving things with Thelma. I wanted to finish talking to her. I know I said tomorrow, but there is a situation that has to be dealt with and tomorrow won't do it for me." Pastor grabs his chest. "I haven't been feeling too well today, Mary. I could hardly study for thinking about my baby. She is very heavy on my heart. There is definitely something going on with her, and it's my job as her father and a man of God to get to the bottom of things."

Mary tries to distract him and bring up another subject. "Honey, you really need to make a doctor's appointment to see about those chest pains. You know what, why don't you just rest tonight and we can handle things tomorrow, besides… what's going on with Mother Patten? Did the doctors tell Benny and Sister Martin what's going on with their decision?" Mary was trying really hard to distract her husband and change the subject off of Thelma.

"I don't know, and truthfully, I can't really think about anyone else until my baby is okay. I think I better go upstairs and see Thelma." Pastor starts walking towards the stairs.

"Wait!" Mary yells, stopping Pastor from proceeding up the stairs. "There is something that I need to talk to you about, honey."

"Well, can it wait until later?"

"No, it can't, it's about Thelma, honey."

"What's wrong? You look serious."

"It's pretty serious, honey. I don't know where to start." Mary paces the floor, trying to figure out how to tell him.

"Mary, what's going on?" Pastor McKinney gets frantic.

"Well, honey, Thelma and I kind of had an argument, and I'm so sorry. I'm afraid I didn't handle things the correct way, I was just so upset."

"Upset about what, Mary?"

"I overheard Thelma telling TiTi that she is…"

"She is what, Mary?"

Mary sits down in a chair. "She told TiTi that she is…"
Pastor turns around to the wall, holding his chest. Mary decides not to tell him about her pregnancy. "Mary, what is it?"

Mary grabs his hands, and pulls him to sit down. "Thelma found that letter from Estelle." Mary places her hand on Pastor's leg.

"The letter? Oh my God, when?" Pastor leans to the side of his chair.

"I'm not clear when she found it, honey. I just know she was very hurt and upset and feeling as if we both lied to her."

"Well, where is Thelma now?" Pastor asks, walking over to the window, looking out.

"I don't know, she left a few hours ago," Mary replies.

"Oh my God, you mean that my baby is out there alone and feeling like this?"

"I'm sure she's ok, and I don't want you to get your blood pressure up. You need to just calm down and we will figure this out together." Mary tries to keep Pastor relaxed.

"My main concern is my child, everything else can wait."

Mary gets upset. "And your health is important to me, Greg. Thelma is eighteen years old and we all make mistakes in life, and there are consequences with them."

Pastor grabs his chest again. "Mary, do you care at all what is happening to our little girl? For God's sakes, she is out there hurt, and all alone and all you can talk about is the mistakes she's made, what about the choices we've made? I mean, we all have made them. I made the mistake not..." Pastor catches himself from saying something else.

"You made the mistake of what, Greg? Not marrying Estelle instead of me? Is that what your mistake was? Oh, come on, it doesn't take a rocket scientist to figure that one out."

Pastor stands there, looking at Mary with no response.

"Oh. Now it's clear, is that what this is all really about?" Mary turns to Pastor, with hurt in her eyes.

"What are you talking about, Estelle?" Pastor catches himself, and realizes he just called his wife Mary, his ex's name. "I'm sorry, Mary, I really am. I didn't mean to call you her name, it just seems like everything is so crazy at the moment."

"Oh really, Greg? You called me just what you meant to call me, and furthermore, you promised that the letter would be destroyed. I need some air!" Mary walks outside, shutting the doors.

Pastor looks up to the ceiling. "God, where are you? Please help me, I haven't been perfect, because only you are, but...I've been faithful to your word, faithful to your people, and most of all, faithful to you. Please return the favor, Lord. Help my family, God... we need you!"

TiTi and Word come downstairs. "Daddy, is everything okay?" Pastor is sitting in his chair, rubbing his head.

"Both of you come and sit down next to me, I don't know how much you're aware of, but I want you both to know that I love you all very much. I am sorry for any hurt I may have caused to our family, and I know that God will work it all out!"

Word and TiTi are standing in the family room with their dad. "We love you, too, Daddy." They both hug him.

"I love you both, too," Pastor replies.

"Hey, Dad, I want to go look for Thelma, I can't rest until I see that she's alright." Word walks over to the closet to get his coat.

"Yes, son, I think that's a wonderful idea. I'll come with you!" He turns and looks at Tonya. "TiTi, I'm going to call Ms. Jerkins across the street and send you over there for a little while, okay?"

"Daddy, I want to come with you guys and look for Thelma, too." TiTi replies.

"I know you do, honey, but just in case your sister comes back, you need to be around home so she will know what's going on. And usually you all know to go to Ms. Jerkins' in case of an emergency, right? We won't be gone long, princess, okay?"

"Okay, Daddy." TiTi goes to get her jacket from the family room closet.

"Now, TiTi."

"Yes, Daddy."

"Tonya, what has happened to Thelma should only stay between our family. The devil is busy, and people, especially church folk, love to gossip. So not a word, not even to Ms. Jerkins, until I come back, and then if I decide to say anything, I will."

"But, Daddy, why would church people act like that?" TiTi asks.

"Well, because, honey, church folks are just regular folks who know the Lord, but are not exempt from bad behavior. So, just you remember that, sweetheart."

"I hear you, Daddy!"

"Let's head out. Tonya, get your coat, it's a little chilly outside, and close the door behind you."

"I got my jacket already, Dad." TiTi heads out the door with Word and Pastor McKinney.

Pastor knocks on Ms. Jerkins' door across the street.

"Just one minute," Ms. Jerkins calls from the other side of the door. She peeks through the peephole before opening the door. "Oh, Pastor McKinney, it's you. Is everything okay?"

"Oh, yes, I just was wondering if you could allow Tonya to hang out with you for a little while?"

"Well, Pastor, of course, but it's 11:45pm, are you sure everything's okay? And where is Sister McKinney?"

"Ms. Jerkins, with all due respect, I really need to know if she can just stay," Pastor McKinney replies.

"Of course she can, come on in, child. I'll just get you a blanket," she says, closing the door.

"You hungry, Tonya?"

"No, ma'am."

# Chapter 8

# The Search

It's Sunday morning and there is no sign of Thelma. Her mom is upstairs getting ready for Sunday school. Pastor McKinney is in his study, praying. TiTi and Word are in Thelma's room talking everything over, wondering where their sister is.

"Man, this is crazy. I wish she would call us," Word says, sitting on the edge of Thelma's bed.

"She will. I'm sure she just needed time to process it all," TiTi replies, while looking out of Thelma's room window.

"Yes, I guess you're right; she probably will be home today," Word replies.

"Word, you know what really bothers me?"

"What's that?"

"How Momma is acting. I mean, you should have heard her. She said some really mean things to Thelma, and now she acts as if she doesn't even care that she's gone." TiTi's voice cracks because she's so upset.

"I know, Sis, but people make mistakes. Even adults do. Sometimes they don't know how to apologize... and after all, this situation is not your everyday situation either."

TiTi nods in agreement as she drops the bedroom curtain in Thelma's room.

"Well, come on, Sis. It's almost time for Sunday school."
"Word?"

"Yes, TiTi."

"I don't want to go to church without her. I don't feel like being bothered with those people. Besides, we're always together. What's it going to look like if Thelma doesn't come to church with us?"

"I feel the same way, sis. But remember the Bible says that 'The joy of the Lord is our strength.'"

"Ok, Word, let's not do all of the preaching right now."

"Well, it's true." Word walks towards Thelma's door with his Bible in his hand.

"I know, but, please, Word!"

Pastor Call's TiTi and Word downstairs. "Can you both come here please?"

"Yes, Daddy, were coming." They both replied, running down the stairs.

"Yes, Daddy," Word says.

"You both have a seat, please. Your mother and I need to speak with you both about what has happened and how the enemy is trying to destroy our family, but God is on our side. My job as your father is to protect you from anything that will harm, hurt or cause confusion; so I would like to apologize for everything that has happened. I'm sorry!"

"Yes, Daddy." TiTi and Word turns and look at their mother.
Mary stands up and grabs Pastor's hand. "Well, I would like to apologize as well. I'm afraid I did not handle any of this the way a mother should have. I guess I let my emotions get in the way, so I'm sorry, too. You both know that I love you, right? And I love your sister Thelma with all of my heart."

"Of course we do, Momma. We know this," Word replies.

TiTi just sits there looking at her mom. Word hits TiTi on the arm to respond.

"It's okay, TiTi. I understand you're angry that your sister left, but I am still your mother and deserve some respect, Tonya?"

TiTi stares at her mother and replies. "I just don't like what you said to Thelma, Mom. You made her feel like everything was her fault. And you called her the devil."

Pastor interrupts. "Now, I don't know what took place last night because I wasn't here, all I know is all of my children are a blessing to me and is certainly not the devil, which is who's causing all of this confusion in the first place. Now let's get it together, we are running late to Sunday school. Now, like it or not, you all are preacher's kids, and most importantly, God's children and others are looking up to you. We have to make sure that our house is in order so we can all be that light to a dying world."

Mary grabs her coat and walks towards the door. "I will meet you all in the car." She is still upset at how disrespectful Titi is being.

"Wait, honey." Pastor gets his blessed oil, and begins to put some on each of their foreheads. "Now I'm ready. The master's work must continue. Let's go." Pastor McKinney and the rest of the family head towards the car so they can leave for Sunday school.

When they arrive at the church, Pastor asks his wife to come into his office. "Mary, you know how much I love you and our family. I am praying for God's strength today. My heart is so heavy. I need to know that you and I are on the same page, or I cannot preach to anyone until I'm sure. This is hard for me...the stress of it all. My baby is gone and us fighting is a bit too much."

"Of course, honey. We're alright. I know it is hard, Greg, but this one thing I know: we are a strong family and we can conquer anything with the help of God. I love you. I know I'm a work in progress. I pray that you can have a little more patience with me. What does the song say? 'Please be patient with me, God is not through with me yet'?"

Pastor smiles at Mary. She walks over and kisses her husband before she walks out and closes the door.

Sunday school ends and there is a knock on Pastor's door. "Come in," Pastor says. "Well, good morning, Deacon."

"Good morning, Pastor."

"What can I do for you this Sunday morning, sir?"

"Well, Pastor, I was coming to ask, can I do anything for you?"

"Oh?" Pastor McKinney looks surprised.

"Yes, Pastor, there is lots of talking going on that Thelma has run away from home, is this true?"

Pastor puts his glasses on. "Well, Deacon, I'm not sure how to answer that."

Deacon says, "Now, Greg, we've been friends for years. In fact, when your daddy passed away, I promised him that I would take care of you. This is why I moved here to Arkansas when you did, because of the promise I made to my good friend, your father!"

"Yes, I know, Deacon. Since Daddy died, you have been like a father to me, and I know I can depend on you." Pastor sits on the corner of his desk in front of Deacon.

"Son?" Deacon looks at Pastor.

"She knows, Deacon. She knows about Estelle, her biological mother." Pastor looks up at Deacon with hurt on his face! "I don't even know where my child is, and that's not the worst part of it. Thelma and Mary, got into an argument."

Deacon drops his head.

Pastor McKinney gets up and goes to put his robe on. "Look, Deacon, I'll have to talk about this matter later. I really need to go over my notes and pray before I come out. I hope you understand."

Deacon shakes Pastor's hand. "You know I understand, son. Just know that I am here for you. God will be with you. You just go on out there and speak what God has given you. Talk from your heart, son."

"God bless you, Deacon, and thank you!" Pastor stands up and shakes Deacon's hand again. "Deacon, can you tell Sister Marcus to have the choir sing 'I Feel Like Going On'? I think that's the message that God wants me to deliver today." Pastor McKinney looks down at his notes.

"Okay, Pastor, I will let her know." Deacon walks out of the office.

"Well, God, it's me and you. I give you all of the glory and the praise. I trust that you will make everything today alright. AMEN." Pastor McKinney grabs his Bible, takes a deep breath, walks out of his office into his pulpit, and kneels down in front of his seat to pray. The choir sings the song that Pastor requested, "I Feel Like Going On." As he hears the words, the Spirit moves and he gets very emotional. After the choir sings, Pastor McKinney walks up to the microphone and begins to speak.

"Well, after that number from the choir, who in this room feels like going on?"

The audience responds by saying "Amen."

Pastor speaks to the crowd. "Today is a very different day for me because even though I'm the Shepard over this church, the Devil fights me as well. In fact, I think he comes at me sometimes even harder; but even though my trials and my tribulations come...I am determined to go on in Jesus name! I have been going through something very difficult with my family, and last night I was lost for words because the hurt that life itself can bring us, can get difficult. But I want to encourage you to hold on, a change is coming after a while. Can the church say Amen!"

The church replies in unison, "Amen!"

Pastor McKinney finishes his sermon earlier than usual and is eager to get home to find Thelma. As church lets out, he notices that some of the church members are saying, "We're praying for you, Pastor." He realizes that the word must be out about what has taken place with his daughter.

Upon arriving at home there is a commotion outside, there stands Thelma with the parents of Johnny Ramsey, the boy that Thelma is pregnant by. Thelma is crying. Pastor walks towards the commotion. "What's going on here? Thelma are you okay? I've missed you, baby, we all have." He kisses Thelma on the forehead.

"What's going on is your daughter has been sneaking in and out of our home trying to see our son Johnny. All due respect Pastor, we don't tolerate this type of behavior around our home and certainly not with our son. I'm not judging you on your parenting skills, but...something is wrong when a young lady conducts herself in such a way, and her very own father is supposed to be one the finest Pastors in our city."

Mary McKinney arrives. "What's going on here, Greg?" She sees Thelma and runs and hugs her.

"Deacon and Sister Ramsey seems to think that Thelma—"

Pastor McKinney is interrupted by Sister Ramsey. "We don't think, Pastor, we know your daughter is sneaking in and out of our home, and we will not have it! Deacon, are you going to ever say anything on behalf of Johnny and what's going on?"

Deacon Ramsey, clears his throat. "Well, dear, I think we might be jumping into this whole matter a little fast and there are definitely two sides to every story, so just calm down!"

"I don't know what's going on, but we will get to the bottom of it all," Pastor McKinney replies to Sister and Deacon Ramsey.

"Well, I sure hope so. Can we come inside, Pastor?" Sister Ramsey says.

"No, Sister. I'm sorry, but we need to speak to our own daughter right now. Take no offense, but Thelma is our responsibility, no one else's!" Pastor, Mary and Thelma walk inside of the house and closes the door.

"Take a seat Thelma." Pastor says as he pulls out a chair for her. He takes her hands and kneels to the side of the chair. "Where have you been? Is this true that you were over Deacon Ramsey's house? Baby, you have your own house and own family, never feel like you have to escape from your own support system, which is all of us, your family." Pastor hugs Thelma tightly.

"I know, Daddy, and I love you all for it, but it honestly didn't feel like I had too much support last night. I'm sure you heard about it all, right?"

"Yes, I did, baby, but I want to know why you were over at the Ramsey's house. And what was Sister Ramsey talking about?"

Mary McKinney looks at Thelma, trying to let her know that her dad wasn't told about the pregnancy.

"Well, Daddy, I was just over there to talk with Johnny, he's a good friend. We talk sometimes.

"Oh?" Pastor McKinney replies to Thelma. "I didn't know that, I mean, I know you both go to school together, but I wasn't aware you were close friends. I always thought that we were close enough that you could talk to me about anything, baby? Lately you haven't been acting like yourself. Is it anything else that I don't know, baby girl?" Pastor looks at Thelma, with a concerned look on his face.

"Daddy, it's not that big of a deal, like Sister Ramsey tried to make it to be. But to tell the truth, Daddy, I haven't been happy for a very long time now, but finding the letter put the icing on the cake for me. This is way too much to handle." Thelma walks over to her mother, and grabs her hands.

"Momma, I'm sorry for any problems I may have caused you. Thank you for taking me in as your own. I realize now that it couldn't have been easy, so I want to say that I'm sorry. You're the only mother I have ever known."

Mary starts to cry and replies, "Stop talking like that, Thelma. You are my baby and I love you. I'm the one that's sorry this all has happened to you, baby. We're so glad you're home."

"Thank you, Momma but it all makes sense now. I mean, everything does! I had time to think about a lot last night while I was away. Daddy, you know how much I love you, you are my rock and everything in between. I thank you for always supporting me, and I love you both."

"Baby, why are you sounding like this? We know you love us. I know you all too well, what else is going on? Well, Thelma?" Pastor is looking at Thelma, trying to figure out what's going on.

"Daddy, everything that has happened up until now has been no one's fault but my very own, I have brought shame to this family, I have let down my baby sister and brothers. I have completely messed up my entire life. God doesn't even want me anymore."

"Baby, what are you talking about, how have you brought shame upon this family? You haven't done anything sweetheart. It's my fault this all has happened. All you've done is found that letter that has hurt you so very deeply. Thelma, God loves you always. No matter what you do, don't ever forget that! There is a calling on your life, and the enemy is trying to make you think you're not worth God's time. The devil comes to kill, steal, and destroy us, but you don't have to let him, honey. You just don't! We are your family and we will get through this whole thing together, okay, sweetheart?" Pastor McKinney is visibly upset and still is not aware of the entire story.

"No, Daddy, all due respect, and I know that you all love me, but I have to do this one on my own. My mess, my decision!" Thelma says, looking down at the ground!

"Thelma, what are you talking about?" Mary says to Thelma, looking confused.

"I'm talking about moving away from home, Momma."

"Thelma…What do you mean, moving from us? What have we done to you that bad that you have to leave? You can't do this, what will you do with no support? You don't have a job or any-thing."

"Mom, STOP! It has nothing to do with you or Dad. Look, I have made up my mind, and I'm moving!"

"I strongly disagree with you moving out of the house."

"Daddy…I'm not just moving out of the house, I'm moving out of town!" Thelma becomes emotional.

"Now, Thelma, you just calm down. I will not let you go. You can't leave." Pastor grabs his chest and falls to the ground. Everyone screams.

"Daddy, Daddy," Thelma screams.
"Thelma, call 911!!"

Thelma runs outside screaming… "Help, help somebody help my dad, PLEASE!"

Thelma and Mary McKinney are frantic. Pastor McKinney is laying on the floor and not responding.

# Chapter 9

# *Love Hurts*

The family is at the hospital. The doctor tells the family that Pastor McKinney has suffered a massive heart attack and is in ICU. Things are not looking good for him! First Lady Mary is standing in the hallway waiting for church and family members to come. Thelma, Tonya, and Tim are all there as well.

Thelma walks over to the nurses' station. "Excuse me, I need to see my daddy, please."

The nurse looks down at her clipboard. "I'm sorry, what's your dad's name?"

"It's Greg McKinney."

The nurse looks in her book and replies. "I'm sorry, honey, you can't see him right now. Just take a seat and we will let you know when it will be a good time. I promise!"

Thelma walks away from the nurse, rubbing her hands together and worrying about her dad.

Mary McKinney walks over to Thelma, puts her hands upon her shoulders and messages them lightly as she tries to prevent her voice from cracking through the tears. "Thelma, no one can go in there. We have to wait until they get your father stable, ok?"

Thelma drops her head, asking her brother and sister to step outside with her. The siblings walk outside of the hospital.

"Hey guys, how are you two holding up?"

"I'm scared, Thelma. I don't want Daddy to die," TiTi replies.

"I know, TiTi. I know just how you feel. All we can do now is pray just the way Daddy has taught us, right?"

"Yes, I know," TiTi replies.

"Man, Thelma, I'm so glad you're back. We all were so worried about you. I have never prayed so hard in my life. We were worried, Sis." Word expresses himself to Thelma.

"Look at you, Word. Standing there looking just like Daddy. Wow, I mean, you look just like him. Especially today. Listen, you guys, I want to apologize for everything I've done. Being the oldest, I'm supposed to set an example for you, and I think that I failed you terribly and I'm sorry."

"No, Thelma, you haven't let us down," Word replies. "You are one of the most loving sisters I could ever have. Now what we're not going to do is allow the devil to come in and destroy us. John 10:10 says, 'The thief cometh not, but for to steal, and kill, and destroy: I am come that they might have life, and that they might have it more abundantly.' So, since we know what he is trying to do, we have to pray now more than ever, and allow the Lord to move in this situation. Daddy has raised us to be God-fearing, but also to have faith. And I have faith, that Daddy's going to be just fine. Amen?"

TiTi and Thelma both smile at Word, and reply, "Amen, Word."

74

Thelma looks at her sister and brother and smiles. She walks over to the bench outside the hospital door; looking like she has more to say to them. "Tonya, Tim, come here."

They both walk over to Thelma. "Oh Lord, she's calling us by our names. This must be serious," TiTi replies.

"Yes, I'm afraid there is something else I have to tell you both."

"What's wrong, Thelma?" TiTi replies. She sits down next to Thelma, and Word stands in front of both of them.

"I think I'm the cause of Daddy having the heart attack."

"What are you talking about?" they both reply to Thelma.

"Well... I was telling Daddy and Momma that I was moving away, when Daddy grabbed his chest! I'm so sorry, you guys. It seems I'm just a big ole mess up no matter how you look at it." Thelma starts to cry. "I keep having this dream about Daddy." Thelma's voice cracks as the tears began to roll down her face.

"Tell me about it, sis." Word tries to get Thelma to talk about the dream.

"Word, I really don't want to talk about it right now."

"Tell me, sis. I may be able to help you." Word stands, wanting to help his sister.

"Yea, Thelma, tell him. You know Word is good with dreams and the meaning of them."

Thelma thinks about it for a moment and then shakes her head. She opens her mouth and speaks slowly. "Well, in this dream,

Daddy is on one side of a road and I am on another side. There is traffic going both ways. I keep trying to get to him, but… Daddy keeps telling me to go on without him. Word, I seem so far away from him in this dream."

"Is that it, Sis?" Word asks Thelma as he looks in deep thought.

"Pretty much, in a nut shell." Thelma leans forward and grabs Word's arm.

"Word, what do you think it means?"

Word has a worried look in his eyes.

"Word, what's wrong?" TiTi replies.

Word looks at Thelma as if he wants to say something. "Nothing, Sis, nothing at all. Let's just stop for a moment and pray, okay, y'all?" Word grabs his sisters' hands and begins to pray. "Father God, in the name of Jesus, we come to you right now claiming the victory in this very situation. Lord, you said in your word, that you won't put more on us than we can bare. Lord, we trust you even right now, in the name of Jesus. Do it, Lord, for there is nothing impossible for you. Your word also says, that 'By your stripes we are healed,' so we claim healing today for our dad, in the name of Jesus, and we claim restoration and peace for our family. And, Lord, touch my sister, Thelma, right now, Lord. Let her know that in everything, there is a purpose and that you're in control of it all. We thank you, and we love you, Lord. In JESUS' name we pray. Thank God, AMEN!" Word continues to clap his hands and give God praise, then walks closer to his sisters and grabs them and hugs them.

"Wow, Word, that was a powerful prayer. I feel so much better," Thelma replies.

"Like I said earlier, Sis, you're the best big sister that we could ever have. Don't blame yourself for this happening, that's a lot to carry, ok? Always know that we got your back, and most of all... God does!" Word replies.

"Thanks, Word. I love you guys, group hug?" They all put their arms around each other and hug again.

Their cousin Bobby comes outside. "Hey, you guys, your Mom is looking for you. She says you can see your dad now."

"Okay, we're coming," they reply. They all hold hands and walk into the hospital. As they enter, there is a large crowd of people, including church folks, friends, and family.

"Man... look at all of these people here," Thelma says.

"Well, you know that Daddy is loved by everyone," TiTi replies.

Thelma walks over to Mother Thompson, one of the church Mothers. "Hi, Mother Thompson, have you seen our mom?"

"Yes, baby, she is in the room with your daddy at the moment. How are you holding up, baby?"

"I'm doing okay, ma'am."

"We're all praying for you and your father. You know GOD is a healer," Mother Thompson replies, patting Thelma's hand.

"Yes, ma'am." Thelma takes her brother and sister by their hands, and they walk towards the ICU area. Mother Thompson walks with them for support."

"I think Daddy is in room three." Tonya starts sobbing as she backs away from the others. "I'm scared. I don't want to see him like this."

"It will be alright, TiTi," Thelma replies. "NO, I can't. I just can't!"

Mother Thompson walks over to TiTi, placing her arm around her. TiTi lays her head on Mother Thompson and begins to cry. "It's okay, baby, it's alright." She rubs TiTi's back.

"Thelma, I'm going to take your sister out in the family room. And when she's ready to see him; I'll bring her back."

"Yes, ma'am." Mother Thompson walks down the hall with Tonya. Thelma and Tim walk into their dad's hospital room. Thelma sees her dad lying there with tubes attached everywhere and a very large one going down his throat. "Oh my God," Thelma says.

Thelma and Tim begin to cry.

"Daddy!" Thelma runs up to him and lays across him crying. "Daddy, I'm so sorry. Oh, Daddy, it's all my fault you're here."

Tim runs out of the room.

Their mom tries to console Thelma. "Thelma, none of this is your fault, honey." Mary places her arms around Thelma for support.

"Don't say that, Momma, it is my fault. You saw how I was acting. If I hadn't caused all of this trouble, then Daddy wouldn't be lying here fighting for his life. I'm so sorry, Momma. I'm sorry for everything!"

"I know you are, honey, and the thing is...we all make mistakes, okay? Now is not the time for anyone to blame anyone, now is the time..."

Thelma finishes her mom's sentence, "to pray, and thank God in advance."

"Amen, baby, and that's what we are going to do. We will thank God in advance for your Daddy's complete healing, right?"

"Yes, Momma," Thelma replied. "I better go and check on your brother and sister, okay, hun?"

"Yes, Momma."

Mary kisses Thelma on the forehead and says, "Be strong, baby." She kneels down to Pastor and kisses him. "I Love you, Greg, my dear heart. I'll be right back, you rest now!"

As her mom walks out of the room, Thelma stands beside her dad's bed. "Daddy?, It's Thelma, Daddy. Please wake up. I will do whatever it is you want me to do if you would just wake up. You're always singing that song 'Have a Little Talk with Jesus Makes it Right,' well, can you please talk to Jesus and tell him to let you wake up, Daddy?" She begins to cry. "I can't live without you, you're the only one who truly understands me. Please don't leave me, I'll just die, Daddy. I know I will!"

One of the nurses walks into the room. "Are you ok, sweetheart?"

"No, I'm not ok, I need him to wake up."

"I know, honey, but these things take time. I know it's against company rules, but...would you like me to pray with you, sweetie?" The nurse takes Thelma's hand, while looking at her. "Yes, Ma'am. I would."

"Okay, well, let's pray!" The nurse holds hands with Thelma and prays. "Dear Heavenly Father, we are asking you that you hear this prayer on behalf of this young lady concerning her dad. We are asking that you would send your healing power and for it to begin to move from the top of his head to the soles of his feet. We know that all things are in your hands. We say to you to let your will be done, in his life, Lord, in Jesus' name, Amen!"

The nurse turns toward Thelma, "Do you feel better, sweetie?"

"Yes, ma'am."

"Well, I'm glad you do." The nurse pats Thelma's hand and smiles as she walks away. "Be encouraged, little lady," she says while leaving the room.

"Well, Daddy, everyone is praying for you everywhere. People from all over are sending prayers your way and Pastor Stevenson says his whole congregation is praying for you, isn't that great? We all are!" Thelma lies across her dad's chest and sings, "I feel like going on, though trials come on every hand, I feel like going on."

# Chapter 10

# The Decision

It's Tuesday morning and the doctor is calling for a family meeting to talk over Pastor McKinney's condition.

"Thelma?"

"Yes, Momma."

"I'm heading back to the hospital to meet with the doctors about your father. Your Aunt Linda will be coming here at ten o'clock this morning to help you out with your brother and sister, okay?"

"Momma, what kind of meeting is it, is it bad?" Thelma asks. "Because I really want to come."

"No baby, I really need for you to stay here for your brother and sister. I will send someone to pick you all up later and bring you to the hospital, but right now isn't a good time!" Mary calls all three of her children together. "I really need to let you guys know how proud I know your father would be of you all."

Word gets upset at his mother and replies, "Momma, why are you talking like Daddy is dead? Why are you saying how proud Daddy would be, instead of how proud he is? Dad is not dead, Momma, he's not!" Word begins to walk the floor.

"Word, I know your dad is not dead. I didn't mean to upset you, honey. Listen, I am trying my best to hold my own self together, and I know this is difficult for us all, but God is going to take care of us!" Mary begins to break down crying a little.

"Momma, I'm sorry. I didn't mean to upset you." Word hugs his mother. "We will get through this, and yes, Word, your father IS very proud of you all, and he loves you very much! I'll be back later, and Thelma, don't forget that your Aunty is coming over, and your brother Mickey is trying to fly home.

"Ok, Momma," Thelma replies.

"I love you all, can Momma get a hug?" They all hug their mom, one by one. "I will see you all later."

"Bye, Momma." TiTi turns to Word, upset that Word got upset with their mom. "Man, Tim, why you have to go off on Momma like that, as if she don't already have enough pressure on her?"

Word gets upset with TiTi. "Shut up, TiTi."

"No, you shut up, Tim." Thelma steps in, to calm her siblings down.

"Both of you, stop it, and I mean NOW! We are all worried about Daddy and under a lot of pressure, but you heard Momma, God will take care of us all." A sharp pain rushes over her stomach and Thelma bends over in pain, "OUCH!"

"What's wrong, Thelma?" TiTi ask Thelma, with her hand across Thelma's back.

"I'm fine, Tonya. Just a little pain, that's all, I'll be just fine! You guys get your chores done and I will fix you something to eat."

"We thought that's what Aunty is coming for?" Word replies to Thelma.

"Just do as you're told, I don't have time for all of this jibber-jabber."

There's a knock at the door. Thelma goes to answer it. It's Johnny, the father of Thelma's baby. "Um, what are you doing here?" Thelma is standing at the front door, holding it slightly cracked.

"I heard what happened to your father. I also know what went down between you and my parents. I just wanted to see if you're okay."

"I'm fine and you can't be just coming over here whenever you want."

"Listen, Thelma, you don't have to be rude. Can I come in?"

"No, you cannot come in. My little brother and sister are here and my Aunt is on her way. You have to leave!"

"Thelma, why are you being so mean to me?" Thelma is standing in front of Johnny, trying to keep him from entering the house. "Look, Johnny, I'm sorry, I have a lot on my mind right now and…"

Johnny interrupts her. "And what, Thelma, you don't have time for the likes of me? Is that what you want to say?"

Thelma puts her hands on her hips. "Take it like you want it. My dad is very sick, and I'm dealing with all of this other mess around this town. That's why as soon as my dad gets better, I'm taking my baby and I'm…" Thelma catches herself.

"And you're what, Thelma? Finish what you were going to say."

"I'm leaving this town! Now there, is that what you wanted to hear?"

"No, that's not what I wanted to hear, but that's what you said! Wow, really, Thelma? So, when was I going to find this news out?"

"Why? I don't owe anything to you, Johnny. It's not like we're together or anything."

"You're right, we're not together, but you're carrying my child. And because of that, you owe me that much!"

"Why you acting like you even care, Johnny? You have never cared before, you've known that I was pregnant for a month now, and all of a sudden, you want to play daddy of the year? I don't think so. I don't need you, I just want to be left alone." Thelma begins to close the door a little more. "I'm only concerned about my daddy getting well, and then I'll be gone so fast it's going to make everybody's head swing!"

"Why are you being this way with me, Thelma? You are evil. I haven't done anything to you for you to treat me like this."

"Oh, you haven't, Johnny? Well, since you don't believe you've done anything wrong, how about I heard that you were down at the camp house talking about me to Tracy, Martin, and Shari? Saying that I'm nothing and I'm never going to be anything. I shared with you the letter that I found, thinking you were my friend and I could trust you...now you have everybody walking around talking about me, talking about I'm adopted and I'm probably more like my real mother because everyone else in my family isn't crazy like I am! What do you have to say about that, Johnny, huh? What's wrong? Cat got your tongue?"

"I'm sorry, Thelma, I never meant to hurt you."

Thelma gets really angry and begins to yell at him. "JUST LEAVE, NOW!"

"Thelma, I."

"GO, JOHNNY!"

Word and TiTi runs down the steps, startled by Thelma yelling.

"What's going on?" Word asks, looking from Thelma to Johnny.

"Nothing at all, Word. I'm just taking the trash out," Thelma said, looking at Johnny and rolling her eyes,"

"Oh, now I'm trash, Thelma?"

"JOHNNY, LEAVE!" Thelma demands again.

Word gets upset and defends his sister. "Say, man, didn't you hear what my sister said?" Tim walks up to Johnny, staring at him.

"I heard her, but you better get out of my face or…"

"Or what?"

"Thelma, you better get your little brother before he gets hurt."

"I wish you would put your hands on my brother. You have totally lost your mind." Thelma is yelling at Johnny, and walking up on him.

"Thelma, I got it handled, sis." Word gets closer to Johnny, right in his face and says, "You are going to leave this house like my sister asked you to, or get thrown out."

Johnny looks at Thelma, and replies, "Fine, this is how you really want things, huh, Thelma?"

Thelma turns her back to Johnny.

"Oh okay, all I know is, you better not leave town with my baby without me knowing!" Word closes the door in Johnny's face, totally missing the last part of his comment due to the high emotion of the situation.

"You alright, sis?" Word hugs his sister with great concern.

"Yea, I am, thank you, little brother, trying to act all tough!"

"I am tough, but really, sis, you're really going to move away from us?" Word said, sitting down on the family room couch, shaking his head.

"Word, please don't say it like that, I'm not leaving you guys. We will always be together. You're my brother and my going away will never change our relationships we have for each other. And just think of it this way, you could always come and visit me."

"Visit you where? Do you even know where you are going? You need to be with your family, so we can look out for you."

"Aww, thanks, Word. Look at my little brother trying to grow up." She grabs Tim's face, smooshing it together with her hands.

"Stop it, Thelma, I'm serious. You don't have a job or anything; how will you make it or survive?"

"Like Daddy always says, 'God will take care of his own.'"

"I know, Thelma, but God also helps those who help themselves, and who makes wise decisions."

Thelma looks at her brother, with a proud look. "Wow, Word... you have really grown up, and it warms my heart to know how much you care for me."

"Of course I do."

Tonya comes in the room, clearing her throat. "Enough of all the mushy stuff Aunty is here, and I'm starving!"

Back at the hospital, Mary waits in the Family Room with Pastor McKinney's brother, Thomas; Mary's mother, Linda; and two of the deacons from the church. They are all sitting and waiting for the doctor to come to discuss Pastor McKinney's condition and options.

The doctor enters the room. "Good morning, folks."

"Good morning, Doctor," everyone responds.

"Is everyone here so we can start?"

"Yes, Doctor, this will be all," Mary McKinney replies.

"OK, if everyone is here. Mrs. McKinney, your husband has suffered a massive heart attack, and I believe he is suffering from coronary artery disease, also called coronary heart disease."

"Doctor, what does all this mean?" asks Mary McKinney.

"Well, Mrs. McKinney it is simply a result of plaque building in the arteries, which blocks blood flow and heightens the risk for heart attack or stroke. In your husband's case, he suffered a heart attack."

"Oh God." Mary leans up closer to the edge of her seat. "Doctor, what can we do to make him better?"

"I would suggest coronary bypass surgery. It would be the best move to take for his situation. The good news is, it's a procedure that restores blood flow to your heart muscle by diverting the flow of blood around a section of a blocked artery in the heart."

"If his artery is already bad, how can you fix it?" Mary McKinney replies.

"Good question, Mrs. McKinney, we can take a blood vessel from the leg, arm, chest, or abdomen and connect it to the other arteries in his heart, so that the blood is bypassed around the diseased blocked area. We have been very successful doing this procedure in the past; we will just have to see how he responds to everything."

Thomas, the pastor's brother says, "Can you explain why my brother isn't responding or waking up?"

"Actually, I can't. Right now, we are in a waiting period. Your brother has suffered a massive heart attack and sometimes the body just needs to recuperate from the trauma. I will let you all talk things over and we will check back with you for your decision."

"Thank you, Doctor!" Thomas is standing next to Mary. As the doctor leaves the room, Mary breaks down in tears again.

"It will all work out, Mary," Thomas assures her.

"I know it will, Thomas. I just feel so helpless because I can't help him."

"You can pray for him, honey?" Mary's mother says. "After all, remember prayer changes things."

"Thanks, everyone, for coming here with me. The support really made it all a little better. I don't know if I could have taken that all in by myself!"

"We will always be here for you," Thomas replies. "I would like to go and spend some time with Pastor in case he wakes up, I need to be there."

"Mary, honey, have you had any rest, anything to eat?" Mary's mother asks.

"No, Momma, but I'm fine."

"Listen, honey, if you don't take care of yourself, you will be no good for anyone else. Go and get you something to eat."

Thomas steps in and says, "I'll go down to the cafeteria and get you some food, Mary."

"I'm really not hungry, but I'll try," Mary replies.

"And that's all we can ask you to do."

"Oh, Thomas, after you step in and see Pastor, could you go and pick up the children from the house? I promised them they could come and see their dad."

"Of course, I will!"

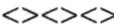

A few days have gone by and the family has decided to go ahead with the surgery. Prayers are coming from everywhere and the family is overwhelmed with the love and support they feel.

Mary is visiting Pastor in the hospital, standing by his bed and praying over him. "Father God, I don't know what's going on or why you are doing this, but I pray it is all going to be for your glory. As Greg lays on that bed, Lord touch his mind and his heart both in reality and with your word. Let his blood begin flowing the way it should, Father God. Be his healer, his provider, and his redeemer. Lord I come against all the enemy is doing to try to break my family up. I stand against death, hatred, anger, rage, and sadness. I stand against division and poor health. Father God, heal my husband. Heal Greg today. He is your son Lord...your son. Don't take him yet, Daddy. Don't let him leave this world. Father let him wake up soon and let him be healed to better than he was when he came into this place, that he may be able to be a living testimony of your saving grace and healing power. In the name, of Jesus, I pray and trust you will all my heart, mind, body, and soul to answer these prayers of your daughter Lord, Amen."

As she opens her eyes, she looks down and realizes that while she was praying, Greg's eyes had opened and he was staring at her with tears streaming down his cheeks. They see one another for the first time in too long and Mary's eyes flood with tears. She bends down and hugs him tightly and he winces. "I'm so sorry, honey. Oh Jesus! Hallelujah!!!" She begins dancing around the room and praising the Lord. Suddenly she realizes she needs to get the nurse in to the room. She peeks her head out of the room toward the nurses' station, "NURSE! Nurse, come in here! My husband has opened his eyes. Glory hallelujah! Lord, you are so worthy," Mary shouts with excitement.

The kids hear their mother's shouts from the Family Room. As they come running in their dad's room, praising God for his healing power, the doctor and nurse walk in.

"Well, hello, Mr. McKinney," the doctor says with a big smile across his face, as if he is witnessing a miracle. "Did you have a nice long nap?" He pauses as Greg tries to respond. "It okay Mr. McKinney. Squeeze my hand one time for yes and twice for no, okay?"

Pastor squeezed one time. "Very good. How are you feeling, do you know where you are?" Pastor squeezed his hand one time.

"Oh, honey, you had us all so scared," Mary says.

Pastor tries to point to the respirator he has on. "I know, Mr. McKinney," says the doctor. "I'm sure that's very uncomfortable for you, but we must leave it in until further notice." Pastor squeezes the doctor's hand one time to confirm he understands.

Thelma goes out in the waiting room to notify everyone that Pastor has opened his eyes. The doctor and Mrs. McKinney stayed to talk with the Pastor and inform him that he has to be prepared for bypass surgery, and how important it is that it's done! The doctor turns to Mary McKinney. "Ma'am, I will leave you alone with your husband for a few minutes before they come to take him to surgery, okay?"

"Yes, I would really appreciate that," replied Mary. "Thank you, Doctor!" Mary takes Pastor McKinney's hand. "Hey, dear heart, I'm so glad that you're awake. Heaven only knows how much I've missed you, we all have. The good Lord must have heard my cry, because living without you is not an option for me. I can't even imagine it! Do you understand that since you woke up they can now do surgery and so they have to take you right now to do it?" Pastor squeezes her hand one time. "Oh, honey, I love you so much and I'm so sorry about everything. When you get out of here, it's going to be vegetables and smoothies for you!" Mary says, smiling at him.

Pastor squeezes her hand twice for no, and Mary squeezes his hand one time for yes. She laughs as she lays her head on his chest. The nurse knocks on the door.

"It's time," the nurse says. "Wait one moment. I need to go and get my family so we can pray," Mary says. "Okay, Mrs. McKinney. Why don't you stay with your husband and let me go and get your family?"

"Thank you so much," Mary replies. She turns to look at Pastor, "Well, honey, I know that God is going to really perform a miracle, and you're coming out of surgery a brand new man. I love you, honey, and everything is going to be alright!"

Thelma, TiTi, and Word along with Bishop Taylor walks in the room.

"Look, honey, it's the kids. And Bishop Taylor flew in all the way from Tampa, Florida to see about you." Pastor tries to lift his hand up but TiTi stops him.

"Hey, Daddy," she says. "Don't try to move…just lie still and let us come to you!"

Bishop Taylor walks over to Pastor McKinney. "Hey Greg, I'm here, and I've got a feeling, that everything's going to be alright. Let's all lift our hearts towards heaven." Bishop begins to pray for Pastor McKinney. After he prays, the nurse lets everyone know it's time to go so Pastor can be prepped and brought into surgery. Everyone goes up to the pastor and hugs him.

"We love you, Daddy," Thelma says, holding back her tears.

"And so do I, honey, and we will all be here waiting for you when you come out." Mary reminds him as she gently kisses his forehead and holds his hand. Pastor squeezes once and Mary tells the nurse that he is ready.

"We will take great care of him, Mrs. McKinney," the nurse says.

"Yes, please do. After all, he's all that I have!"

The Bishop, Mary, and the kids head down toward the family and friends waiting in the hallway and waiting room to share what is going on. After they deliver the news, they head into the Family Room. After an hour, Thelma walks over to her mom.

"Momma, can I speak with you outside?"

"Sure, baby. What's on your mind, sweetheart?"

"Momma, after this is all over, I'm in need of some really sound advice."

"About?" Mary asks Thelma.

"About my situation." Thelma is fanning her face because of the heat.

"Your situation? Thelma, I really don't think it's time to talk about your situation."

"I didn't say now, Momma."

"Thelma, I think your situation has caused enough—" Mary stops herself from finishing her sentence.

"Caused enough what, Mom? Enough trouble, is that what you wanted to say?"

"Now, Thelma, what I mean is—"

"Never mind, Mom, I know exactly what you mean. Just forget it." Thelma walks away.

"Now, Thelma, wait a minute." Mary reaches out to grab Thelma's arm but Thelma pulls away.

# Chapter 11

## The Confrontation

Two weeks after Pastor McKinney's surgery, he is doing very well recovering. Things with his health are progressing well and he is praising God for sparing him from going to the other side prior to resolving things with his family. Things will Thelma, however, continue to get worse. The rumor has gotten out about her pregnancy and she has been doing everything in her power to keep the rumors as well as pressure off of her family, especially her dad!

After the youth picnic, Sister Ramsey approaches. "Excuse me, Thelma, may I have a word with you?"

"Yes, Sister Ramsey?" Thelma says nervously, seeing the older woman's body language.

"Look, Thelma, I don't know quite how to put this, but you are destroying everyone's lives around here. My son didn't have to tell me anything, but the entire town sure did! What is your problem? Running around here portraying to be this nice little preacher's daughter while all the while acting and carrying yourself like a slut! I'm very ashamed of your actions and to drag my son into this just really did it for me. The whole town is talking about you and your poor parents. I know what I'm saying to you sounds cruel, but I think if someone would have taken the time and showed you how to act in the first place, most of this wouldn't have happened! But after all, you are probably acting like your real momma did, huh? Well, chile what do you have to say for yourself?"

Thelma fights back her anger and speaks very purposefully. "What I have to say is that you have a lot of nerves talking to me this way, Sister Ramsey. And to think, I've always looked up to you. I am not the only one involved in this, Sister Ramsey. Your son is not perfect either. I know I've made some mistakes, but my daddy says that we will work this all out! And you're in church testifying about God's mercy and his grace, but you talk to me as if I'm dirt on the floor and I don't know God—"

"The way you're acting, Thelma, I'm not sure that you do!"

Feeling her blood pressure raising and the heat in her face getting hotter, Thelma replies, "He who is without sin, cast the first stone, and how dare you talk about my real mother, who are you to judge me? I may have done some things wrong, Sister Ramsey, but what I'm proud of the most is that I still have a chance in life. A chance not to judge people and a chance to help someone when they are going through something they can't help. Unlike you, I will not beat them up while they're already down! I'm not going to disrespect you, Sister Ramsey. No… instead I'm going to carry myself like the young lady my daddy raised me to be. Furthermore, I will pray that God has mercy on your soul. And I'm asking God to make me a better Christian than what you have demonstrated with me today!"

"Thelma, if I had a violin, I would play it for your speech you just gave me. The truth is, your father is a great man of God and will try to do whatever he can to make anything right. You shouldn't have allowed any of this to happen."

"I'm not just anything, I'm his daughter!" Thelma's eyes well up with tears out of anger.

"You are trying to be disrespectful, young lady, but you need to get rid of that baby before the word travels out of state and your father's whole reputation that he's worked so very hard for is destroyed. Take it in consideration of my family, too. My son is not ready to be a father to your baby, or to any baby!"

Thelma looks at Sister Ramsey, and begins to walk away.

"Oh, and Thelma, before you leave, I wouldn't mention our little conversation to your dad. He can't take any more pressure on his heart, but I'm sure that you know this already!"

"As for your son not being ready to be a father to any baby, he should have thought of that before he slept with me. Maybe you should be talking to your son the way you have spoken to me. But I wouldn't expect any of those stones in your hand to be available for your own blood. As for me Sister Ramsey, I am going to be okay. What you and Johnny do is up to you, but this baby is not going to be thrown out like trash. Your son's sin will be just as visible as mine is and I pray Sister Ramsey that the fine church folk of this town who have been acting like I did this to myself will be kinder to him than they have been for me." Thelma start to walks away again but stops to look back at Sister Ramsey. "And about telling my father about this conversation... go to hell."

Thelma can't shake the feelings that rise up within her after the conversation. The next few weeks are a tragic mix of depression, anger, and wondering where God is. She begins to contemplate whether Sister Ramsey was right in what she said. After many prayers that felt like God was nowhere to be found, she considers terminating the pregnancy so no one will get hurt anymore. If she terminated the pregnancy, others would look like liars and her secret would remain between Sister Ramsey, Johnny, and her family. But the more she thought about that, the more she was convicted that no daughter of God would be able to live with a secret like that for the rest of her life. It seemed the only thing to do would be to leave town and hopefully not kill her father in the process. In a moment of desperation one evening, she cried out to God in prayer.

"My Lord, I can't get Sister Ramsey's words out of my head. Why aren't you answering my prayers? Why have you left me? Is she right? I've been trying to pretend as if things are normal, and they are not! I now know that the mother that I've always known as my momma is really not my momma. I've made a mess of my life running off an' getting pregnant, letting my siblings down, breaking Momma's and Daddy's hearts. God, how in the world can I teach my siblings anything, especially my baby sister TiTi? Oh, God, I have messed my life up, but I refuse to cause my family any more damage. Sister Ramsey is right, Daddy couldn't take any more from me. I am hurting him and have broken him with the pain of knowing his baby girl isn't perfect. And as soon as he's well enough to get out of the house, the people are going to start talking more, and he will be totally humiliated! Dear God, I've got to leave. Everybody will be a lot better without me. I know they will! And Lord, please forgive me, I know I've let you down the most. I'm really a good person and I have a kind heart. I never meant to do any of this! I take full responsibility for my actions. Please stay with me, Lord, because I'm really scared. I need you Lord and I know to KNOW that you are with me. I hope that you won't leave me, too!"

After praying she sits on her bed, still feeling absolutely empty inside. She breaks into tears, convinced that God has left her and she is alone.

# Chapter 12

## Walking Alone

Monday night while TiTi is in her room going over last minute homework and Word is reading his Bible, Thelma decides to talk with her parents, who are getting ready for bed. She knocks on their bedroom door.

"Come in," Mary says.

"Hi, Momma. Hi, Daddy."

"Hey, baby, what's going on?" Pastor McKinney replies. "We thought you had turned in for bed already, baby."

"No, I'm still up," Thelma replies. "Are you ok, baby?" Pastor raises up from laying down, seeming concerned for Thelma.

"Yes, Daddy, I'm fine. But it's not about me, how are you feeling, Daddy?"

"Oh, sugar I'm doing just fine. God has certainly been good to me," Pastor says, putting his glasses on.

"Amen, Daddy."

Thelma thanks the Lord quietly for healing her dad. She smiles at her father, the man who always has her back no matter what - her hero, her everything. She wonders to herself how she would make it without him, he is her strength and uses his determination to hold her up when she is weak. She looks over at her mom, who is brushing her hair while looking in the mirror. Thelma reflects on her mother's elegance and how the fragrance she wore always smelled of soft flowers. She feels very proud that her mother loved her even though they had those rough times. The love her mother gave her was beyond those arguments even if she did feel overlooked at times. It didn't matter because she still loved her. She has taught her to always carry herself as a lady, to always look at the bigger picture of things, and to always give second chances. As Thelma looks at them, her eyes fill with tears and she heads toward the door quickly.

Her mom puts her brush down and turns around, "Thelma, stop baby. You looked like you wanted to say something to us. What's going on sweet girl?"

"No, not really, Momma. I just wanted to say good night and see you. That's all."

"Well, we love you, too!"

Thelma leaves her parents' bedroom thinking that it feels like everyone has forgotten she is pregnant ever since her father had his heart attack. That could be a good thing since she wasn't showing yet, but it was weird how it wasn't talked about or questioned. As she walks down the hall, she hears TiTi coming out of the bathroom singing. She driers her eyes so Titi won't see her tears.

"TiTi, please save the world and stop singing."

"Shut up, Thelma," TiTi says with a giggle.

"No, sis, you sound great. Why don't you ever want to sing at church?" Thelma asks, following TiTi to her bedroom.

"T, you know I'm the next Aretha Franklin, but I ain't singing at church."

"You can sing, but going as far as saying Aretha Franklin is taking it to a whole 'nother level. You know there is only one queen of soul," Thelma replies smiling at TiTi.

"Tonya, come sit and talk to your big sister for a minute." Thelma crawls into TiTi's bed and grabs a pillow. TiTi follows and grabs another pillow. Something they have always done growing up.

"Okay, is everything okay?" TiTi asked.

"Sure it is, and why are you always asking is everything okay? Besides, is it okay for me to talk to my own sister?" Thelma says, grabbing a hair brush from the corner of TiTi's end table. She reaches over and removes the rubber band from TiTi's hair and begins brushing it.

"Yes, it is, but you seem sad to me. Plus, you called me Tonya, and you only call me by my name when it's something serious."

"No, TiTi I'm okay, as long as you're with me," Thelma replies.

"And I'm okay, as long as you're with me, too," TiTi replies back.

"I love you, Tonya, you will always be my little brown baby doll."

"Okay, you're getting too mushy for me, Thelma. I love you, too, but, what's going on?"

"Everything is really good, don't worry about anything, TiTi. Everything is going to be alright."

"Thanks for brushing my hair, sis. It feels much better," TiTi replies.

"Good night, girl, and you're welcome. Get some rest."

Thelma walks away from TiTi's room and gently pulls the door shut behind her, realizing that she is slowly telling her family goodbye. She begins to walk towards Word's room, wondering if she is making a mistake by leaving her family? *Will I make things worse or better for my Dad? Lord, please help me to do the right thing, this hurts so bad!* Thelma approaches Word's room and knocks lightly before pushing the door open.

There sat Word, the little preacher, reading his Bible just like their dad. "Hey, boy."

"Hey, Thelma, what are you doing up?"

"Who me? I'm grown, now the question is, what you doing up?"

"Reading my Bible," Word says, looking down at his Bible."

"I can see that. You look like Daddy sitting there! Listen, Word, I just wanted to come and tell you how proud of you I am, and that you have always been one of my best friends."

"I feel the same way, sis...but where is this all coming from?"

"Oh, I just wanted you to know it," Thelma says, turning her head really quick towards the wall, so Word couldn't see her tear up.

"Thanks, Thelma, that makes me feel good," Word says, reaching for his glass of water on the table.

"What are you reading, Word?"

"I'm reading about Moses, and how when God told Moses that he had called him and that he was chosen. How Moses doubted his capability because he had a stuttering problem. God reassured him that if Moses would go and do his work, he would speak for him; all he had to do was just believe in him! Man, Thelma, I think that's what God is saying to us with our situations. No matter how bad it may get, or what people may think of us, God will step in on our behalf because this battle is not ours, it's the Lord's!" Word looks over his glasses at Thelma, who is smiling.

"Wow Tim, that was deep."

"I'm not trying to be deep, sis, only speaking the truth; and God's word is the truth."

"Yes, it is, Tim. Yes, it is!" And at the moment, Thelma knew that God was speaking to her, through her baby brother. All she could do was cry and lay her head on her little brother's shoulder, and for one moment, she felt as if God did care!

"Tim, will you pray for me?"

"Yes, Thelma, I will pray for you. Anything specific? And why are you crying, what's really going on with you, Thelma? You only call me Tim, if something's wrong."

"Just a lot with Daddy and all." Thelma would try to cover her problems from her siblings, because it was always her job to take care of them, not them of her; but at that moment, it felt good to spiritually let her guard down and watch God use her little brother, her baby.

She bowed her head. While Word prayed, the God that Thelma has been taught about all of her life was in the room with them. She felt his presence at that very moment. She felt and knew God was saying to her that he would carry her through. "Thank you, Word. You are your father's son, I love you so much."

"I love you too, Thelma."

"I better go and let you get some rest." Thelma rubs Word across his chin.

"Yes, you know I have to get my beauty rest for all of the ladies."

"Oh Lord, boy," Thelma replies while laughing.

"Oh Thelma, you know that Mickey will be here on Thursday morning."

"What? I thought he didn't have any more leave?"

"Well, he worked something out with the military because of Daddy's illness, but Momma said he will only be here for one week."

Thelma walks out of her brothers room conflicted. *I can't leave tonight if Mickey is coming. I need to see him. He would be heartbroken to know I knew he was coming and still left before seeing him. Why is*

*God making it so hard to leave? I am the problem and my job is to limit my family's problems so that means I need to leave so they can be freed.*

Thelma lay in bed that night crying, thinking, and wondering why God had come so powerfully during Word's prayer only to then drop the bomb on her that Mickey was coming. She needed to leave, because terminating her baby's life wasn't an option. That much she knew from the last few days of prayer and tears. She decided she needed to write her dad a letter. He would be so heartbroken if she left without saying anything.

> *Dear Daddy,*
>
> *I'm so sorry that I couldn't say this in person, but I was afraid to. I'm really sorry for all of the trouble I've caused you and Momma. You didn't raise me to be like this. I don't know what happened. I want to make it right, and the only way I can think of is leaving. Please know that I didn't want to leave you, I just don't want to let you down anymore, Daddy. It seems like lately, everything I touch or do, I mess up! So for now, I'm leaving and going to New York City. I have a little money saved and I'm going to stay with Gloria. I will be okay! I love you so much, and please tell Momma that I love her, too.*
>
> *You are both wonderful parents. I will remember what you taught me and will carry my Bible everywhere I go. I promise Daddy. The 23rd Psalms will be my guide. Please forgive me for hurting you by leaving, but I'll be back one day! Until I see you again, your little girl forever. Thelma!*

After completing the letter, Thelma continues to ponder her situation. *Man, I am so confused about myself, my Grandma used to always say,* "If you don't know what to do in a situation, be still and wait on God." *I want to wait on him, but I don't feel like God wants to help me right now, I know that sounds silly and it's probably the devil telling me this, but it's how I feel at the moment, and the weird thing is for the first time, my biological mother has crossed my mind. I wonder if I am the way that I am because of her? Did I get pregnant because I'm cursed with her generational curse? And will I ever know who she is? I am angry at myself for even one second, allowing her to enter my mind, that woman has lost all privileges to have any space, thoughts or anything concerning me. I hate her!*

At that moment, she caught a surge of adrenaline and rose up off the bed. Thinking about her biological mother made her angrier. With that rush of energy, she took the little bit of money she had saved up, grabbed the bags she packed the night before and left. Thelma went downstairs and out the back door quietly, and ran as fast as she could! She left the home that she was secure in, her dad's church that she loved, and her family that she needed so very badly! Thelma wasn't sure of her decision, but for some reason, her feet wouldn't stop moving, and she couldn't look back. It's dark and very cold out, and Thelma misses her dad and family already. Thelma goes down to the church to gather her thoughts. It is two o'clock in the morning.

"I sure hope that emergency key is still under the broken freezer in the back," Thelma speaks aloud to herself. "Oh, Lord, please let it be there. I really need to sit down, I'm not feeling so good."

Thelma takes her hand and feels under the freezer. "YES!" Thelma says with joy. "Thank you, Lord."

She opens the door to the kitchen of the church. "Well, Lord, I'm here and I'm so tired. I wish I could rest my eyes, but I can't stay for long." Thelma hears a sound like feet walking. "Who's there?"

"Thelma, it's me." TiTi had followed Thelma down to the church.

106

"Oh my gosh, TiTi?" Thelma runs and hugs her sister. She's happy to see her. "What are you doing here?"

"I should be asking you the same thing, why are you trying to leave me?"

"How do you know what I'm doing, TiTi?"
"I'm not stupid, nor am I dumb, all of that 'I love you, TiTi, you're always going to be my pretty little brown baby doll,' told on you!" TiTi replied.

"I am so sorry, Sis, I have to go."

"But why, Thelma? I don't understand."

"I know, and there will be lots of things in life you won't understand. I really don't understand why these things are taking place right now in my life either, but I have to do what I think is best, Sis. I'm never going to leave you, Tonya. But right now I need to go away to make things right, just for a little while, okay?"

"But where will you live, Thelma? Who will take care of you and the baby?" TiTi says wiping her eyes.

"I have to believe that God will, just like he will take care of you while I'm gone. And your big sister does have about three hundred and ten dollars saved up from my allowance, and helping Ms. Chiles with her laundry from time to time. It will be enough to take the train, and to maybe carry me for a short while. I would love to go to a place like New York City; somewhere brand new. Plus, Gloria moved there with her pops and says I can visit anytime, she loves it there. I spoke to her last month, and I think I'll visit there; although that will be a long train ride. See, I have her number and address right here." Thelma pulls the paper out of her purse that has Gloria's phone number and address written on it. TiTi looks skeptical.

"So is that where you are going?"

"I think so, TiTi, and at least I'll be with family.

TiTi begins to cry, begging her sister to stay. "Thelma, is there any way I can change your mind?"

"No, TiTi, I'm afraid not, but what you can do for me is tell Momma and Daddy that I'll be okay, and I'll just be away for a little while. Will you do that for me?" Thelma grabs TiTi hands facing her.

"Of course, I will. I'll do anything for you, sis," TiTi replies, looking at Thelma with tears in her eyes.

"Now, I'm counting on you to make me proud, and I promise when I get settled, I will make you proud, too, OK?"

Thelma is trying her best to hold back her tears. "Oh, TiTi, give me a hug." Thelma breaks down and starts to cry, hugging her little sister. "Now you get home, so I won't worry about you, okay?"

"I just really don't want to leave you, Thelma. I'm going to miss you terribly."

"I'm going to miss you even more. I will be fine, TiTi, I promise you. Go home right now."

"I love you, Thelma."

"And I love you, too!" The sisters hug each other and TiTi is overcome with sadness as she leaves the church.

Thelma watches her walk away. "Lord, this has to be one of the hardest things I've ever had to do. That little girl is my heart, and I will miss her! God, it's me and you, please direct my path and tell me what to do next!" Thelma leaves her father's church and heads towards the train station, which is approximately three miles away. Thelma buys a ticket to New York City.

Thelma's train leaves at 5 am and she is exhausted. As Thelma sits on the train, she is deep in thought. *God, I can't believe that I'm on this train. I've made a move that I never dreamed I would. My family that I love so much I left behind me, shoot who am I fooling? My family that I need, for heaven's sake. My momma still buys my bras for me. I couldn't even say what size I wear, I've never had to do any of those things for myself. But I just couldn't bring any more shame upon them. Thelma looked around, noticing the weird looking people on the train. The smell was very damp and old. Thelma had only been gone a short time and she's homesick already. Lord, I hate to admit it, but I think I made a mistake.*

She continues to pray as she looks around at the other passengers. Older folks who were probably just on their way to visit family. She wonders if anyone realizes she is running from something instead of to someone.

As the days continue on, she realizes she is traveling through states she has never been to. The driver stops and announces, "We have fifteen minutes until we proceed to leave again." *I have to really use the restroom, but I don't know these people. My daddy would have a fit if he knew that I was out here in No-Man's land. Boy, am I sorry I did this. I think we are a day away from New York, and I'm very nervous about this, but I'm praying that things will work out for me. I just need a break!*

The next day, Thelma awakes and could see the dreary weather. There was a lot of concrete everywhere, she hardly saw any dirt roads or grass. They finally arrived in the city. She couldn't contain her excitement as she looked out the window. A smile filled her face and for the first time since leaving the only home she'd ever known, Thelma felt a sense of peace.

# Chapter 13

# The Arrival

Thelma arrives in New York and jumps in a cab so she can reach Gloria's before changing her mind and taking the next train back home. As she rides in the cab, she takes in her surroundings. Nothing looks familiar to her. The city is bigger and it doesn't feel like home. Thelma realizes she is homesick and wants her dad. Though it is ten in the morning there, but she isn't sure what time it was at home. *I wonder what Momma cooked this morning, Thelma thought as her mind drifted back to her family. Oh my, Momma sure makes the best biscuits and those fresh eggs straight from Mr. Martin's farm are so good. I wonder what TiTi and Word are doing, too. Oh my Lord, I hope that I can make it for more than a week away from my family! God, please give me the strength to do this. I have never been away from them and other than spending the night over Lana's house.* The cab driver interrupts her thoughts and alerts her of her arrival.

"Is this 19200 Elsa Road?"

"Why yes, it is, little Miss Lady. It's that white house right there," the cab driver replies, pointing to a rather lavish looking home.

"Wow, my friend didn't tell me how big her home is!"

"You talk like you're not from here," the cab driver says.

"That's because I'm not from here, I'm from Pine Bluff, Arkansas." Thelma replies, smiling.

"Well, isn't that something! Now why would a young and very pretty girl like yourself come all this way just to visit a friend?" the driver says in a flirtatious way.

"Please, stop with all of the compliments, and I'm not exactly visiting. I've moved here." Thelma turns towards the window.

"I'm sorry if I've upset you," the driver says.

"I'm fine, and I apologize if I seem rude. I just have a lot on my mind." Thelma looks at the houses in the neighborhood while sitting in the cab.

"No need to apologize, it's cool! Well, welcome to New York City."

"Thank you, umm…" Thelma puts her hand out to shake the drivers hand.

"My name is Michael, and your name is?" Michael shakes Thelma's hand back.

"Oh yes, I'm Thelma. Thelma McKinney."

"Well, let me help you with those bags, Thelma McKinney," the driver replies with a huge smile.

"Oh, no, I don't need any help, I can do it."

"I really don't mind at all, Thelma. Let me help you."

"Thank you, Michael." Thelma smiles.

Thelma watched this young, very strong, man help her get her bags. He was quite cute, too, and didn't look much older than she was. "I sure hope that they are home," Thelma says.

"I'm not sure they are. Mr. Williams is a very high paid attorney and his daughter Gloria works for his firm," Michael replies.

"Wait a minute, you know Gloria?" Yes, I sure do. Gloria's friend Terry is my friend and sometimes we all hang out together."

"Cool, Michael. Well, maybe I'll see you around then," Thelma says, checking Michael out as he walks down the steps.

"I'm sure you will," Michael replies winking his eye.

"Well, let me see if they're home," Thelma says, knocking on the door.

A little old woman came to the door. "Hello, may I help you?"

"Yes, ma'am, is Gloria home?"

"No, she isn't. Did you call first before you came over here?" the little old sweet lady asked.

"No, ma'am, I did not. I'm here from out of town; Pine Bluff, Arkansas," Thelma explains.

"You wouldn't happen to be Thelma McKinney would you?" When the old woman said Thelma's name it felt like heaven to her, it felt like she wasn't so alone; that someone actually knew her in this very strange place. This little old lady was the prettiest little woman Thelma had ever seen, she had texture in her voice as if she was black but she looked very white. All-in-all she had the kindest smile. It felt as if she had met her before. "Why yes, ma'am, I am."

"Well, come on in here, sweetheart. I feel like I know you already," the old lady replied.

"Gloria talks about you all of the time. Oh, I'm sorry, where are my manners. I'm Ms. Shepard, but you can call me Grandma Shepard or Granny. I'm Gloria's grandmother."

"Pleased to meet you, ma'am," Thelma replies with the biggest smile on her face.

"Pleased to meet you, too. Why come over here and give me a hug, honey. You look like you need one," the old woman said.

Thelma was so happy when she said that, she walked over to her and hugged her; it was like hugging her Nana when she was alive. And oh, she smelled so good, like perfume and baked goods; if that makes sense.

Thelma turned around to Michael and told him thank you. He smiled at her and said in a very sweet voice, "You'll be okay." And Thelma felt in that moment, that she would be!

"See you, Michael," the old lady says.

"See you, Ms. Shepard," Michael replied back.

"That's Grandma Shepard to you, too, honey."

"Okay, thanks, ma'am. Oh, and I would love to see you again, Thelma. I would really love that," Michael says, standing there in a daze as if he's seen an angel.

"Alright, now, Michael, you take care," the little old lady, now called Grandma Shepard says, leading Michael out of the door smiling.

"Looks like you have a little admirer, lady." She laughs. "Anyways, Thelma, you look hungry. Are you, baby?"
"Yes, ma'am. I am."

"Come on in the kitchen so I can feed you something. Gloria will be home very soon."

"Ms. Shepard, I mean, Grandma Shepard, I'm a little nervous about just showing up here unannounced like this."

"Well, honey, I don't mean any harm, but usually, people contact the other person. Especially when visiting from another state. Are you in some trouble, honey?" Grandma Shepard asked with concern in her voice.

"No, I mean, yes. I don't know what to say," Thelma says, scratching her head.

"Well, sweetie, as long as it isn't trouble with the law."

"No, ma'am, I'm not in trouble with the law." The phone rings.

"Excuse me for a minute, baby."

"Yes, ma'am." While Ms. Shepard answered the phone, Thelma walked through the house heading towards the living room. *WOW! This house is beautiful! The beautiful crystal chandeliers shined like glitter, and there was an elegant stairway that extended to the upper floors like Thelma had only seen on TV. I could only dream of owning a home like this one day!*

"Thelma?"

"Yes, Ms., I mean, Grandma Shepard," Thelma says smiling.

"Come on in here and sit down, take a load off. Do you like tea?"
"Yes, ma'am, I do."

"Okay, then I will make you some tea, and how about some leftover pork chops with mashed potatoes and green beans?"

"Yum, sounds really good, but I don't want to cause you any trouble."

"Oh, you're no trouble, honey. Just relax. Gloria is on her way!"

"Really?"

"Yes, she is, and I didn't tell her you were here either. I thought that it would be a pleasant surprise. I can tell by looking at your face that you must be tired after all that traveling, honey. Let me show you to your room so you can get settled. Then after you can eat you can rest a little!"

"Rest? What's that, I haven't had a good nap in what seems like months." Thelma laughed. "I really appreciate you, ma'am."

"Oh, honey, it's no problem at all. I have always felt as if God placed me on this here earth to serve."

"Well, you sure are a breath of fresh air to me, thank you."

"No, sweetheart, thank you. And thank God for all of your blessings, because he is the only one that can supply us with all of what we need, and a lot of times what we want!" Ms. Shepard leaves the room.

Thelma places her face in her hands and begins to pray and thank God for sending her some encouragement after going through so much. "Lord, I know that I have not been the daughter that my daddy has raised me to be. In fact, I have completely made a mess of most things in my life, but I promise you if you will get me through it all, I will make you proud of me and make a change."

A few hours pass and Thelma falls asleep in the guest room. Gloria arrives home and calls out to her grandma. "Hey, Grandma."

Grandma Shepard comes downstairs. "Hey, honey, how was your day? I thought you were coming home a little earlier today?"

"I was, but work can get very hectic sometimes," Gloria says, kissing her grandmother on the cheek.

"Yes, honey, you're so right, but the good thing is that God has blessed you with a good job."

"Yea, you're right about that, Grandma." Gloria walks over and gives her grandma another kiss on the cheek.

"Granny?"

"Yes, baby?"

"Do you have any more pork chops left? I'm starving, I didn't get any lunch today."

"I sure do, you know that Granny is always going to make sure her baby eats well." They both laugh together.

"Oh, Gloria, before you eat, go up into the guest room I have a special surprise for you."

"Granny, you're always doing something for me."
"Go on upstairs, baby, and see. I think you're going to love this one."

"Okay, Granny." Gloria runs up the steps as if she was a little girl full of excitement. She gets to the top of the stairs, walks into the room, and looks around. She yells back downstairs, "GRANNY?"

"Yes, sweetie?" Granny yells from downstairs.

"What's the surprise?" Gloria walks towards the stairs. As she does, Thelma comes out of the bathroom and yells with excitement as she sees her friend walking down the hall.

"GLORIA!"

Gloria turns around and screams, "THELMA MCKINNEY!" They both hug and cry. "What...when...how?"

"I just got here a few hours ago," Thelma says laughing.

"Oh my gosh, I just can't believe you're here. You look good, girl." Gloria is twirling Thelma around with one hand.

"You ain't looking too shabby yourself, chick," Thelma replied.

"Man, Thelma, it's been what, over seven years since we last saw each other, huh?"

"Yes, almost seven."

"How's Momma and Daddy and everybody?" Gloria asked, sitting on the bed and crossing her legs.

"Girl, we have so much to catch up on."
Thelma touches her stomach and replies, "We sure do!"

"I have some friends I want you to meet, girl. We're all going out tonight to hear my friend Loren sing at the Wind Spot," Gloria says, standing in the middle of the floor snapping her fingers and dancing in place.

"What's the Wind Spot?"

"Oh, it's this cool spot we all go to hear live music, spoken word and just rap with each other."

"Oh, cool." Thelma says. "I don't have anything to wear."

"Yea, right."

"No, really, Gloria. You know I'm a country girl straight from the church. I wouldn't want to embarrass you now."

"Don't you worry, I got you. I have lots of clothes for you to choose from, and if that doesn't work, I'll just take you shopping."

Thelma looks up at Gloria and smiles. Gloria grabs Thelma hand and says, "I'm so glad you're here, Thelma."

"I'm glad to be here with you, too."

"No, you don't understand, Thelma. It's going to be nice to have someone around that you can trust."

"Trust, what do you mean by that, Gloria?" Thelma asked, looking confused. "I mean, it seems like you have lots of friends."

"I do, but you remember that song we use to sing when we were little from camp?"

They both begin to sing, "Make new friends, but keep the old, one is silver, but the old one's gold." Both of the girls laugh.

"Girl, I get it, I totally understand," Thelma says.

"If you don't mind me asking, I know we've always talked about you visiting me, but I truly never thought that you would, so what brought you here? I mean, way to New York City and away from TiTi," Gloria asks. "You know that little sister of yours worships the ground you walk on."

"I know she does, and I her," Thelma replies, looking down at her hands.

"Okay. What's wrong, Thelma? You seem sad."

"Man, Gloria, it's just so much…I mean, sometimes it seems as if I'm under water—"

Gloria finishes her sentence. "With no oxygen, right?"

"Exactly right," replies Thelma. "See, girl, that's why I love you so much; you were always able to understand me."

"Yes, because that's what best friends do, we understand each other," Gloria says with pride.

"Girls." Grandma Shepard calls.

"Yes, ma'am?" They both reply.

"I'm stepping out to the store for a while, I'll be right back."

"Ok, Granny!" Gloria says, answering her Granny.

"Girl, your Granny is something else," says Thelma.

"Yes, she is, and you talk about a praying woman." Gloria shakes her head. "That's my Granny. Chile, her prayers have really gotten me out of some serious crunches," Gloria says.

"Well, I do know one thing, yawl don't have a worry in the world, I mean, look at this house! It's beautiful and so bright," Thelma says, looking around and walking through the living room.

"Yes, but money isn't everything. Trust me, sometimes, the more money you have, the more stress comes with it. My dad and stepmother argue all of the time."

"Your dad remarried?"

"Yes, chile, he did. I mean, for the most part she's cool, but she has a power trip, and loves to shop; things of that nature. And she travels a lot, I think that's what my dad doesn't like. I really try to stay out of it, though. I have enough problems of my own."

"I hear you," Thelma replies.

"But I have no problem with her."

"That's good, I'm always happy to hear families working things out!"

"Yes, but it has not always been that way."

"What do you mean, Gloria?"

"I mean, she's cool and all, but she can be a little demanding on Dad. From my understanding she has not always had all of this. I heard she had a pretty dark past."

"REALLY?" Thelma asks, leaning forward for more information.

"Girl, yes, but my dad can't see anything negative about her."

"Well, love is blind, right?" Thelma says.

"I guess so, Thelma. When they first got married, she tried to come in and completely change our lives around, trying to act like she was my birth mother or something. Yea, but you know me, I had to put her in her place quick and in a hurry."

Thelma laughs at Gloria. "Gloria, you don't have a mean bone in your body, let alone putting somebody in their place. Girl, stop it."

"No, for real, I did, Thelma. We had a real heated argument about my dad. I told her that my mother was dead and she was not coming in changing things; my dad and I were just fine before she came along."

"What did she say?"

"Thelma, girl, she tried to tell my dad that she felt we should upgrade to a much larger home, because she didn't like the country side of New York."

"What country side?"

"That's what I said, Thelma. Just because Daddy is more of a private person and loves more of a country feel, and besides, my Momma picked out this house! I try not to worry about her anymore, she don't even have to like me, just treat my Daddy well."

"Girl, what a mess," Thelma comments.

"So tell me, Thelma, what's been going on with you?" Thelma looks at Gloria, with anticipation, wanting to share her story with Gloria but ashamed.

"Okay, spill the beans, Thelma. I know you have stuff to share; we haven't talked in like forever."

"Well, you know that Daddy was really sick," Thelma starts, looking down at the floor. "Yes, I heard about that, is he okay?"

"Yes, thank you. He's much better now, he just has to take it easy. He's on a strict diet and has to remain stress free."

"Your dad, stress free? Yea right!" Gloria replies.

"I know, but he's trying."

"I'm sure glad to hear that he's doing better, he gave us quite a scare. We were going to fly back there, if he—" Gloria catches herself from saying the wrong thing.

"I know, Gloria. I'm so grateful to God that He didn't take my Daddy away from me. I couldn't take it! God is good, but Momma is an entirely different story. I don't know, but the last couple of years, she just pushes all of my buttons. I mean, every last one of them. She is always passing judgment on me. It's always 'Thelma you should be more like this person and that person,' and oh, her favorite thing to do is embarrass me in front of people." Thelma is talking with her hands, and getting more upset.

"Girl, now that's just wrong," Gloria says, shaking her head. "Thelma, I'm so sorry."

Thelma continues, "It's like she hates me at times. You never know how she is going to act from one minute to the next."

"Thelma, from what I've observed, I think she's jealous of your relationship with your dad."

"You think so? You're not the first person to say that. Shortly before I left, Momma and I really had a falling out, Gloria. It was bad. I have never disrespected my momma in any kind of way before in my life, but this time…"

"What happened, Thelma?" Gloria goes over and sits next to Thelma.

"It got so bad, she said things to me that I will never forget."

"WHAT Thelma, WHAT?"

"Truthfully, Gloria, I don't want to relive that incident."

Gloria gets upset. "ARE YOU SERIOUS? I thought we were best friends, we have shared everything since we were little!"

"And you are my best friend and I love you, it's just—"

Gloria interrupts with her mouth crooked over to the side, getting irritated. "It's just what, Thelma?"

"I just don't want you to be disappointed in me."

"Thelma, I would never be disappointed in you. We're like sisters and we cry, grow and survive whatever it is together."

"Yes, you're right, and thank God that you are here and always have been."

"That's right, and I got your back, T."

"And I got yours!" Thelma replies to Gloria, reaching out rubbing her hand.

"We will talk later. You want to get unpacked so we can plan our week?" Gloria asks.

"Yes, that sounds good. I'm so tired. Do you think it will be fine for me to stay here for a while?"

"What kind of question is that, you know you're like his other daughter, and besides, he knew you would visit soon," Gloria reassures Thelma.

"Okay, I'm just checking." Thelma starts to head upstairs, to unpack her clothes.

<><><>

Later that day, Gloria's dad comes in. Gloria meets him at the door with excitement. "Dad, look who's here to visit." Thelma walks out of the kitchen.

"Well, I'll be, little Thelma McKinney! Girl, look at you. You have grown up to be a very beautiful young lady."

"Hello, Mr. Williams." Thelma puts her hand out to shake his hand.

"No handshakes with family members." He reaches out to hug Thelma, they embrace. "Wow, Thelma! Welcome, sweetheart."

"Thank you so much, Mr. Williams."

"How's your father doing? You know we were all worried sick about him. In fact, we were going to fly home to see about you all."

"Yes, that's what Gloria told me. Thanks for all of your prayers and support, it was needed!"

"How long will you be visiting, Thelma?"

"Well, I'm not sure —" Gloria interrupts Thelma.

"Daddy, we will worry about that all later, right?"

Mr. Williams looks at his daughter with curiosity and says. "Yes, I guess you're right! There's one thing I do know and that's that Gloria missed you every day you two were apart, and I'm glad you're here. How in the world did your dad let his baby girl leave, even for a little while? You know how he is about you girls, especially you, Thelma," Mr. Williams asks.

"To tell you the truth, Dad did very well with me leaving, because he knew I was coming to see you all!"

"That's great, I've been meaning to give him a call. This weekend would probably be best, with his busy schedule."

Thelma gets very nervous about the two men talking and speaks before thinking. "Daddy is out of town on a business meeting, so you probably won't get him," Thelma says very quickly.

"Oh, okay. I'll just try the next weekend then." Thelma sighs quietly with relief.

"Well, I will see you both later, long day. Make yourself at home, Thelma. Our home is your home. How old are you now, Thelma?"

"I'm eighteen, sir." That's right, you and Gloria are three months apart! That's great. Well, see you later, going to have supper and then go to bed!"

"Thanks again, Mr. Williams."

"No problem, Thelma!"

# Chapter 14

# *Not Yet Home*

The very next day, Gloria wakes Thelma up. "Hey, girl, rise and shine."

"What time is it?" Thelma asks.

"Oh, it's seven thirty," Gloria replies, looking at her watch.

"You going into work today?" Thelma asks, sitting up in the bed.

"I wish I would on a Saturday," Gloria replies.

"Cool, so what are your plans for today then, I'm so tired I would love to go back to sleep."

"Chile, go back to sleep. It ain't nothing to do today, besides, you have had a long travel. I have to fly. Me, on the bus? No way!" Gloria replies, pulling her hair back into a ponytail.

"Honestly, 'Miss, I Can't Ride a Bus', it wasn't that bad. Besides the smell, and the weird people, and the incredibly long ride," Thelma says, smiling at Gloria.

"See, that's what I'm talking about," Gloria says laughing. "I thought you and I could get up, get out of this house and do some shopping."

"Shopping? I don't have money for that, Gloria. Can a girl get on her feet first?"

"Did I ask you if you did?"
"I will earn my own dollar, I won't have you taking care of me, it's not fair to you."

"Don't you worry about that, I got connections," Gloria says, winking her eye at Thelma.

"Oh, okay. I see, you have it like that."

"Just like that," Gloria replies. "So, get dressed and meet me downstairs. Granny has breakfast all ready, unless you still want to sleep in?"

"Naw, girl, if you got it like that, I'm getting up and getting dressed. I'm not missing my blessing. I'll be downstairs shortly," Thelma laughs.

Gloria, walks out of Thelma's room, closes the door, and heads downstairs.

<><><>

"Good morning, Dad. Hey, Granny, how is everyone today?"

"Good morning, Gloria. How did you sleep, baby?" Granny asks, stirring the grits on the stove.

"I kind of didn't sleep. Thelma and I stayed up most of the night talking."

"I thought that you two would," Mr. Williams said.

"Yes, Daddy. I have to say, I really missed her a lot. It's going to be nice to have Thelma here for a while."

"Gloria?"
"Yes, Dad," Gloria says, rinsing off the fruit for breakfast.

"What is really going on with Thelma? I mean, it was clear that she panicked when she thought I was calling Pastor. Is she in some kind of trouble, sweetheart? I know that's your friend, but sometimes it's best to help them the right way, that's telling the truth."

Gloria looks at her dad, with hesitation. "Daddy, all I know is, Thelma needed a break from home. We all know how much pressure she carries at home. It was that way even when we were younger. She has a lot on her, remember, Dad, you said so yourself."

"I know, honey. I remember, but at the same time, she is still young and her parents have a right to be included in her decisions. I know…I'm a parent myself. Plus, her dad is crazy about that girl. I know if he doesn't know where she is, he has to be going crazy! I know I would."

"You're right, Daddy, but I'm sure that Pastor and First Lady Mary have to know she's here. I didn't get the impression that they didn't."

"Well, honey, I agree with the both of you. However, sometimes even children need a break from being overwhelmed, but your father's right that her parents should be called. Just to make sure everything's all right," says Granny, taking food off of the stove.

"Momma, you usually pick up what's going on with people from your first interaction with them. What happened with Thelma? You haven't said much about what God has shown you."

"Who's to say I didn't, Thomas? I knew it when she walked through that door," Granny replies to her son, patting him on the shoulder.

Thelma walks in the room and interrupts the conversation. "Good morning, everyone."

"Hi, sweetie." Granny greets her with a hug and kiss on the cheek. "Thelma, we were just talking about you, honey. And I made you a big breakfast this morning."

"Thank you, Jesus. And thank you, too, Granny. So you all were just talking about me, huh?"

"Yes, we were," Granny said, placing a glass of orange juice in front of Thelma.

"I sure hope it was good talk." Thelma smiles.

"Honey, sit down and eat something. I made some homemade biscuits, omelets, ham, and hash browns, grits, too. There's some fresh sweet tea and you already have our fresh squeezed orange juice. I want you to eat, baby."

"Wow! Thanks, Granny. Do you cook like this all of the time?"

"You're welcome, honey, and yes I do. I feel that a family that prays together, stays together. But a family that eats together, completes together. Table time is important for the soul."

"Yes, chile. Granny makes it impossible to lose any weight around here," says Gloria, with a biscuit hanging out her mouth.

"You be quiet, Gloria. Keeping me up all night." The girls laugh.
"Girl, I'm so tired," Thelma says yawning.

"Looks like you girls were able to play catch up," Mr. Williams commented.

"Yes, we did, Mr. Williams, but your daughter tried to catch up with my past and future. It was a long night!"

"Whatever, Thelma," says Gloria.

Thelma holds her stomach and leans up against the table. "Are you okay, Thelma?" Granny says with a concerned voice.

"Suddenly, I don't feel very well, I think I may be coming down with something. I'm going to go lie down, maybe that will help. Sorry, Granny, I know how hard you worked on breakfast."

"It's okay, honey, but can't you eat something?"

"Maybe later, Granny. May I be excused?" Thelma stands up, holding her stomach.

"Yes, but of course, honey. I hope you feel better. The blood of Jesus," Granny whispers, while rubbing Thelma's forehead.

Thelma quietly walks out of the room.

"She may just need some rest. That poor child looks like she has been through, but she's going to be just fine," says Granny.

"Yea, Granny, I think you're right. I'll go and check on her."

Thelma's family sits in the living room looking for answers about Thelma's disappearance. Pastor and First lady McKinney are worried.

"I just don't understand. This makes no sense. Where could she be?" Pastor says, pacing the floor.

"Daddy, I wanted to let Thelma get settled before I said anything. I have to tell you something." Titi looks afraid to speak.

"What do you mean, TiTi? You mean to tell me, you knew where your sister was this past week and said nothing while the entire family worries ourselves sick?"

TiTi nods. "I'm sorry, Daddy. I really am, I should have said something."

"Where is she, Tonya?" Pastor McKinney questions TiTi.

"Greg, try not to get yourself too upset. Remember your heart, honey." Mary McKinney touches Pastor on the shoulder while handing him a cup of tea.

"Thelma's alright, honey," Mary McKinney responds, trying to keep Pastor calm.

"How do you know, Mary? Did you speak with her?"

"No, I'm just trying to keep you calm, for the benefit of your health, Greg."

"I don't care about any of that, and I'm not going to play any games. TiTi, where is your sister?" Pastor demands, with a scowl on his face.

"She's in New York, Daddy." TiTi begins to cry. "Daddy, please stop getting upset, I don't want you to get sick again."

"I'm going to really be upset if somebody doesn't tell me where my baby is."

"New York, Daddy. She's in New York City."

"What do you mean New York? Lord, have mercy." Pastor sits down, and begins to cough intensively.

"Honey, please calm down. Everything is fine."

"How can you say that, Mary? Everything isn't fine. My child is way across in another place, and you're saying for me to calm down? You should be just as concerned as I am."

"And I am, honey, but getting all wound up isn't going to make the situation better," Mary says.

Pastor is getting upset, feeling as if no one is concerned but him. "TiTi, who is she staying with?"

"She is staying with Gloria and her family, and she told me to tell you and Momma that she will be fine. And as soon as she gets settled, she will contact us."

Pastor looks at Word. "Did you know about this too?"

Word sighs. "She came to see me the night before she left and her spirits were very down."

"Why didn't you come to get me, son?"

"Dad, us kids are all very close and we talk often, and honestly, I thought it was just another chit chat session like we have all the time. Anyway, she asked me to pray for her and that was it!"

"Oh my Lord, my baby didn't even think she could come to me for prayer." Pastor McKinney hangs his head, feeling like he has the weight of the world pressing down on his shoulders. He is feeling really hurt that he was not there for his baby girl.

"No, Daddy, it's not that at all," Word replied.

TiTi begins to cry. "Daddy," TiTi calls her dad's name with tears coming down her face.

"Baby, what's wrong?" Pastor walks over to TiTi and places both of his hands gently on her shoulders.

TiTi sadly looks up into her dad's worried eyes. "Daddy, Thelma's pregnant!"

"What did you say?" Pastor asks in disbelief. "Yes, Dad, she is. She wanted to tell you, but she couldn't bring herself to say it." Pastor McKinney leans up against the table, holding it with both hands, with his head down.

"Did you know about this, Mary?" Pastor McKinney, turns and looks at his wife.

Mary drops her head. "Yes, Greg, I found out the night that Thelma and I had that argument."

"And you weren't going to tell me? No one feels that I can handle anything around here. But I manage to take care of all of you, and I can't even receive common respect as the head of this household." Pastor was furious.

"Greg, honey, you were so upset and I was worried about your health. I didn't think it was the right time!" Mary shrugged.

"Maybe if you had shared this information with me about my own daughter, maybe I could have tried to prevent her from leaving. Now, look at this mess!" Pastor shook his head, trying to make sense of it all.

"Greg, don't go blaming me for this. Look, we all are upset, let's just calm down and regroup."

TiTi reveals one more thing to her Dad. "Daddy, there is something else I think you should know."

"Oh Lord, what is going on here. Dear God, give me strength! What is it, Tonya?"

"Well, at the youth picnic, Sister Ramsey confronted Thelma about her destroying everyone's lives. She told her that everyone would be much better if she just left. Especially you, Daddy. So, Thelma left so she wouldn't bring any shame to you or our family."

Pastor rubs his chest, and sits down in his chair. "How dare she tell my daughter that! That was not her place!" Pastor frowns.

"No, it wasn't, and I'm talking to her about this when I see her," Mary says sternly.

Pastor pauses for a few seconds and shakes his head. "No, Mary, I'll do better than that!" Pastor walks over to the phone and attempts to call Sister Ramsey.

"Honey, no. Now is not the time, just wait, you are too angry." Mary walks over to him, and takes his hand, forcing him to hang the phone up.

"You are darn right. I am more than angry, I'm furious. You wait until I get my mouth on her. People have a lot of nerves when it comes to passing judgment. No one goes around talking about their son Johnny, and we all know he's had some problems, but what do we do? We pray for him... for all of our youth. I just really don't understand why Sister Ramsey even got involved with our family's affair. Thelma's not her daughter." He pauses trying to understand why Sister Ramsey would know Thelma was pregnant but he didn't. "I'm very surprised at Thomas Williams. We've always had a good understanding when it came to our girls. Why wouldn't he call me and tell me she's there and that she's okay?" Having had enough, he starts to walk toward the stairs and turns back to the family as Titi begins speaking again.

"Man, I am so angry at Sister Ramsey. I tried to tell Thelma that it didn't matter what that old trouble-making woman said to her, but she wouldn't listen."

"Yea, Tonya, I wish Thelma hadn't listened to her either, because if you think about it, Sister Ramsey wasn't concerned about Daddy's ministry, she was worried about her own reputation." Word glanced around at his family, then continued. "So quick to point her finger at my sister, but what about her own raggedy son! That's the problem with church people today, always meddling in other people's affairs, but not taking care of home first. Thelma didn't get pregnant by herself!"

Pastor's jaw drops. "What did you just say, Son?"

Word realizes that he just spoke too much. "Daddy, I just... well...he came to the house one day before Thelma left and was trying to talk to her about the baby. Thelma thinks I didn't hear about it because I didn't respond when he commented about her pregnancy. I figured it wasn't my place to talk about it. As he left, he told her that she wasn't going nowhere with is baby."

Pastor becomes infuriated. "That's it. Everyone knew what was going on but me?! Does the entire town know? The church? I am sitting back here thinking I am dealing with my baby girl finding out about her mother and she is learning that as she is about to become a mother. Now my baby girl is out there, what…more than 500 miles away? Maybe thousands of miles? And I am supposed to just believe my children that it is going to be okay?" He looks up to toward the ceiling, "My God, what did I do for my family to begin falling apart? All these years of service and NOW I have to pay for a decision made 18 plus years ago?"

TiTi starts to cry again, frantically, and whispers a little too loudly to her brother. "It seems as if everything is crumbling in front of me too. Word, I want my Thelma back home."

"I know, Tonya. Me too, Sis, me too!"

Mary McKinney, was sitting on the couch, listening to Word and TiTi talk. She begins to try to encourage them. "I know that Thelma's really been acting strange lately, but we have to hold it together as her family, you both hear me? We all make mistakes, God knows I wish I had handled things differently, but this is where our faith is tried. Do we let the enemy win, or do we fight? And above all, we have to try and keep your father calm, you both understand?"

"Yes, Momma," Word and TiTi replies.

Pastor hears his wife's words and decides against calling Thomas Williams that evening. Instead he heads up the stairs and prays. "Father God, I know I made mistakes. I know I made decisions that affected others. But Lord, why now? Why my baby girl? Why my family? This is too much Lord. My heart hurts, physically and spiritually. What are you doing? What are you trying to teach me? Let this lesson be learned so I can have my family back. I need my family back Father."

The next morning, Pastor gets up and calls Thomas Williams.

"Hello?"

"Yes, good morning, Thomas. It's Greg, Greg McKinney."

"Yes, hello, Pastor! You know it's funny, I was going to call you the other day, but Thelma said that you were out of town for a week. How is the trip going?"

"I'm not travelling, Thomas. I'm still recovering from the surgery. I've been told by my doctor not to travel for a while. I have to admit I was a little confused about why you didn't call me about my daughter staying at your house. I felt that our families are close enough to keep the flow of communicating going. Wouldn't you agree?"

"Absolutely, Greg. I would have called but I had no reason to doubt that Thelma was telling me the truth so I was waiting until next week. However, hearing your voice and words, I think you're trying to tell me something. What is it, Greg?"

"It's very complicated. Thelma left without us even knowing it. She took off in the middle of the night about a week ago and Titi just told us tonight that she was with you. Mary and I have been worried and have been trying to put the pieces together about where she could be."

"You're kidding me, right?" Mr. Williams face looks like a man who has just seen a ghost.

"You mean to tell me, Thomas, you didn't know either?"

"Greg, now, we've been friends a long time, you should know me better than that. If I knew that Thelma was here without your permission she would have called you with me standing there watching. She is upstairs right now and I can go get her so you two can talk," Thomas says.

"No…if she lied to you she is probably very scared. I have peace of mind knowing she is with you Thomas. I can sleep tonight knowing she is in good hands. But tell me, what did Thelma tell you was the reason for her visit?"

"Actually, she hasn't said much. I was under the impression that she was visiting and you and Mary understood that she was in New York. I'm sorry, man. I really didn't know. She looks tired and in need of a break, so I figured being that she just graduated at the top of her class and has some big college decisions to make that perhaps you sent her up here to get a break from the other kids and the small town. I remember how everyone had an opinion about how you should live your life, the poor girl is probably drowning in opinions from everyone on where she should go and what she should study," Thomas replies, feeling Greg's pain. He could only image what Greg must be going through. He loved his baby Gloria so much and he knew if she had pulled a stunt like that, he would be devastated.

"Oh Thomas, I wish that was all this is. Listen, it's not your fault, and I have to say again that I'm grateful that you all were available for her to feel safe to come stay with."

"No problem, sir. That's what family is for. So now that you've discovered where your daughter is, and I've discovered she somewhat ran away, what should we do?"

"I would like to speak with her by tonight. Please have her call me, Thomas."

"I sure will."

"Oh, and Thomas, thanks again."

"Please, Greg, it's okay. It really is my pleasure, I'm sure that you would do the same for me."

"I absolutely would, and I'm feeling much better. I'll talk with you soon, good bye!"

Pastor McKinney hangs up the phone and thanks God for the assurance that his baby girl is safe and with someone he trusts. Thomas Williams is a long-time family friend who he trusted with his life, so he felt relieved that Thelma at least had the wisdom to go somewhere that she would be safe and well-loved. And if Grandma Shepard still lived with them, well…his baby girl was in for some true growth for however long she was away. The Lord spoke through that woman in ways that you read about in the Bible, he thought to himself.

Back in New York, Thelma is still lying down not feeling well. Mr. Williams and Gloria spoke about the phone call and tried to come up with a plan for how they should talk to Thelma. They agreed it was clear the situation must be serious for her to have run away and lied, which goes way beyond her character.

"Gloria, I think I need to speak with Thelma," Thomas says, wanting to get to the bottom of things.

"Daddy, please don't go too hard on her, she has already been through a lot."

"Gloria, I'm concerned for her. I'm a father, too, and it's not good that Thelma left home the way she did."

"I agree, Daddy, but—"

"Alright, honey, I'll go lightly, but I still need to speak to her."

"That's fine. She is still up in the guest room lying down. And, Dad, is it okay that I talk to her first?" Gloria says out of concern for her best friend.

"Yes, sure, baby, but hurry up. Her father wants a call by this evening and I don't want to make Greg wait too long. I would be a mess and I can feel his pain. We need to have her call as soon as possible so he doesn't have another—"
Gloria interrupts him, "I'm going now Daddy. I will have her down in a few minutes." She heads up to their guestroom to talk with Thelma. "Knock, Knock. Thelma, it's me."

"Hey, come in, girl."

"How are you feeling?" Gloria asks Thelma, as she sitsat vanity set.

"I'm feeling a little better."

"Well, that's good. Look, Thelma, I won't beat around the bush. Your dad called my dad."

Thelma raises off of the bed feeling very nervous. "What? Oh my God, what happened?"

"Thelma, I don't know what all was said, but I do know that Dad is aware how you left home. It would have been nice that someone knew, don't you think?" Gloria asks solemnly. "Thelma, why did I have to find out like this? I thought we were closer than this."

"We are, Gloria. I'm so sorry. Man, it doesn't matter where I am and who it is, I always seem to mess things up. I'm just tired, I'm tired!" Thelma replies, as she lies back down and turns her face towards the wall.

"I'm sorry, Thelma. I don't know what's going on, but my dad wants to speak with you," Gloria says as she backs up against the bedroom door.

"Gloria, I don't know what to say to him."

"I know you don't, but you better think of something and fast because it sounds like he decided I didn't get to have a few minutes with you first!"

Thomas Williams is at the bedroom door. He knocks softly.

"Come in, Daddy."

Thelma looks at the door. Thomas Williams walks into the room, and begins to speak to Thelma. "Thelma, I wanted to talk to yo—"

Thelma cuts him off. "Mr. Williams, let me start off by saying that I didn't mean to mislead any of you. I have just been under a lot of pressure lately. I'm depressed and there is so much going on at home and in my life right now. I didn't know who or where else to turn. I apologize."

Thomas Williams walks over to a chair in the room and drags it in front of Thelma. He straddles it facing her. "Thelma, I haven't always been my age, I've been where you're at right now. Well, maybe not exactly, but I can relate. But what I don't agree with is you running away and not letting your parents know where you are. That's never good. Do you understand that your parents love you and are concerned about you? The last thing parents want to feel is that our children can't talk to us about anything, especially us dads."

"I'll leave, Mr. Williams."

"Now, did I ask you to leave?"

"No, but I'll probably end up disappointing you all here, too. That's seems to be the story of my life," Thelma says quietly, her voice cracks as tears push to the surface. She wipes her eyes quickly with the back of her hand.

Gloria sits beside Thelma on the bed and takes her hand. "Thelma, things will get better, you are my best friend and WE will get through it all, okay?"

"Yes, and thank you, Gloria."

"Girl, please! There is no need to thank me, that's just what we do," says Gloria, playfully shoving Thelma in the arm.

"Now, Thelma, I need you to know that my doors are open to you as long as you have squared things away with your parents. I can't come between you and them. Am I clear?" Thomas Williams says to Thelma.

"I understand, sir. I'll call them tomorrow."

"No," Mr. Williams says firmly. "You will call them today, and to be clearer, here's the phone!" Mr. Williams hands the phone to Thelma. "We will be downstairs if you need us, okay?"

"Okay," Thelma replies, reluctant to call her father.

# Chapter 15

# Growing Pains

"Dear God, what's going on? I thought that you were giving me a fresh start to make things right. I even messed this up. Why am I even here? Just kill me already. My life is already destroyed. I mean, YOU don't even understand me. Please, just end this for me. I don't have any fight left in me anymore. God, please!" Thelma sits there with the phone in her hand.

She dials her home number and the phone rings. "Lord, please help me," she thinks as she hears the second ring. Her heart begins racing so fast she can almost feel it in her throat.

"Thomas? Is everything okay?"

"Hello, Dad?"

"Baby, how are you?"

"Daddy—"

"Wait, Thelma, before you say anything, I want you to hear me out. First, I want you to know that Daddy loves you and nothing you do will ever change that. Second, I want to tell you that I'm hurt that you couldn't come to me and let me know what's going on with you. We've always been close, at least, I felt we were!"

"Daddy, we are close," Thelma said softly. "I just felt that I've created some problems that couldn't be fixed. Plus, you've been sick, Daddy. I couldn't put any more on you."

"Thelma, I am your father, and that's my job—no one else's. Please come home, baby."

Thelma heard what her dad asked, but she couldn't answer him. She just couldn't go home now. But it was breaking her heart to hear the disappointment in her father's voice.

"Thelma, did you hear me, baby?"

"Yes, Daddy. Daddy, I can't come home right now. I can't bring the family any more trouble, and I don't want to damage your ministry either."

"My ministry? What kind of ministry do I have if I can't minister to my own daughter and make a difference in her life?" "I hear what you're saying, Daddy, and believe me, I love you so much. You are the best father any girl can ever have, I mean that!"

"Baby, what if I fly in and come and pick you up?"

Thelma interrupts her dad. "Daddy, I can't come home right now. I hope someday you will find it in your heart to forgive me."

"I don't understand, but I'll give you till next week to come home, okay?"

Thelma couldn't say anything because she knows her dad's heart. He has always taken such great care of her and has always been her protector, but this time he can't fix what is broken, so she just answers him and tells him what he wants to hear. "Yes, Daddy, I just need some time to think. They are taking great care of me here."

Thelma chokes up and has to hang up so her father doesn't hear her cry. "Goodbye, Daddy. I'll call you later, okay?"

There was total silence on the phone, Thelma could hear her dad's voice beginning to crack as he speaks to her.

"Baby girl, always know that everything I have done has been for you children. I have tried to be the best dad that I know to be, not perfect, but I've done my best. Always remember that, I am so proud of you and I know that God has a bigger plan for your life. You will tread on ground that I could only dream of. You are special, baby, you are. My prayer is that God will one day show you your worth and who you are in him, and I pray that you know how important you are to me. Never forget it, okay?"

"Daddy, I know this. Why are you saying all of this to me?"

"Because we as parents take it for granted that our children already know how we feel, so I want to make sure that you heard it from me. You are my angel and Daddy loves you no matter how far you go or what you have done. My love does not change based upon your actions. It is consistent and always available to you, unconditionally."

"Wow, Daddy, thank you so much."

"No, baby, thank you for bringing such joy into my life. Now promise me this, promise me that if I'm not around that you will always trust, believe and have faith in God, okay?"

Thelma pauses on the phone. "Where are you going, Dad? What are you talking about?"

"I'm not planning on going anywhere, I'm speaking in general."

"Well, of course I will, that's how you've raised me. I know that God is my source, it's just sometimes I feel so alone."

"Baby, that's normal to feel that way, Jesus even felt alone when he was in the Garden of Gethsemane. His heart was heavy and he wanted out of the deal, but he also knew that his father had placed him in a place to fulfill a purpose. It's the same with us. We have a purpose to fulfill, too. Our purpose is to follow the paths that God has set before us."

"But, Daddy, how do we know that we are following the path correctly?"

"We don't, baby, but all we have to do is keep walking. He is holding our hands and will always order our steps. He will not let you down, baby. I promise. You are not in a place that I or others haven't experienced, so remember 'This too shall pass.' It always gets better."

"Thank you, Daddy. I really needed to hear what you shared. Only you can make me feel better."

"No, baby, only God can make you better. Thelma, know that I love you, and I will check in with you in a couple of days. I wish you were home, however, I do feel much better knowing you are safe with the Williams."

"OK, Daddy, oh, and, Dad?"

"Yes, honey."

"Thanks again, for everything. I am sorry I worried you."

"You are so welcome, now get some rest!" Pastor and Thelma hang up the phone both feeling relieved.

<><><>

Later that night, Gloria comes into the room to check on Thelma.

"Thelma, I know you have been through a crazy day. I think you will feel much better if you got dressed and go with me."

"Gloria, I'm pregnant!" Thelma says, her eyes swollen eyes from crying.

"What did you say?" Gloria gets up to close the bedroom door.

"You heard me right, I am—."

"Oh, Thelma, who is the dad?"

"It's Johnny Ramsey."

"JOHNNY? Johnny… Johnny, in church when we were little Johnny?"

"Yes, Gloria, Johnny; in church when we were little Johnny."

"Oh, Thelma, I'm so sorry you are going through all of this." Gloria hugs Thelma.

"Thanks, girl."

"Do your parents know?"

"My mother does. And Tonya and Word, but not Dad."

"WOW!"

"I know, right? I told you that I was a magnet for trouble."

"No you are not, you are just going through the valley. Remember your dad used to preach about the valley?"

"Yea, Gloria, you remember that?"

"I sure do, in fact, it's what got me through some of my trials," Gloria says, walking over to the mirror."

"What trials do you have, Gloria?"

"Girl, please, everyone has trials."

"Yes, I guess you're right. I guess when you are going through, it feels like you're the only one!"

"True, but as long as you know you're not alone in this, okay?" Gloria says, walking back over to Thelma on the bed.

"Thank you. I appreciate you, Gloria, I really do," Thelma says, wiping her eyes.

"There's dinner downstairs for you. Granny cooked some fried catfish," Gloria says.

"Yum, sounds good," Thelma replies, slowly getting out of the bed.

"You know what? I can do better than that, I'll fix you a plate and bring it to you."

"Thanks, Gloria."

"Oh, girl, you're welcome! Now what are your plans, about your baby and all?"

"I really don't know. I'm keeping it, though."

"Oh, yes, of course. I meant about everything else," Gloria replies.

Thelma just stares away. Gloria sees that Thelma is stressed and walks towards the bedroom door. "You know what? I'll let you rest and I'll fix your plate, I love you, girl."

"I love you back!" replies Thelma to Gloria.

# Chapter 16

# Take the Pain Away

Thelma sits on the bed and writes in her diary, the one place she always loved to write her thoughts out.

*Dear Diary,*

*It's me again. Wow! What a mess, right? My dad found out where I'm staying. I never wanted to hurt him, that is why I left in the first place. Yes, you guessed it...I manage to still bring hurt to him. I could hear the disappointment in his voice; his heart was shedding tears. My daddy does not deserve this, but I don't know how else to handle things.*

*My heart almost stopped when Mr. Williams and Gloria came to talk to me. I felt as if I betrayed them by keeping the truth away. But one thing about it: God never lets me get by with much of anything! It seems I always get caught. When you're a little girl, you tell yourself that you can't wait until you grow up, but a word to all the young children out there: STAY YOUNG as long as you can, being an adult is definitely for the birds.*

*I don't know what my plans are for the future, but I do know that I can't take any more stress. I do miss my family – my sister and brother. I hate that I didn't get to see Mickey. I miss my mom, too, but most of all, I miss my best friend, my Daddy. But I am thankful that my dad ministered to me, I really needed that.*

*I wish I could lay in his arms, and he could tell me that everything will be alright! I'm asking God to work a miracle in my life, and show me what way to go, because I'm fresh out of ideas!! I hate to sound as if all I do is complain, but I really don't know what to do. Even though I'm going through a lot, I still believe in God and I know he loves me. I have to believe! My Grandma always told me, "Baby, God don't make no mistakes. We have to give thanks at all times, because it can always be worse!" And I try to remember that, but sometimes it gets a little hard, but yet, my faith is still alive!*

Thelma closes the book.

# Chapter 17

## His Will Be Done

Pastor McKinney asked his wife to sit down next to him on the bed. "Come here, honey. I want to share with you something that's on my heart."

"Sure, Greg." Mary sits next to him.

"Mary, I've spoken to Thelma and she is okay for now, however, I want her home."

"I know, honey. I would have loved to speak with her, but I wasn't aware of your call, I mean, you didn't tell me."

"I know, dear, I just needed to speak to my little girl."

"Greg, she's my child, too."

"I know, honey, and I didn't mean any disrespect, it's just that—"

Mary cuts him off. "I know you two share a special bond, but, Greg McKinney, she is still my daughter, and you never leave any room for me to ever reach out to Thelma, or to fix any problems she may have. You're always there to fix them."

"Perhaps you are right, Mary. But my objective is only for my daughters to know—not just Thelma, but Tonya as well—that their father loves them, and I accept them for who they are. They will hear it from me, their father, and not have to search in life from the approval of any other man because their Daddy spoke it into their lives first. Now, as their mother, you'll have to ask God to show you what to do or how to reach out. But for now, this is how I choose to handle it!"

"I get that, Greg, and I'm not taking that from you, either. You are a good father to all of our children and I appreciate you so much!"

"Well, honey, it's been a strange night for me anyway," Pastor says.

"Strange? What do you mean, Greg?"

"I'm not sure myself, but I want you to call Thelma on Monday and see if you can get her to come home."

"Sure thing, honey. I really miss her, too, so, no worries. I'll call."

"Thanks, honey," Pastor replies. "Mary McKinney?"

"Yes, Pastor Greg McKinney?"

"Have I told you lately that I love you?"

"Yes, you have, but you can say it again, and again if you like," Mary says, blushing. She can't help smiling.

"I love you, Mrs. Mary Lydia McKinney."

"And I love you, too, Mr. Gregory Edward McKinney."

"You have been such a help to our ministry, even things you didn't agree with me on, you always supported, and I thank you." Pastor says, taking both of Mary's hands in his and looking her in her eyes.

"Where is this coming from, Greg? I know you appreciate me, and I you."

"I just think it's nice to give flowers while you can smell them, right?"

"Yes, sir, you are right, and I don't mind the live flowers either." She couldn't resist a grin.

"You got it, honey," Pastor replies. They both laugh and hug each other.

"Greg, what did Thelma say was wrong?" Mary asks, concerned for her daughter.

"Just life, honey. That's all. I'm a little tired and my head is hurting just a little bit, I'll just take a couple of aspirin and some hot tea."

"Of course, Greg. I'll be right back." Mary walks towards the door.

"Mary, God has been good to us. We have been married for over twenty-six years and I'm still in love with you." Mary looks at her husband and smiles. "I'll share more with you later, honey. I just need to get some rest."

"I understand, Greg. You rest now, honey." Greg reaches out to hug his wife.

Mary kisses him on the forehead. "I love you, Greg. Now rest, honey."

It is early Sunday morning. Word and Tonya are getting up and arguing as usual. Mary is in the kitchen cooking breakfast and Pastor is not feeling well. Tonya comes downstairs. "Good morning, Momma. Where is Daddy?"

"Your dad is not feeling too well this morning. He's been up most of the night, so I'm going to allow him to rest as long as he needs."

"What's wrong with Daddy, Momma?"

"Well, baby, I'm not sure. He spoke with Thelma and he's been pretty upset, so that could have a lot to do with it."

"Is Thelma coming home soon, Mom?" TiTi says, grabbing a piece of toast and talking a bite of it.

"Your dad says Thelma isn't ready to come back, but he wants to give her the time she needs to gather her thoughts; he feels she will be home soon! So I need you and your brother to help out and keep things calm as possible around here. I'm really worried about your father; in fact, Word, go upstairs and check on your dad for me."

"Yes, ma'am!" Words heads upstairs, to check on Pastor.

"I think I'm going to call Deacon and see if they can carry on church without your dad today. He really needs to stay home and rest." Mary walks over to the table and sits down.

160

"Momma, I've never known him to miss church."

"I know, but he has to take care of himself first. The church will be just fine."

"I'll get the phonebook for you, Mamma." TiTi walks over to the kitchen drawer, to get Mary the church directory.

"Thank you, baby!" Suddenly, there is a scream coming from upstairs and it's Word. "Momma, Momma!" Word is running down the stairs crying and leaning up against the wall.

Mary McKinney stands up and begins to run towards the stairs. "Oh Lord, WHAT'S WRONG?" Mary asks frantically.

"Daddy won't wake up! Oh, Momma!" Everyone runs up the stairs. When they enter their bedroom, Mary screams.

"WORD CALL 911...."

The family and church members are gathered at the hospital where Pastor McKinney was pronounced dead due to a massive attack while he slept. Mary and the kids are besides themselves with grief.

"I can't breathe, I can't think. I just want to see my Daddy." TiTi is crying and pleading with her mother to let her see her dad.

"Momma, can I go see him? He will wake up for me." Tonya closed her eyes to stop the flow of tears. But they wouldn't stop falling. She couldn't believe her dad was gone.

Mother Martin, one of the church mothers, grabs Tonya and hugs her.

"NO, I want my Dad!" Tonya is crying frantically.

Mother Martin begins to hold TiTi really tight and pray.

Word is kneeling on a chair in the Family Room, as Mary McKinney sits in a chair and stares. Mary stands up and calls her children by her side and asks them to accompany her into the hospital room where Pastor McKinney's body lays. She begins to quote the 23rd Psalms, as they walk into his room. "Yay though I walk through the valley of the shadow of death, I will fear no evil, for you are with me, Lord." Word holds his mother up to keep her from falling on the floor.

Monday morning Sister Ramsey heads to the house to make phone calls for Sister McKinney. The house is full of people. Sister Ramsey goes up to Mary's room, she knocks on the door. "Come in," Mary says.

"Mary?" Sister Ramsey replies, opening up the door.

Mary is in bed, her eyes swollen and red from crying.

"Mary, have Thelma and Mickey been notified yet?"

"Oh my goodness!" Mary begins to cry again.

"Don't worry about anything, Mary. Now you just lay down here and rest, myself and the sisters from the church will take care of everything for you, okay?"

Mary stares as if she is in a dream. *Is she really standing in my house as though she is not at the root cause of my family falling apart? How dare she ask me about Thelma! Lord help me from saying what is on my mind.*

"It's alright, honey. You just rest!" Sister Ramsey says with reassurance.

"Sister Ramsey?" Mary says very calmly, sitting on the edge of her bed.

"Yes, First Lady?"

"I will call my own children. I have to be the one to tell them. After all, you have done enough. Don't you think? Why don't you just head home. We have everything under control here." Mary catches Sister Ramsey off guard.

Sister Ramsey stutters over her words. "But of course... I, I understand." Sister Ramsey quickly leaves the room, closing the door.

"Dear Lord, why have you allowed this? I have never questioned you before, but this I just don't understand. I can't make it without Greg, I can't! This cross, I can't bear!" Mary begins to cry.

Later on that evening, Tonya and Word are in the living room. They look up as they see their mother walking down the stairs. "There is food in the kitchen, Momma. We came up to see if you were hungry but you were asleep. Are you okay, Momma?" Word asked.

"Baby, I can't lie to you, I'm not doing well at all. How are you two holding up?"

"Momma, this is like a bad dream," Word states.

"I can't believe, that Daddy is gone." Tonya begins to cry again, wiping at her eyes with a crumpled up tissue.

"I know, baby."

"Momma, Sister Martin called Mickey."

"What? I told Sister Ramsey that I would like to notify my own children!"

"Momma, I just think everyone is trying to help out. Would you like me to call Thelma?" Word says.

"No, baby, I really think I should be the one to call her, Word. But I thank you, baby! In fact, I need to call her right now!" Mary walks upstairs to make the phone call that she is dreading having to make. She dials Mr. Williams' home phone.

"Hello."

Mary sits on the phone, not able to speak.

"Hello."

"Yes, hello. Is this the Williams' resident?" Mary says, trying to pull herself together.

"Yes, it is."

"Thomas, it's Mary...Mary McKinney."

"Oh, Mary, how are you? I just spoke to Greg the other day and I can reassure you that Thelma is alright, and staying here isn't any problem for me. We love her as if —"

Mary interrupts. "Thomas, I need to say something to you."

"I'm sorry for babbling on, Mary." Thomas chuckles.
"Thomas." Mary begins to weep.

"Mary, what's wrong?"

"Thomas, Greg passed away last night!" There is total silence on the phone.

"What did you just say, Mary?" Thomas is in disbelief.

"Yes, Thomas, my husband is dead." Mary begins to cry.

"Oh my God. Mary, I'm so sorry, I mean, I don't know what to say."

"I know, Thomas. I feel so numb I can't even think straight. Although I know I'm talking to you, it doesn't seem possible that I'm even telling you this. Is Thelma around? I need to speak with her."

"Yes, of course. Mary, since I'm right here with her, do you want me to tell her? And please understand I'm not trying to do anything but help."

"No, I need to tell my daughter, but I would appreciate if you could be there in the room with her for support," Mary says.

"Of course, I will. I'll get her." Thomas puts the phone down, and walks into the guest room where Thelma is staying.

"Thelma, sweetheart."

"Hey, Mr. Williams."

"Yes, sweetheart, your Mom is on the phone for you. She needs to speak with you now."
Thomas Williams is trying to keep any emotions he is feeling from Thelma.

"Aww, man, I thought that Daddy said he would give me until next week, at least. Mr. Williams, I don't want to talk to Momma right now. I'm really not feeling well, and all due respect, she's going to want to argue and I can't right now."

"Thelma, take it from me, you're going to need to take this call." Mr. Williams holds Thelma's hand as he speaks to her, with a look of sorrow in his eyes.

"Mr. Williams, what's going on?"

"Just come downstairs, please."

"Okay," Thelma says reluctantly. Suddenly feeling a release of anxiety, she begins to weep.

Gloria comes to Thelma. "Thelma, what's wrong?"

"I don't know, but I don't want to take this call."

"Daddy?" Gloria looks at her dad.

"Come with her, Gloria."

"Daddy, you're scaring me," Gloria replies.

They all walk down the stairs. Thelma walks over to the phone, with tears in her eyes.

"Momma?"

"Thelma, baby, I'm so sorry to call and tell you this—"
"NO!" Thelma couldn't even let her say the words. She already knew, her heart told her before she got to the phone. It seemed like time stood still. Thelma could see Mr. Williams and Gloria calling her name, but she couldn't hear one sound. At that moment, she knew that her life was over.

Pastor McKinney's funeral is held the following week. Thelma arrives home in time to be there, but isn't present when the family is gathering to enter the family car. Mickey is holding his mother's hand as Word and Tonya walk outside to leave.

Mary notices that Thelma has not come downstairs yet. "Mickey, I'll be right back. I need to go and find your sister."

"No, Momma, I can do that for you," Mickey replies.

"Are you sure, son?"

"Yes, Momma, it's the least I can do. I'm sorry that I couldn't be here more to help out."

"Are you kidding me? Baby, you are out there serving our country and making us very proud of you. So there is no need to feel bad about anything, alright, son? The point is, you're here now!" Mary McKinney says with a weak smile.

"Thanks, Mom. Let me walk you to the car." Mickey links his arm with his mother's.

"No, baby, I'm okay. Your little sister probably needs you right now!"

Mickey goes upstairs to check on Thelma. "Knock Knock! Hey, Thelma, are you in there?"

"Mick? The door is open."

"What's going on, are you okay?"

"I can't go, Mick."

"What do you mean? You have to go, Sis." Mickey walks over to the bed and puts his arm around his big sister.

Thelma releases an onslaught of fresh tears. "Mickey, I don't know if I can see Daddy like this." She sniffles and wipes her eyes with the back of her hand.

"Mickey, it's all my fault this happened."

"That's foolish talking, Thelma. God doesn't allow things to happen if it's not meant to."

Thelma widens her swollen eyes. "God? Don't talk about God to me." Thelma looks at her brother with tears in her eyes, but anger on her face!

"Now wait a minute, Thelma, we are all hurting here. We all are going to miss Daddy terribly, but we can never be angry at God. Besides, you know it's not what Dad would want, right?"

Thelma closes her eyes and sighs deeply. Mentally, she is exhausted. Physically, her body feels as if it is about to give out. She has no more fight left in her.

"Come on, Sis. It's all going to be alright, I promise."

A few days later, Thelma decides it is time to have a discussion with Momma. She walks up to her mom's bedroom and knocks softly.

"Hi, Mom."

"Hey, baby, come and sit next to me." Mary holds her arm out for Thelma to sit beside her.

"How are you holding up, baby?" Mary asks, moving Thelma's hair off of her face.

"I'm not, Mom."

"I know just how you feel, believe me, I do."

"Momma, I have to tell you something."

"Yes, baby?"

"Momma, I was having these dreams for a long time about Daddy being away and I couldn't get to him. I didn't know what they meant, now I think I do."

"Yes, sweetheart, when you were a little girl you would dream dreams, and most of them would come true. However, they kept you so upset most of the time, and so your Dad and I prayed for

169

you, and after a while, they stopped. But we always knew that you had a special gift. You could see things before it happened. You dreamed of being separated from your dad, that couldn't have been easy."

"No, Momma, it wasn't. I kind of felt what it was when I would dream it, I tried to pray them away but they wouldn't leave."

"Sometimes, honey, God has his way in preparing us for what is to come, I'm sorry, Thelma."

"Momma, I hate to say this, but I'm really angry with God for doing this to us!" Thelma has tears coming down her left cheek.

"Baby, I know just how you feel, but I have to hold on to God's word. When he tells us in his word that he will never leave us, or forsake us."

"Momma, there is no other way to put this, and I really hate to say this to you especially right now, but I'm going back to New York."

"Thelma, why? You have a family and you can stay here with us. It's what your Dad would want."

"Mom, I know this time is hard for us all, but I have to make things right. I feel if I go back, it will make things better for you all," Thelma says, looking at her mother. "Thelma, if you stay it will make things better for us. We need you here, as a part of our family. We have to help each other get through this," Mary replies. "Mom, I have made such a mess of things. I have to go. What can be worse than losing your Dad?"

"I love you, honey, and I want you home," Mary says holding Thelma's hands.

"Mom, we can talk about it tomorrow, okay?"

"Just say you're staying home," Mary tells Thelma.
"Mom, I hate what has happened to our family, I just cannot be here. I can't live without him, Momma. I can't live in this house and Dad's gone."

"Have you forgotten that was my husband?" Mary says, grabbing her Bible, stroking it and looking down.

"No, Mom, I haven't forgotten. I know that it's hard on you and I'm sorry, Momma."

"Well, you seem to only be concerned for yourself. If you really feel that way, Thelma, then go. If that's what you want. I honestly thought that you would want to be here for your own siblings."

"Momma, I have my own life and only God and I can fix it. Look, Mom, I thought that I at least owed it to you to tell you."

"Thelma, I can't do this right now. Just be courteous enough to tell your brothers and sisters that you're leaving this time, because apparently I don't matter!" Mary gets up to leave the room.

"See, Momma, it has nothing to do with you, my sister or brothers, it wasn't even Daddy. It's me. Me, Momma. I'm the one that has messed my life up. I'm the one that has all of these problems, so why should my problems bring a burden upon my family? Because of me, Daddy is dead. Go ahead and admit it, Momma. If I had not gotten myself into all of this mess, finding that stupid letter, getting pregnant, running away…need I say more?" Thelma is very upset, and is getting emotional.

"Thelma, I understand."

"Understand? What is it that you understand, Momma? My Daddy is dead, my world has crashed, and my life is completely over!"

"Your life is never over, Thelma, when you have God in your life. Remember how your Dad would always preach on God's love?"

"I can't take you using Daddy's name in past tense, it's too hard."

"I'm sorry, Thelma, I'm only trying to help you." Mary tries to hug Thelma, but Thelma pulls away.

"Well, maybe I don't want any help, and I certainly don't want to hear any talk about God or his love!"

"THELMA, how can you say that?"

"I don't know, Momma. It's just how I'm feeling right now. How can God love us, and take Daddy away when he knew we needed him so much?" Thelma walks to her mother's dresser, picks up a crystal vase and throws it against the wall, causing it to shatter.

Mary runs over to Thelma, and grabs her. Holding her in her arms. "I got you, baby. It's alright. The pain you're feeling is valid, baby. Trust me, it is, but, honey, God doesn't mean for this part of life to be cruel. It's just a process we have to go through to be with him. And most of all, we all know where your Dad is, he is with the Lord, he is, honey."

"Oh, Momma!" Thelma falls across her mother's lap and begins to weep. They both cry and embrace each other!

The others come running from upstairs and the entire family embraces once another as they weep together.

A week later, as the family prepares for Mickey and Thelma to leave, Mary cooks a family dinner. She is in the kitchen with Tonya and Thelma, who are helping to prepare the meal.

"Hey, Momma." Mickey kisses his mom on the cheek. "Good morning, son," she says, smiling at her oldest son. "Mickey, I can't tell you how much I'm going to miss you. I wish that all of my children could stay here with me." Mary looks over at Thelma.

"Yes, I know, Momma. I wish I could stay here longer, too," Mickey says.

"Mom, who's all coming over for dinner?" TiTi asked, looking over her mom's shoulder at her pies.

"No one but us, Tonya. It's just dinner for me and my babies today."

"Well, Momma, why so much food? Your cooking everything that..." Tonya pauses for a moment, "...that Daddy loves," Tonya continues. For a moment, the room goes silent.

"Hey, everybody." Word walks in the house.

"Where you been, boy?" Mickey puts his brother in a headlock.

"Man, you don't want any," Word says jokingly to his big brother.

"What you got, Word? Come on with it." Mick slugs Word in the arm.

"Now you guys be careful. Boy, it's been a long time since I've seen you two play like that."

"Momma, let me stop. I wouldn't want to hurt Mick."

"Really?" Mick replies. "OK, little man, I'll let you think that!"

"Now that I'm here, what can I cook, Momma?" Word teasingly asks his mom.

"NOTHING!" everyone replied.

"Haha, very funny," Word giggles and says.

"Word, you can make the punch or something," TiTi says.

"You know what would be really nice? If you could make a hot fire for us, Word. I'm a little chilly."

"Sure thing, Momma."

"Tonya, can you go and set the table?"

"Of course, Momma."

"And, Thelma, can you help me with the food?"

They look over at the table. Thelma is seated at the table with her head down. Mick walks over to her. "Hey, big head. Thelma?"

"Yea, Mick."

"Girl, don't be scaring us like that!"

"I'm sorry, I didn't mean to," Thelma says, talking really slow.

"You okay?" Mick places his hand across Thelma's forehead.

"Yes, I just don't feel so well," Thelma replies.

"Why don't you go and lay down, baby," says Mary.

"No, Momma, I'll be okay. I just need a moment.

"Okay, you sit there, Thelma. I'll help Momma with the food."

"Thanks, TiTi," Thelma replies, proudly smiling at TiTi.

"Everyone come and let's sit at the table." Mary calls the family together. They all sit down, recognizing that the person that means everything to them was not present! Their dad, and Mary's beloved husband. "Well, let's say grace," Mary says, holding back her tears.

"Momma, if it's alright with you, and everyone else, I would love to pray the blessing."

"Word, we would love that." Mary pauses for a moment. "Wait, honey, before you pray, I have something to say to all of you." She looks around the table at all of her children. "Mickey, I want you to know how proud of you your father was. He always bragged on you and he prayed every night for your safety. He said that he knows you will be the kind of man that will change the world." Mick looks at his mom, and smiles. "Tonya, your dad and I always said that you would be the one that would see the world and parts of it that he or I could only dream of; you are so smart. You made your daddy smile, and he loved you so very much."

"Oh, Momma, I miss him so much," TiTi says breaking down crying.

"Mr. Timothy, you are a mirror of your dad, you were called while you were in my womb. The knowledge that flows out of you when you speak, your dad would always say 'That Timothy will tread on the devil's territory and tear his kingdom down.'"

"Amen," says Word, wiping the tears away.

"Finally, Thelma, you were your dad's heart. Just me saying your name made him smile. One thing he always said about you is that God has called you to the ministry and the trials that you would endure in life would benefit the Body of Christ. You will bring many to believe in the gospel which is the good news of Jesus Christ. He loved each and every one of you, and honestly, I don't know why this happened. I am so lost without your father, but all I know is, I don't have a choice, but to trust that God knows what's best. Does it hurt? Yes! And it is hard to understand? But as a family, we will make it. That I promise you!"

After Mary spoke to the kids, they all cried and reflect on their father's memory, and that moment they all were together, just the way Pastor always wanted!

# Chapter 18

## My Brother's Keeper

Later on that night, TiTi and Thelma were hanging out in TiTi's room when they heard their mother crying in her room. "Thelma, can't you just stay home for a while? Listen to Momma, doesn't that bother you?"

"TiTi, you know that this entire situation hurts me, but there is nothing I can do about anyone's hurt. Heck, I can't even help my own hurt. You mean you want me to stay here with you, just say that," Thelma says, wrapping her arms around TiTi.

"Will it keep you here if I tell you that I want you to stay?" TiTi says. "Mmm, probably not, but you know I'm never far away from you – from any of you for that matter. I just feel that it's time for me to go, that's all! And TiTi, you will be out of school soon, then you will feel the same."

"No, I don't think that I can leave Momma after Daddy passing away, it's not right. Thelma, you know it's wrong." TiTi says, removing Thelma's arms from around her neck.

"I love you, but right now, no one's opinion matters, because this walk that I have ahead of me, only one pair of shoes was given and I got them to wear. TiTi, you know that I love you, all of you. We are sisters and we've always understood one another. We all are given different paths in life, like Daddy use to say when we stand before that great white throne, and have to answer to God.

Momma, not even Daddy, can answer for us. It's you and you alone, this is kind of like the same thing."

"I get it, Thelma. I guess everything is changing so much, I don't have time to process it all."

"Yes, lil sis, it's hard, especially with Daddy leaving us behind," Thelma says.

"You know what, Thelma? For some strange reason, I feel Daddy is working on our behalf from heaven."

"What do you mean, TiTi?"

"It's like the family dinner that we had, when was the last time we even done that without having a disagreement?"

"Yea, I see your point, TiTi. It was nice and I even felt Daddy's presence there just like he was sitting at the table," Thelma admits. "Word said that same thing, and I have to admit, I'm a little scared. Life is not going to ever be the same, this is so not cool. I am going to miss you, girl, but you can come and visit soon. At this time, I just need a fresh start, and the thing is, I can always come home if things don't work out."

"I want you to stay home, but I pray that things work out for you there, too, Thelma!"

"Thanks, TiTi." The two sisters embrace each other.

The next morning, Gloria arrives from New York City. "You okay, T?" she asks while helping Thelma pack her bags.

"No, not really. This is one of the hardest things I have ever had to do, I feel like I'm abandoning my family at the crucial time in all of our lives." Thelma sits on her bed with both arms wrapped around her childhood blanket.

"I'm sorry, Thelma. I can't even imagine what you are feeling. What is your heart telling you to do, Thelma?"

"I don't even know, Gloria. I want to leave and I know that I'm running away from my problems, but I don't know how else to handle it." Thelma begins to cry, and apologizes for crying to Gloria.

"It's okay to cry. Come here, Thelma. I'm here for you. I truthfully don't know what I would do if the shoe was on the other foot, but I do know this, what you are going through is just a test that you will pass. It's almost time, you ready?"

"Yes and no," Thelma replied quietly.

"Well, our flight takes off in a couple of hours, but we need to get there a little early."

Everyone is downstairs waiting for Thelma's to say goodbye before her departure. Word and TiTi are sitting together and Mary McKinney is sitting next to Mickey. Thelma comes downstairs with Gloria. "Hey, yawl, it's time for me to go," she says as she puts her luggage down on the floor.

"How's your grandmother, Gloria?" Mary kindly ask Gloria.

"Oh, Sister Mary, she's doing well."

"You know your grandmother is a real jewel. I just love her," replies Mary.

"Thank you, Sister Mary," Gloria says.

"So, my baby girl is going with you back to New York, huh?" Mary is talking to Gloria, trying to hold back the tears.

"Yes, ma'am, she is," Gloria says, walking towards the front door.

"Thelma?" Mary holds her arms out towards Thelma, looking at her daughter with tears in her eyes. "Oh honey, Momma wishes you would stay, but for now, I respect your decision," she cries as she holds Thelma tightly in her arms.

"Momma, I don't know how this is going to pan out for me, but I know I can't do too badly. After all, I was raised by two wonderful parents who have given me the best upbringing that they could have. Momma, anything that I've ever done or said to disrespect you, I didn't mean it. I know at times I made it hard for you."

"Thelma, baby, you are a wonderful and beautiful daughter that any woman would be proud to call their daughter!" They embrace, and cry.

"Promise you will call me every day, oh and write."

"I will, Momma."

"Oh and..."

"Momma, I'll stay in touch, I promise." Thelma kisses her mother on the cheek.

"Come here, Word. Give me a hug, boy."

"I'm going to really miss you, sis," Word says hugging Thelma.

TiTi begins to cry, and runs up to her big sister and hugs her.

"I love each and every one of you, please know that I feel I'm doing the right thing." Thelma begins to walk out the door.

"I'll be praying for you, sis," Word says.

Thelma looks at Word with tears in her eyes. "Prayers are always welcome, little bro."

Thelma blows a kiss to her family and walks out the door.

"I'll walk you outside, Thelma," says Mickey. "Thanks, Mick." Thelma replies.

"Thelma, I want you to know, that I stand behind your decision. I know it's not an easy one, but I understand."

"Thank you, Mick, that really makes me feel better."

"I wish that I could make it better for all of us. This will be a journey, but we will make it."

"Yes, Mick, we will. We have to deal with the cards that's dealt, but we'll win the game."

"I've always loved the way you viewed things, Sis."Mickey reaches in his pocket. "Thelma?" He hands her an envelope from his pocket.

"What's this?" Thelma says, taking the letter from Mick as he hands it to her.

"This is a letter from Daddy."

"Daddy?" Thelma is surprised and shocked.

"Yes, it's from Daddy. When he got sick the first time, he mailed this to me and made me promise to give it to you if anything ever happened to him."

"Oh, wow, Mick, I don't know what to say." Tears roll down Thelma's face.

"Yes, I know what you're feeling, sis. Just don't open it until you get settled, okay?"

"Thanks, bro," Thelma said through her tears.

"You're welcome, T. And remember, I will always be here for you; family is forever. Come here, girl. Mickey hugs his sister.

"Oh Mick, I don't know what I'm doing."

"Well, like Daddy use to always say, 'Look to the hills,' right? Well, you better go, and don't worry about Mom, the military is giving me personal leave, so I will be here to help Momma out for two more weeks. She doesn't know yet… I figured I would tell her after you left so she would have some good news. I'm helping to get Dad's affairs in order, and you know that's a lot."

"Mick, I'm sorry, I just couldn't stay. I can't…"

"Shh, sis." Mick puts his finger over his sister's mouth. "You have been holding it down while I was gone, now it's my time to help out. I'm the man of this family now."

"And you're doing a great job. I love you, Mick."

"I love you, too!"

Gloria walks over to where Thelma and Mick are standing. "Thelma, our cab is waiting."

"You don't get away without hugging me, Ms. Gloria."

Gloria accepts his embrace. "Oh, I'm so sorry, Mick."

"Love you, girl."

"I love you, too, Mick."

"Promise me you will take care of my sister."

"I got it, I promise!" Thelma turns around and her family is at the door.

"I love you all. I will miss you but you are in my heart forever. I am just a phone call or letter away," she says, waving at them and blowing kisses.

# Chapter 19

# A New Chapter

Three months later, Thelma is working at a local coffee shop. She has made some friends at her job and is enjoying meeting new people there. Michael, the taxi driver that she met when she first moved to New York, has become a very good friend.

"Good morning, Ms. Thelma," Michael says, walking into the coffee shop.

"Hey, Michael, to what honor do I receive this visit? Let me guess, you were just in the neighborhood, right?"

"Aww, you got me, I'm guilty. So what time are you taking lunch today, Ms. Thelma?"

"I'm not, Michael."

"Oh come on, why do you have to give me such a hard time, huh?" Michael says, leaning on the counter in front of Thelma.

"Michael, you're cool and I consider you a great person to hang out with, but…"

"But what, Thelma?"

"But I'm not looking to be in any relationship with anyone right now, I have too much on my plate." Thelma turns around and helps another customer.

"Wow, is this how you treat your friends in Arkansas? I don't want to marry you, I only want to hang out every now and then, but every time I come around, you act weird, or have some kind of excuse."

"Look, Michael," Thelma says, trying to explain herself to Michael.

"Never mind, Thelma, I get it. It don't take sign language for me to see you don't want to be bothered, and your point is clear – CRYSTAL!" Michael walks away to leave.

"Michael, wait a minute. I get off for lunch in fifteen minutes, will that be okay?"

Michael smiles. "It's perfect! I'll be outside waiting for you, don't keep me waiting long."

"I won't!" Thelma says, shaking her head and blushing.

As Thelma walks up to the courtyard where Michael is waiting, "Wow! You're breathtaking! Hey beautiful!" he says as she walks up to him, looking flustered.
"Hey, Michael. Sorry I'm running a few minutes late, I had one more customer before my break. She refuses to allow anyone else to help her but me. I think it's kind of cute, though. She has to be around eighty years old."

"Eighty?" Michael replies.

"Well, maybe not eighty, but she's old, though," Thelma says laughing.

"Don't worry about the time, Ms. Thelma, I would wait all day for you."

"You would, huh?" Thelma replies, sitting down across from him.

"Yes, ma'am, I would. These are for you." Michael hands Thelma a beautiful set of flowers he picked while waiting for her.

Thelma gasps at them. "Thank you so much, Michael. These are so beautiful. Why would you give these to me? No one has ever given me flowers before."

"Really? Well, looks like to me, you need new friends then. I love flowers. My mother had a flower garden when I was growing up. They always signified to me the meaning of beauty, and Thelma, you are just that!"

Thelma looks down at the ground, a tear trickles down her face. "MICAHEL, they are beautiful. You know my Dad use to do things like this for my Mom, just because. I was just thinking about that. You brought up good memories for me." Thelma smiles at Michael.

"Good, I was hoping they would make you smile. Thelma, you make me smile. Are you crying?"

"No, I'm fine, Michael, it's just…"

"Just what?" Michael inquires.

"Nothing. Hey, Michael, I heard that you were at some grand opening for a club, doing an open word session or something like that and the report was...you got skills."

Michael blushes and laughs. "Who told you that I got skills?"

"Oh, a little birdie told me. The birdie said that you got a standing ovation."

"A huh? Could this little birdie's name be Gloria?"

"Yes." Thelma laughs.

"Hey, Thelma, why don't you ever come around and hang out with us? I mean we're a cool group of pretty well-rounded young people. I'd like to think that we have our heads on straight."

"Oh, really?" Thelma says, laughing, looking at Michael.

"Yes, especially mine," Michael says, winking at Thelma.

"You have your way of bragging, but in a non-bragging sort of way," says Thelma.

"I've been wanting to ask you something."

"Ask me what, Michael?"

"How are you, Thelma? I mean, how have you really been since your father died?"

"Well, it's been really hard. I miss him every day, he always was there for me. It's not the same; my life seems empty. I really miss him." Thelma turns her head away, so Michael won't see her tears.

"You may not believe it, but I can identify with your pain. I lost my mother five years ago to cancer. The pain is sharp and it hurts. I remember crying and the pain getting worse."

"I'm sorry, Michael. I didn't know."
"How would you?" Michael gives Thelma a sideways smile.

"Yes, you're right. How did you cope with losing her?"

"To be truthful? There is no coping, you just have to live without them and it's very hard, but it does get better, that I can promise."

"Better how? I am ashamed to say, but I've been pretending that he is still alive and just on a very long vacation."

"Been there, done that, too. And sad as it is, that even stops working. I'm sorry, babe!" Michael realizes what he just called Thelma. "Thelma, I'm so sorry, I didn't mean to say that."

"It's okay, Michael. You know, as I sit here talking to you, it makes me really sad."

"I didn't mean to upset you, I just had been wondering, and I've also been driving Gloria crazy asking about you."

"Yes, I've heard. Michael? I know that you're a real nice guy, but what exactly do you think is happening here? I like you as a friend and I'm not looking to be in any relationships at this time. I'm fat, pregnant—"
"And beautiful. Hey, Thelma, relax, pump your brakes; I just want to be here for you that's all. Are we cool?" Michael puts his hand out for Thelma to shake.

Thelma smiles. "Yea, were cool."

"Good then, when will I see you again?"

"MICHAEL!" Thelma yells playfully, hitting him in the arm.

Michael laughs jokingly.

"Look, I will talk to you later. I better go before I have no job," Thelma says.

"Well, thanks for your time, Ms. Thelma."

"Man, Michael, you sound so old, just call me Thelma or T, anything other than Ms. Thelma."

"Alright, T." Michael helps Thelma off of the bench.

"Thank you, Michael, I'll see you later."

"See you, can I call you later on?" Michael asks.

Thelma hesitates. "Yes, I guess so, see ya, later!"

Gloria comes home and goes straight to Thelma's room. "Umm, open up this door, Thelma."

"Girl, just come in," Thelma says, looking at a magazine.

"Well, hello," Gloria says, grinning at Thelma.

"Hey now, girl, what's up and how was your day, Gloria?"

"Never mind about my day, how about yours?" Gloria says still smiling at Thelma.

"Oh, I just had a regular ole day, and what's up with all of this smiling?"

"Did you have a delicious lunch?" Gloria's says, beating around the bush.

"Yes, it was alright. Wait a minute, what are you talking about? Who told you what? Did Michael tell you that we had lunch together? We didn't even eat, we just talked."

"Michael didn't tell me anything, you just did," Gloria says, cracking up laughing.

"Aww, man, Gloria, stop being so nosey."

"Girl, I won't ever stop being nosey; that's what I do the best. I'll be in my casket and while everyone's walking around to view my body, I'll be raising up talking about 'Where y'all going to eat after this?'" Thelma and Gloria laugh together.

"You aren't lying, you are very nosey."

"Enough of this talking about me being nosey. Soooo?"

"Gloria, I'm not telling you anything."

"Oh, come on, girl, you have to tell me because I tell you everything."

"Don't even try it. I don't tie your arms behind your back and force you to speak!"

"Please." Gloria is begging Thelma to tell.

"All we talked about was everyday things. And he asked me why don't I hang out with you guys on the weekends and..." Thelma hesitates.

"And what, Thelma?"

"He gave me flowers!" Thelma says with a big smile.

"Girl, shut up. Did he really?" Gloria replies, smiling back at Thelma.

"Yes, and it felt so nice to get them, and I have to be honest, Gloria. I think he is the sweetest guy. Mild natured and he seems very caring!"

"Oh, Michael is the sweetest guy. A lot of my friends have had a crush on Michael, but he always told me, that he was waiting on God. Ooh, Thelma, do you like him?"

"No, I don't. I just happened to think he's a really nice guy, and I might add not bad on the eyes either."

"Thelma, Michael is one of the nicest people I know, and I'm telling you that every girl on this side of town tries to get with him!"

"I bet he goes out with them, doesn't he?"

"No, you're wrong, he doesn't, honestly. Michael has been my boy for a long time now and I've seen women throw themselves at him. And he's not moved, but with you, T, he's different. I mean, he really likes you!" says Gloria, trying to play matchmaker.

"I think he's great, too, but I'm just not ready for any relationships."

"Who said anything about that, shoot, just be friends. Some of the best relationships are formed from friendships. I wish I could find someone these days!"

"Well, there you go, why don't you try and date him, then?" Thelma says to Gloria.

"Girl, Michael is too nice for me, I like them bad boys, you know, someone to slap me around a little bit."

"GLORIA!" Gloria and Thelma laugh.

"Girl, I'm just playing. It's the weekend, what are you going to do tonight, Thelma?"

"You know what, I think I'll go out with you, I guess. It will be better than sitting in the house."

"Awesome, Thelma. I'm just hanging out with some friends. I think we're just having game night over at Tia's house, so you down?"

"Yes, I'll come. Umm… is Michael going to be there?"

"Well, look at you, asking about him already," Gloria says teasing Thelma.

"Not what you're thinking," replies Thelma, brushing her hair in the mirror. "I don't care, I think it's cute! Anyways, Ms. Thelma, I'm going to go lay down for a minute. Will you be ready to go around 8 o'clock?"

"First off, don't call me Ms. Thelma, you sound like…"

"I sound like Michael?"

"How did you know that he called me that?"

"I knew because he told me about your lunch." Gloria starts laughing. "GLORIA, I knew it."

"Well, like you said, I'm nosey."

Thelma threw her pillow at the door as Gloria walks out.

Thelma sits in her room thinking about her family back home; her Momma, TiTi, Word and Mick. It seems so weird not being with them, but what she really can't get over is that her Daddy is gone. *Oh my goodness, what has happened to me? I have tried to act as if he's on vacation and will be back soon, but my heart reminds me that he's not coming back, ever. I've watched Daddy do lots of funeral services at our church, and I've heard him say several times before* "To be absent from the body, is to be present with the Lord." *I just hate that saying. Yes, I know it's true, but I don't want him with God right now, I'd rather have him here with me. None of this seems fair, at all! I've also been feeling a little guilty about leaving Momma and the rest of my family, but I had no other choice but to leave. My stomach is getting bigger and for some reason I haven't allowed myself to bond with this baby, adoption has crossed my mind! But I don't want to do to this child what my real mother did to me. Abandoning a child is not what I call a* "Mother of the Year." *To have my child grow up wondering if I ever loved them would just break my heart! I really don't know what I will do. Daddy, why did you have to leave me, I need you.* As Thelma sits on the edge of her bed deep in thought, a letter falls to the floor. She walks over and picks up the piece of paper, and realizes it's the letter from her dad. Thelma could not hold back her tears, because at that moment, she felt her daddy was saying, "It's time, to hear my voice again."

Thelma picked up the envelope and her hands begin to shake. She couldn't see through all of the tears. She sat on her bed and slowly opened the letter. *Lord, help me. I feel so overwhelmed.* Thelma immediately brought the paper up to her nose and inhaled the familiar scent of her dad. Her daddy smelled so good all of the time. She laid across the bed holding the letter, clutching it with everything inside of her... afraid if she let it go, she would lose him all over again. Thelma looks at the letter, opens it and begins to read.

My dearest daughter, Thelma Marie McKinney. It is a pleasure to write you this letter, but...sadly, if you're reading it, that means I'm home with the Lord. Words can't explain how emotional this is for me, to know that you will one day read this letter and I'll be gone. Baby girl, I love you so much and I want you to remember everything you have been taught, and most importantly...don't turn your back on God. And Thelma, FORGIVE! Yes, life hurts, but let it go; hatred, envy, and resentment will kill you. The people you're holding those things against are moving on in life while you carry it. It's not worth it, Let It Go!!! Don't worry, it will all be fine. Remember the prophecy over your life, it's true, honey, you are called. Things will come to make you want to throw in the towel, but don't! If you will be faithful to God, he will be faithful to you. I'm so sorry, Thelma, for any hurt that I may have caused you, just know when the time is right...you will find your answers. Don't worry about me, I will be fine, what better place to be than with the Lord. 'Some glad morning when this life is over, I'll fly away.' Oh, that song just keeps ringing in my spirit, honey. I am not afraid of dying. I thought long and hard about it when I had the first heart attack, and if God comes for me I'll be alright with it all! Hang in there, love bug, I will miss you, too. But...I will see you again. Just know I'll be with you in your heart forever and always!

Thelma lay across her bed and begin to cry again. "Daddy, I miss you!"

"Thelma, pick up the phone!" Gloria walks to Thelma's room and opens the door.

"Huh?" Thelma answers with a pounding headache.

"Girl, guess who's on the phone?"

"Who, Gloria? I don't feel like playing no guessing game, who is it? And can you please keep your voice at a minimum?"

"What's wrong, Thelma, why are you crying?"

"I'm okay."

"Well, your boy, Michael's on the phone for you."

"Gloria, can you please tell him I'll talk to him later? I really don't feel like talking right now."

"Are you sure?"

"Yes, I am, I just need some time alone right now."

"I'll tell him, I hope you feel better, T!" Gloria closes the door.

# Chapter 20

## From Bad to Worse

A couple of weeks have gone by, and this weekend Michael and Thelma spent the evening together watching movies and talking. They have slowly become good friends. It was just nice to hang out and be with someone that Thelma could trust, no strings attached. That's what she loved about Michael: with him she could just be herself and not have to be fake and be someone she's not. Michael is such a gentleman and he keeps Thelma laughing about something all of the time. For Thelma, is was a good feeling to be happy, even if it was just for a little while.

"So what movies you want to watch, Michael?"

"Well, I kind of thought it would be nice to do something else besides movies. We can always watch movies."

"What 'something else' did you have in mind then?" Thelma turns towards Michael on the couch.

"I would love to just talk, Thelma. Let's learn a little more about one another."

"I'm cool with that, like what would you like to know?"

"I would like to know more about your father, the hero you loved so much. It seems like every time you speak about him, you light up and it makes you smile. Would it be alright if we did?"

"Of course it would be. I would love to share with you about him. What kind of things you would like to know?" Thelma smiles thinking about her dad.

"No special order, just share what you wish, babe. Just tell me what you loved the most about him."

"Wow, where do I start? Man, it's really weird talking about Daddy in the past tense, I mean, my dad was everything to me. We shared a special bond that even death still can't break. My daddy was a God-fearing man, who loved the Lord with all of his heart and soul; he took his ministry very seriously. He taught us all to respect the spirit of God, and to love unconditionally. I remember when I was much younger, Daddy would have these church picnics and he would try and provide all of the food so the families that couldn't contribute, wouldn't have to stress about it. He wanted everyone to just come and enjoy themselves. He was a giver at his best! Daddy and I loved on Sunday mornings. My daddy would stand up in the pulpit and stretch his arms out and say 'If you are sitting out there in the pews and you walked into this church, whether on your own or someone helped you, that means you are blessed to see another day. Turn to your neighbor and say 'Neighbor, the Lord has blessed me and I have a reason to give him praise.'' And the way he would say it, the church would immediately go up in a praise. People would begin to jump with joy and cry out while clapping their hands 'Thank you, Lord.' It was an amazing feeling!"

"Wow, Thelma, it sounds like your dad's church and ministry was awesome. Like he really cared about people."

"Oh, he did! My dad would give you the shirt off of his back, and then go into his closet and give you more! But he was not just a person that would do things for attention or for recognition at all. Daddy has even gone as far as paying people's rent or a utility bill and never said a word."

"You mean they never knew that it was him?" Michael says.

"That's exactly what I mean. Momma would sometimes get upset when he did that, because she would say, 'Honey, they need to know who blessed them.' And Daddy would say, 'God blessed them and that's all they need to know.' I remember asking him, why didn't he want some people to know some of the things he did, and he would say, 'Baby, sometimes people need to believe that God is still in the miracle working business and if they knew I'm the one that paid a bill, they would take the focus off of God. Thelma, remember only what you do for Christ will last.' I'll never forget those lessons Daddy taught me, it's what keeps me going each day. He was truly my hero, my daddy never judged me or made me feel bad about the mistakes I made. He always made something positive out of the situation, no matter how bad it may have been, my siblings and I could always count on Daddy to make us feel better in the end!"

"It's strange, but I feel like I knew your dad just from hearing the stories and how highly you speak of him," Michael says, looking at Thelma.

"Michael, my Dad would have loved you. I know he would have. In some ways you remind me of him!"

"Well, I count it an honor for you to say that to me, thank you, Thelma."

"You're welcome, Michael. You are sweet to me and I appreciate who you are and our friendship. I thank God for you!"

"And I thank God for you as well!"

For the rest of the evening, Michael and Thelma shared things about each other's past, families, their goals, and more. Thelma was happy to meet a man that was not all about himself. One that wants to share with her what's important in her life. Michael got brownie points for that in her book.

It's been seven months since she left home and Thelma is feeling really irritated. She has a lot of blessings to be thankful for: she got a raise and promotion to Manager at the coffee shop, she has her own apartment, and she is feeling independent and stable. She also has a lot of struggles with missing her family. Her baby is about to be born and she's not excited. And to top it off, her family thinks she had a miscarriage! Thelma only told them this because she didn't want them to worry more about her. Gloria thought that it was cruel of her, but, oh well! Thelma really hasn't been in touch with her family as much. She knows better, but talking to them on the phone is all she's done. It's for the best at the moment!

TiTi and Thelma write occasionally; Word has sent pictures. Thelma tried reaching out to her mom, but she always seems too busy. Thelma knew that running the church couldn't have been that easy after her dad passed away. She's feeling very guilty because she knows home is where Daddy would want her to be, but she has to find her own self right now. Thelma has one more doctor's appointment until the baby is born. The due date is October the 10th. Thelma has seriously thought about adoption, but she promised she would be the mother that her biological mother wasn't to her. She couldn't even imagine giving up her baby to have someone else raise her own flesh and blood. She could never live with herself. *NO, if I created this child, I will raise this child; with or without any help from Johnny or his sorry family! He's been calling talking about he wants to be a part of the baby's life, I don't think I want this. I'm so confused on what direction to take, I know if Dad was here, things would be much better for me.*

There's a knock at Thelma's door that interrupts her thoughts. It's Michael. "Hey, beautiful, how are you feeling?" he asks as he kisses her cheek.

"I'm good, and how are you?" answers Thelma.

"Well, since I've spoken to you last, I'm extremely hungry."

"You haven't eaten yet, Michael?"

"No, I was hoping that you and I could grab a bite after your doctor's appointment."

"That would have been nice, but I thought you knew that I have to be back to work by 3 o'clock."

"Oh, I didn't know," Michael replies sounding sad.

"I'm sorry," Thelma says, rubbing Michael on the back.

"No need to apologize, Thelma. It's okay, you didn't know."

"Do you think we can grab a bite to eat tonight?" says Thelma.

"Yes, sure, why not!" Thelma thought it was very weird when she and Michael were together. They both knew they were attracted to each other, but they also knew their limitations. Well, she did anyway. Thelma found Michael to be trustworthy, kind, and very supportive of her. She thanked God for him. Although he knows where she stands in this whole thing, it hasn't changed his treatment towards her and the baby. He is a wonderful man! "Michael, before we go, I just wanted to thank you for being here for me. I know that at times I can be a little grumpy and almost unbearable, but you have proven to me that you care."

Michael walks close to Thelma, and rubs her face with the back of his hand. "I more than care for you, Thelma, and nothing could deter me away from you. You are a special woman in my life!"

"Wow, thank you, Michael."

"Thelma, please stop thanking me. It is my pleasure. Now can we get to this doctor's appointment?"

"Yes, let's go!" They both are laughing together while leaving Thelma's place.

Thelma and Michael take a seat when they arrive to the appointment. As they wait in the waiting room, a lady sitting across from them keeps smiling as she stares. "Ma'am, is everything okay? You keep looking at me and my friend."

"Oh yes, honey, I'm sorry to stare, but you two make such a beautiful couple." The lady smiles again. "It must be so nice having a new baby and starting off your new lives together. Just remember to keep God first, and everything else will come. God Bless you both, honey!"

"Thank you, ma'am, but—" Before Thelma could correct the lady, Michael grabs her hand and smiles, and for that moment, Thelma pretended like he was the father of her child and they were together. Thelma had to admit, it wasn't a bad feeling. It felt amazing!

The nurse calls Thelma back for her appointment. Her usual doctor is away delivering a baby so they see one of the other practice doctors. The doctor performed an ultrasound after speaking with Thelma and hearing how she has been feeling lately. Michael and Thelma head back to the waiting room while the doctors analyze the results.

After what feels like hours, Thelma and Michael are greeted by Doctor Malis, her main OB/GYN. "Hello, Thelma and Michael. It's good to see you again. I am really sorry about the long wait. If you can sit down, I have your results from your ultrasound." He turns to look Thelma in the eyes. "Thelma, how are you feeling?"

"Hi Doctor Malis, I was feeling a little yucky last night, but I just slept it off. For the most part, I guess I must be getting really close to delivery, because the baby hasn't been that active for a couple of days. Is that why they did the ultrasound earlier? What's going on?"

"Thelma, I really need to talk with you for a minute. But before we continue, I need to ask if it is okay for Michael to stay. I know he has been here for most of your visits—"

"Yes, he can stay. You are scaring me...what is going on?"

Michael grabs Thelma's hands and sits next to her on the bed. Thelma's eyes have welled up with tears and she is having trouble breathing. "Doctor Malis, I need you to just be straight with me. What did my ultrasound show?"

"Thelma, there's no easy way to say this. Your baby has suffered Meconium Aspiration Syndrome. This occurs when a newborn infant aspirates or breathes in a mixture of meconium."

"I'm confused, Doctor, talk to me as though I don't know medical terms. What is meconium?" Thelma says, holding Michael's hands with both of hers.

"It means, Thelma, that your baby has swallowed a bowel movement and didn't make it." At that moment Thelma, leans forward and drops to her knees. "What did you say, Doctor Malis?" She asks, looking up at the doctor from the floor.

"Thelma, I'm so sorry," the doctor says, consoling Thelma with his hand on her shoulder.

"Oh, Michael." Thelma begins to weep. "OH GOD WHY ARE YOU DOING THIS TO ME?" She screams through her tears.

"Thelma, I got you. Lay back in my arms, baby, I'm here!" Michael says, sitting on the floor with Thelma laying between his legs, holding her in his arms.

"Doctor Malis, are you sure? I mean, Thelma and the baby were fine the last visit I brought her to. There has got to be something you can do, right? Maybe take another ultrasound," Michael says, with a tear rolling down his right cheek.

"Michael, I am so sorry, but the ultrasound is accurate. I need to talk with Thelma to discuss alternatives."

"I need Michael here. Whatever you have to talk to me about, Michael can stay," Thelma says through her sobs.

"Doctor Malis, I'm in total shock. I can't wrap my mind around what you just told me. I mean, are you sure? I mean she hasn't moved in the last couple of days but couldn't she be resting to prepare for her birth?"

"Thelma, all I can tell you is I'm sure and I'm sorry. This happens often to women, and it's a sad situation. We will need to decide whether you should have a C-section or deliver the baby naturally."

"What do you mean...deliver the baby naturally?" Thelma asked.

"Thelma, you are almost full-term and there is no other way to do it. You will give birth to your baby just as any other mother will, and you can even hold her when she is born. But unlike other mothers, when your baby is born you will not be able to see her take her first breath or take her home. You will hold her to say your goodbyes. And this needs to happen today or tomorrow if you really need one more night with her. We will induce you and you will go into labor. I am so sorry, Thelma. I will give you a couple moments to talk about what is best for you."

"Oh God."

The next moments feel like an eternity. Thelma feels as if she can't breathe, her heart feels like someone put a dagger through it and then yanked it out quickly and carelessly. *What have I done to deserve it all? I can't take anymore!*

"I need to go to the store and check in. I never called in today and they were expecting me by 3 — "

"Thelma, you lay down. I already called you in back when we were in the waiting room. I could see you were distracted so I didn't want you to have to worry about it. I will call now and talk with Karmen about what is going on. I will let her know that you will be out for a few days. All you need to do is relax. You took in a LOT of information today and made a very hard decision. Tomorrow you go in and have a very long, emotional day ahead. I will do whatever it is you need for me to do."

"Oh, Michael! What would I do without you?" She holds back tears, trying to be stoic as she walks into the room.

"It's okay to cry. I'm so sorry, Thelma. If I could take the pain away, I would! Come here."

Thelma walks back to the living room and lays down in Michael's arm for a while. He reassures her that everything will be alright. A few hours have passed and Michael realizes that he's late for his shift. "Oh no! Look at the time. I am so sorry to do this but I have to head to work. I couldn't find anyone to cover my shift when we were at the doctor's office and we got called in and I just lost track of having to find someone. I am so sorry Thelma. Will you be okay until I come back? Would you like for me to contact Gloria or anyone else? I really don't want you here by yourself."

"No, Michael, not right now. I just want to lay here for a while."

"Ok, I'll be right back, babe, OK? You call me if you need ANYTHING."

"Yes, I will be okay. Take your time… I am not going anywhere." Thelma says, closing her eyes again.

*I'm totally numb right now. What am I suppose to do?* Thelma is holding her stomach as she lies on the couch with her eyes closed. *My dear baby, Momma loves you. I know I said I was confused about what I would do after you were born, but I love you! I need you in my life, please wake up, I can't stand to lose someone else that I love. Dear God, please help my baby wake up, this one I don't know if I can bear. Holding her is what I've longed to do, taking care of her, loving her and*

*being there with her the way my real mother was not there for me! Lord, I know that I've made a mess of my life, but please don't punish me, not this way. I'll do anything, God. Please!* She begins singing. "Hush little baby don't you cry, Momma's going to sing you a lullaby, and if that lullaby don't sing, Momma's going to buy you a diamond ring."

Later on that night, Thelma's still at her place on her couch. Michael is in the kitchen making her some warm tea. "Thelma, are you hungry? Thelma!"

Michael walks into the living room where Thelma is finally sleeping soundly. Her cheeks are tear stained and her eyes are puffy from crying while he was gone. He gently places his hand on her back, giving her a soft rub.

"Michael?"

"Yes, it's me." He hands her the steaming mug and motions for her to sit up. "Here I made you some hot tea. Sit up and drink something. I know you haven't moved since I have been gone." Michael kisses Thelma on the forehead.

"What would I do without you, Michael?"

"That's something you will never find out!"

"You know what? I'm going to take you up on that offer, because, Michael, I need you. Thank you for being my rock."

"Thelma, you will, WE will make it through this!" Michael sits on the couch with Thelma and holds her in his arms as she drinks her tea.

The next morning Michael calls Gloria and a few other friends to support Thelma on one of the most difficult days she has faced.

At the hospital, the nurses come into Thelma's room. The one in charge begins speaking. "Good morning, honey. I am Lisa, and I will be your nurse today. We will be getting you ready for delivery. If there is anything you need through this process, just know that I'm here every step of the way."

Thelma stares into space, while the nurse is speaking to her. There's a knock at the door. It's Gloria. "Hey, T." Gloria quietly walks into Thelma's hospital room, walks over to Thelma and kisses her on the cheek.

"Gloria, what are you doing here?"

"You're my best friend. Michael called and told me what happened. I'm here for you, okay?"

"Gloria, I'm scared," Thelma says, looking up at her best friend.

"I know, T. You are not alone. Michael and I are here and most of all, God's got your back!"

"Does he really?" Thelma says, turning her face away from Gloria.

"Of course he does, Thelma!"

Dr. Malis enters the room with Thelma and Gloria. "Hi Thelma, I'm here. They've started in your IV some medicine that will make you feel better, okay? Just try and relax and it will be all over very soon. How are you doing, dear?"

"Not good, Doctor, I'm so hurt."

The doctor looks at Thelma with sadness in his eyes. "I know, dear. This isn't going to be easy but you have a great support system. Rely on them to help you." He turns and walks towards the door. "I'll see you in the operating room."

Thelma is lying in the bed with a blank look on her face. "Where is Michael, Gloria?"

"I think he went to move his car so he wouldn't get a ticket." Michael walks into the room. "Oh here he is!" Gloria exclaims, never having been happier to have Michael around.

Thelma stretches her hands out to him.

"Hey, pretty lady." Michael takes her hand and kisses it. They make eye contact, and Michael kisses Thelma softly on the cheek. "Thelma? I'm here, okay?"

"Yes, Michael...Michael?"

"Yes, hun," Michael answers.

"Will you be in the room with me?"

"I'll be with you all the way," Michael says, standing beside her bed.

"Do you mind, Gloria?" Thelma says to Gloria, making sure her best friend wasn't feeling left out.

"No, sweetie, I'm down with whatever's going to get you through this. And I think Michael is a great choice. I'll be here when you get back. I love you, girl!"

Thelma begins to cry with fear. Gloria goes over to Thelma and leans down, whispering in her ear. "T, it's going to be okay!" Gloria kisses her best friend on the cheek, then starts repeating the 23rd Psalm. "Yea tho I walk through the shadows of death—" Thelma finishes saying the rest. "I will fear no evil." Thelma closes her eyes.

A few hours have passed, Thelma has had the C-section and she's in her hospital room. The nurse and doctor check in on her.

After doing her vitals and checking on how she is feeling, Doctor Manis asks, "Would you like to hold your baby and take some time to say goodbye?"

Thelma answers, crying, "Yes, I would like to see her." As Thelma lies in her hospital room waiting for them to come back with her baby, her body begins to shake. She can hardly see through her tears. Michael is holding her hand as Gloria strokes her hair back off of her face.

The nurse walks into Thelma's room door with this little bundle wrapped in a blanket with teddy bears printed on it. Thelma's hands begin to shake. "Here is your baby, Thelma. Now, you only have about an hour and will be back to get her. If you want us to come earlier, just hit the button and we will be right in?" Thelma could hear the nurse speaking, but she could not release any words out of her mouth. She just wanted to see her baby's face.

Michael turns to the nurse and nods his head yes. Thelma looks down and sees a head of beautiful hair. She pulls the blanket further back and there lay her pretty little girl. She was so perfect. It was hard to believe that she wasn't alive. Thelma holds her tight and kisses her over and over – her skin so soft and her body is so warm.

Gloria walks over. "She's so beautiful, Thelma." Gloria starts to cry and then walks out of the room without saying another word.

"Michael, I love her so much. I never want to let her go, never!"

"I know you do, babe, I know."

Thelma looks down and gently takes her little hands. Her fingers are so tiny, and Thelma's heart is breaking. Thelma wraps her in her blanket to keep her warm, because in her mind, her baby is still alive.

"Thelma, are you going to name her?" asks Michael.

"Yes, I already have. Her name is Joy, Joy Karina McKinney. Joy, you have your grandfather's last name; he would have loved you so much!" Thelma holds her baby close to her heart while the tears fall. The time flies by and before she knows it the hour is up.

"Michael, I feel so guilty because I told my family that I had a miscarriage. I spoke it into existence, it's all my fault!"

"Baby, don't do this yourself, none of what has happened has anything to do with you, it's God's plan, babe, it's his plan!" says Michael.

The nurse returns to the room. "It's time, Ms. McKinney."

"NO! Please don't take her away. Please, I'll do anything, just a little more time?"

"Ten more minutes and then I'll have to take her, I'm so sorry, sweetheart," the nurse says, walking away knowing this is one of the toughest parts of her job.

"Michael? If you don't mind, I would like to be alone with her."

"Of course, I'll be right outside if you need me." He nods toward the door.

Thelma looks down at her baby and feels as if she wants to take her and run away so no one could find them, but she knows that it's impossible. The room grew silent—almost too still.

"Baby, Joy, I want you to know that Mommy loves you so very much. It's going to be hard for me to let you go, but I'll never let you go in my heart, my beautiful baby girl. You will be welcomed in heaven by lots of people that love you – your Poppa McKinney for sure. I know you're in good hands. I don't know why this happened, but I want you to know that I'm so sorry. I will think of you every day, and carry you in my heart until I see you again, my dear angel! I love you, baby girl." Thelma took a little pink ribbon and placed it in her hair, then she kissed her ever so gently. "Goodbye, sweetheart, for now!"

The nurse, came in the room, and Thelma knew it was time. "I'm sorry, Ms. McKinney, but it's time. But I want you to know that I'm praying for you, honey. Things will get better." The nurse takes Thelma's chin and lifts it up. "Keep your head up, for God is with you!"

"Can I kiss her one more time?"

"You sure can, sweetheart," the nurse replies.

"Goodbye, my Angel. I love you!" The nurse takes the baby away.

A few days later, Thelma has a small service for Joy. It was nice to acknowledge her as part of her family...her precious daughter that she would never forget. Michael, Gloria, Mr. Williams and more were there to support her and to say goodbye to her beautiful baby girl!

# Chapter 21

## A Test of Faith

*Lord, this has truly been a year in a half, I know that something's got to give. Losing my dad and next my baby girl, and on top of that just life kicking me in the behind. It has almost been a year, I need a breakthrough! I called my Momma and siblings the other day, and of course, they want me home. But I can't. Not at the moment. I'm feeling that although it's been really rough for me, I'm loving my independence. But I reassured them it will at least visit soon!*

Today is Thelma's day off. She and Gloria have planned a much-needed girls' day that involves hanging out at the mall and doing lunch. The phone rings and it's Gloria. "Hey, kid, what are you doing?"

"Oh, waiting for you to call. What time are we heading out?"

"Tell you what, T, I'll pick you up and we will be on our way. That way you can have a full day to just chill."

"Cool, thanks, Gloria."

"Be there in a few, there is something I need to give you."

"I'll be waiting!"

About twenty minutes later, the phone rings. "I'm outside."

"OK, on my way out." As Thelma heads out towards the car, Michael is pulling up,

"Where are you heading?"

"Oh, I told you, I'm hanging out with Gloria today, remember?"

"No, I don't remember you telling me," Michael replies.

"Anyway, what's up, Michael?" Michael steps out of his car. "I was coming to see if you wanted to have dinner with me?"

Thelma stands there looking at Michael, pondering what to say. "That sounds nice, but not tonight, okay? I'm going to hang out with my girl, but I'll call you later."

"Yea, whatever," Michael says, with an attitude.

"Michael, are you okay?" Thelma says with concern.

"I'm fine!" Michael gets in his car and slams his car door.

"MICHAEL!" Thelma tries to scream his name but he drives away.

"Girl, what just happened there?" Gloria asked.

"Gloria, I don't even know, that was weird. I've never seen Michael so upset before."

"Yea, that's crazy," Gloria agrees.

"Girl, did you hear him?"

"No, but I could tell by his body language that there was a problem. Let's not worry about that right now, this is our day."

Thelma gets upset. "Thelma, why are you crying?"

"Because I've never had a falling out with him and this upsets me! I never want to hurt him, he's been too good to me."

"Oh girl, it will be alright, you're with Michael every weekend and I've stepped back a lot. But I miss you, too. He will be just fine, it's only one day. You alright?"

"Yes, and you're right, girl!" Thelma says agreeing with Gloria.

"Oh, before we take off, this letter came to our house for you. It doesn't have a return address or anything."

"Hmm, from whom I wonder?" Thelma asked.

"I don't know, T, but maybe you can open it?" Gloria says laughing.

"Ok, nosey."

"You know it," Gloria replies. Thelma opens the letter and stares at it.

"What is it, Thelma?" "I can't believe this. Girl, I don't have time for this, it's from nobody." Thelma takes the letter and puts it back in the envelope."

"Thelma, what's going on?"

"Here!" Thelma tosses the letter towards Gloria's direction. Gloria looks down and picks it up to read it.

"Thelma? This is from your mother, your real mother."

"IT'S FROM NOBODY and I don't want to mention this anymore, okay, Gloria? Promise me!"

"Are you sure? Thelma, it's your real mother, maybe you need to—" Gloria was cut off by Thelma.

"Maybe I need to do nothing but forget about her and go on with my life!"

"I get it, but you're going to have to learn to forgive."

"I'm cool, can we just go, please?"

"Yes, ma'am!" Gloria starts the car to drive away, Thelma is mumbling to herself.

"I can't get over this one. Now that took the cake. You been gone all of my life and you think you can just pop back into it? What do people be thinking? How is she just going to interrupt my life because she's ready? Well, I'm dribbling the ball now. It's in my court and I'm not playing this game!" Thelma says.

"Well, T, you have a right to feel the way you do."

"Yes, I do. I mean, all of this time she didn't know if I was dead or alive, and now she's all concerned about me, leaving me for another woman to raise her responsibility!"

"So, it seems she was asking you in the letter, could she see you?"

"Yes, I think that's what she was saying, but not a chance. What do I need to see her for? What could we possibly talk about? I'm not trying to be the voice of reason."

"Thelma, I see this type of situation all of the time on my job, and nine times out of ten, the parent who has deserted the child suffered a trauma in their own life and had to walk away. I'm not for one moment excusing what she did, but I'm just saying—"

"Well, say no more, because I will never see her. I have a mother!" The girls ride in silence for a while. "Gloria, I don't think I can do this," Thelma says, putting her head down.

"Do what, girl, meet your mother?"

"No, I need my baby girl. I see her in my dreams, Gloria. I even hear her crying at night. I'm an emotional wreck!" Thelma begins to cry extremely hard.

"Thelma, I'm here for you, and I'm so sorry, I really am. This is why I wanted you to have this day. You have been through so much,"

"It just hurts so bad, one day I'm pregnant and she is kicking and moving around, and then before I know it, I'm giving birth to her, and I'm given a time frame on how long I can embrace my very own child. Gloria, I had to hand my beautiful baby girl over to a nurse and watch her take her away forever!"

"Thelma, I can't pretend to ever act as if I know what you are going through, and I pray to God above, I never will. You have been through a lot, girl, but God is still carrying you, because that's what he does. I have a suggestion, I know this really sweet lady who is the assistant director of the company I'm working at now. She is a grief counselor. What do you think about seeing her? You know, just to get some of this off of your chest."

"Are you kidding? Gloria, I ain't going to no shrink."

"Look, Thelma, she is a counselor and she's good at what she does. We all can use someone to talk to, so please consider it. Michael can tell you about her. I recommended her to him, when his mother passed away, and he seems to be much better?"

"What do you mean?"

"Oh girl, Michael was a total wreck after his mom passed. You think you were close to your dad? You haven't seen close until you've seen him and her together. She was the apple of his eye, and Michael took it really hard when he lost her,"

"I'm not making any promises, but I'll think about it," Thelma says as they pull into the mall parking lot. She removes her seatbelt and opens the door. She pulls the car mirror down and fixes her makeup, breathing in deeply. "Let's go pretend I am normal for a few hours," she says as she looks over to Gloria.

"Oh, and did I mention this is my treat today?" Gloria asks with a big smile across her face.

"Well, now I feel amazing." Thelma laughs.

The girls put their arms around one another and walk in the mall laughing with one another.

That next day, Thelma is concerned because she hasn't heard from Michael. She picks up the phone to call him, and before she could call, there's a knock on her door. "Who is it?"

"It's me, Michael."

Thelma gets excited that Michael has come over. "Oh, hey, hold on, let me shut the alarm off."

Thelma disarms the alarm system and opens the door. "Hey, Michael."

"Hello, Thelma." Thelma hugs Michael and begins to cry.

"What's wrong, Thelma?" Michael hugs Thelma back.

"I don't know, I just was worried that, you were still upset at me."

"Um, yea, about that. I needed to come and apologize for how I acted yesterday."

"No, you don't have to."

"Yes, I do. Thelma, I don't know what came over me, I am so sorry. I guess I just can't stand not to be with you, and we usually hang out on the weekends."

"Yes, Michael, I wanted to talk to you about that. It's not that I don't want to be with you, it's just I have other friends and I love to spend time with them as well," Thelma says, sitting next to Michael on the couch.

"Is that what you refer to me as, just your friend?"

"Yes, of course you're my friend, Michael. But you're a very special friend that I keep close to my heart." Michael stands up and walks away from Thelma.

"Ok, now that you said that, I'm going to ask you this. What exactly is going on between us, Thelma? Clearly you know how I feel about you, but I am making a fool out of myself thinking that I have a shot at being with you."

"It's not that I don't want us to be together, it's just that my situation is complicated," Thelma says, walking over towards Michael.

"COMPLICATED!" I think that I've proven to you that I can handle any complicated situations, Thelma. Haven't I been here for you?"

"Yes, you have, Michael, but at the same time, I told you from the beginning that I couldn't be more than friends right now."

"Yes, you did, but that's what your mouth says. Your actions, and certainly your heart, say something else toward me! Let me ask you something, Thelma. When you didn't hear from me in a day, how did that make you feel?"

"Well, of course I didn't like it. Look, I never said that I didn't care about you or that I didn't want us to be friends, Michael."

"There you go with that 'friend' word again. I hate it! When you lost the baby, I told you that I would never leave you and would always be here, in so many words, you knew that I was
falling in love with you. Now you're telling me this?" Michael starts pacing the floor.

"Michael, why are you acting like I've never told you?"

"You know what, Thelma? You're right, you have told me, and I was too stupid to get the message. But now I got the message, and it's clear. Crystal! The truth is, Thelma, I don't want to be just your friend, and if that's all I can be at this moment, I have to just walk away."

"What are you saying, Michael?"

"Oh, I think you know just what I mean. You're punishing me, because of all of the other hurt you have been through. But the truth is, I'm the person that's not going to ever hurt you, and you're pushing me away. I need to go for a walk!"

"Michael, I really don't want you to leave!"

"Well, I think it's for the best, Thelma. I'll be around!" Michael leaves and closes the door, Thelma calls him back, but he keeps walking.

Four days pass, Thelma is at the coffee shop and has been waiting to see if Michael would stop by like normal. But he hasn't. Gloria has been out of town on business but is scheduled to return today. Thelma's friend Donavin is working with her and he notices that Thelma's spirits are low.

"Thelma, girl, you just haven't been yourself lately, now I don't mean to butt in…"

"Well, don't, D."

"Oh no you didn't, girlfriend! Now you know your sarcasm is just making me pry more. Now what's up with you, chile?"

"I'm cool, Donavin, I am."

"You're not cool, you've been moping around this coffee shop as if you just lost your best friend, now what's going on?"

"I think I did," Thelma says, looking at Donavin.

"Did what?" Donavin turns to Thelma, anxiously awaiting an answer.

"Lose one of my best friends!"

"Who? It's Michael, huh?"

"How do you know everything?"

"Because I can tell, and you miss him, don't you?"

Thelma starts to clean off of the counter. "Yes, I do," Thelma says, throwing the cleaning rag down on the counter.

"Girl, what happened?"

"Donavin, Michael has been trying to date me since I've moved here, and I told him up front that I wasn't looking to get serious with anyone, but he feels as if I'm turning him away. I really care about him. He has been so incredibly good to me, and now I think I blew it."

"Girl, that man sounds like he has fallen in love with you, and not only does it sound like it, I can tell just the way he looks at you!"

"Really?"

"Yes, girlfriend, really. Tell me something, Thelma, what's holding you back? He is nice, and certainly easy on the eyes, and most of all, has been there for you through thick and thin. I've watched the whole thing and I knew he was falling for you! So what is it?"

"Oh, Donavin, I don't know, I think I'm scared of messing our friendship up. I've managed to mess everything else up in my life!" Thelma sighs, sitting down in a chair.

"Well, Thelma, maybe this is the one thing that you can make right," Donavin raises his hand before Thelma can protest.

"All I'm saying is, you don't have to marry him tomorrow, but it seems like you can use a man like Michael around. And if you don't want him, girlfriend, pass him right on over, honey chile!"

"Donavin, you're so crazy." Thelma laughed.

"I know I am, but this time I'm serious. I think you should just give him a chance."

"Here comes customers, we will chat later!"

"Alright, but I hope you heard me," says Donavin, walking to the back of the Café.

"I did, thank you, Donavin."

"You're welcome, girl," yells Donavin from the back of the Café.

Later on that evening, Thelma goes by Gloria's to see if she has made it in yet. Granny opens the door. "Oh my, I can't believe my eyes, is this Thelma, Ms. Thelma McKinney?" Granny says, opening up the door.

"Granny, I know it's been a while since I've been to see you," Thelma says, looking up at Granny in shame.

"It's been more than a while, this really doesn't make any sense. You get your own place and I don't see you at all anymore." Granny is fussing at Thelma.

"You're right, Granny, and I'm sorry," Thelma says, feeling embarrassed to be called out by Granny.

"Look at you, you're too skinny. I can see you haven't been eating well at all," Granny says, looking Thelma up and down.

"No, I'm fine, Granny. Don't fuss over me, really, I am fine."

"Well, fine or not, you come over here and get you something to eat. I made some butter beans with smoked neck bones in them, fried chicken, corn bread muffins, and peach cobbler!"

"Wow, Granny, that sounds great, but I came by to see if Gloria had made it back in town."

"No, honey, she had a layover. She won't be back until in the morning, if it's the Lord will, and he says the same!"

"Oh, I didn't know. How have you been, Granny?" Thelma removes a cup from the cabinet and pours some tea.

"Oh, honey, I'm blessed and highly favored of the Lord, and just striving to do his will!"

"You look great, Granny. It's always nice to see you."

"Thanks, honey. How have you really been, Thelma? Have a seat and let me fix you a plate. Unless you have somewhere else to go, and you're too busy for old Granny here?"

"I'm never too busy for you, Granny. And to answer your question, I haven't been doing that well, it's been extremely hard."

"You mean losing the baby?"

"Yes, Granny, especially that. I can hear her cry at night."

"Yes, honey, I know that pain all too well."

"You do?" Thelma asked Granny.

Granny motioned for her to sit down as she assembled the plate for Thelma. "I absolutely do. I was a young girl just like you, and I went my entire pregnancy with no complications. This was before Gloria's dad was born. My time of delivery was set on a Tuesday morning at about 9 o'clock. I went in and the labor went fine, and I delivered a beautiful little boy. I named him Lance. I mean, he was the most beautiful baby boy I had ever laid my eyes on. He weighed 8lbs and 14 ounces. My husband and I was so excited, I stayed in the hospital for a week because my blood count was really low, and back then, they didn't kick you out of the hospital the same day. They wanted to monitor me and keep an eye on Lance, too, because he seemed to have a heart murmur. It was not considered too serious, we were released that following Monday. Got home, I can remember that my husband had the house just right. My mother was there and sisters. So Lance and I got in my bed from being so tired from the whole event. A few days went past, and I started noticing that Lance was sleeping a whole lot. I knew that babies naturally did, but he wasn't too responsive. I went to bed that night, and my husband and I woke up that next morning and Lance had passed away. Laying in my bed was this beautiful baby boy that I loved so much, and now he was gone!"

"Oh, Granny, I'm so sorry this happened to you. Did they say what happened?"

"They said that his little heart just stopped. I tell you, Thelma, that was a time in my life that I didn't want to even talk about a God. I felt that he was too cruel to do me like that. But with time, the hurt got better thought it never went away. I still cry from time to time, but the one that I was so angry with, he got me through it all. God's been right there every step of my life's journey. So when I tell you that I feel your pain, believe me that I do!"

"Wow, Granny, I guess we never know what other people have been through, huh?"

"That's right, honey. That's why the Bible says 'That we are over comers by the word of our testimony.' If I tell you my testimony, and you see that I can make it, you will know that the same God that did it for me, he will do it for you!"

"I know that's true, Granny, but it seems so hard. Sometimes I don't even want to get out of bed. It seems so unfair."

"Yes, it does, sweetheart and when you need to cry, you cry. When you feel angry, it's okay. These are all valid feelings you will have, but when you have cried enough and the anger seems to have subsided, you get back up and fight like never before. You see, honey, the devil comes to steal our mind, causing us to slip into a deep depression, to have too many self-pity parties, and to isolate ourselves and push people away that truly love and cares for us. But you have to look that devil in the eye, and tell him 'Greater is he, that is within me, than he that is within the world,' and if that don't work, you tell him that 'I can do all things through Christ, that strengthens me.'" Granny lifts her hands in a praise while talking to Thelma.

"Amen, Granny. You sound just like my dad, moments like this I really miss him! Thank you, Granny, I really appreciate you sharing this with me, it really means a lot. Coming to New York was a very difficult decision to make for me. Leaving my family. My daddy dying on me. It's been a tough journey for me; but like my dad used to always say 'After all I've been through, I still have my joy!'" Thelma replies, with a tear in her eyes.

"Yes, baby, that's it. You have to speak life into your own situation, hold on it still may not all be over, but always remember that our trials will come to make us stronger!"

"Granny, I will cherish this moment forever, thank you!" Thelma hugs Granny.

"Now, baby, don't be a stranger. Eat up that there food so you can gain some weight." Granny says, motioning for Thelma to eat up.

"Oh, after today, I won't, I promise!" Thelma smiles as he picks up her fork to dig into the plate of food Granny placed before her.

# Chapter 22

# *Freedom of Speech*

A few days have passed and Thelma is coming into work, greeting her employee Marie. "Good morning, Marie."

"Hello, Ms. Thelma. You're in early."

"Yes, I didn't sleep too well, so I thought I would come in to start on inventory."

"Oh, boss, I can do it, after all, it's why I come in at 5:00 a.m."

"I know, Marie, if I was thinking I would have called you to let you sleep in."

"No worries, I enjoy it here. I like you much better than that Sarah. Man, I'm glad she's gone."

"Yea, she was a different kind of person all right, always making trouble or stirring up confusion. It is much more peaceful around here with her gone!"

"While it's just us here, I was going to ask you, how are you doing, Ms. Thelma?"

"I'm doing well and you?" Thelma replies to Marie.

"I didn't want to say, but I was just wondering how you were since you and Michael weren't seeing each other anymore."

"And why would you say that?"

"Oh, after you left for work yesterday, he came in here with some girl. I was pretty upset that he would even bring her in your place of work," Marie says, flipping the closed sign to open around, on the door.

"Oh really, he did that? Hmm!"

"Yes, Ms. Thelma. I'm sorry."

"For the record, Michael, and I wasn't a couple so he can see who he wants. And can you please call me, Thelma? The Ms. Thelma makes me feel as if I'm walking around with some granny stockings on, a lopsided church mother's wig, and Certs in my pocketbook."

"Ha ha ha. Okay, point taken, you know I just wanted to show respect towards you. You're my boss, and I respect you."

"And I appreciate you for that, but we don't have to be so formal, okay?"

"Yes, Ms., I mean, Thelma."

"Thank you, Marie. So, Marie?" Thelma says, walking to the kitchen. "What exactly did this girl look like with him? Not that I really care, just curious," Thelma says, with the broom in one hand.

"Curious, huh?" Marie replies with a smile.

"Yes, Marie, and it's not what you think. I can care less about who he's seeing."

"Oh, okay, that means that you really don't need to know then."

"You know what? I don't, I changed my mind. I'll be just fine not knowing!"

"Cool, then I'm going to start in the other room with brewing the coffee." Marie walks away from Thelma.

"Girl, you better get in here and spill the beans!"

"Well, if you have to know, she looks kind of like you well not as pretty. But this girl don't seem at all like Michael's type."

"And what is Michael's type?"

"Don't be mad at me, but you are, Thelma, you are!"

"Oh my Lord, why does everyone keep telling me this? Michael and I are just friends, and I really wish him well. I'm fine with whatever."

"Sure you are, Thelma. If you were so fine about everything, then why are you pouring your freshly made coffee down the sink?" Marie replies, laughing at Thelma.

"Ooops," says Thelma.

"It's okay if you have feelings for him, in fact, I think it's kind of cute. I honestly think that he brought that girl by here just to make you jealous. Thelma, for what it's worth, any man that would go out of his way just to do that, clearly cares for you!"

"Okay, enough talking about him. Is Donavin coming in this morning?"

"Yaaaaas, he will be here in an hour."

"Oh Lord!" Thelma replies, shaking her head.

"I know, right? He is hilarious," Maries says, cracking up laughing.

"Yes, he is! Let me ask you something, Marie?"

"Sure, go ahead."

"Do you think there is something wrong with seeing a counselor like for grieving?"

"Oh, no, of course not. My sister had to go and see one after my dad passed."

"Oh, I didn't know, Marie. I'm sorry, wow."

"It's okay, no need to apologize, besides, how would you know?"

"How did she do after seeing this counselor?"

"My sister was much better after going. She seemed so miserable after dad passed. Now don't get me wrong, I was hurt and very upset too, I just was tired of seeing him suffer; everyone has a different grieving process. I thought about it, but I opted out! It didn't happen overnight, but with time, she was and felt better."

"Why are you thinking about it?" Marie says.

"My friend Gloria, suggested it for me. She says it will help me come to grips. Whatever that means."

"I think it's a very good idea."

"Really? Thanks, Marie."

"No problem, Thelma. Nowadays, people are faced with way too much pressure until it's hard to even focus on your everyday things. I think it's completely healthy to go and talk to someone about problems or what you may have experienced," Marie replies.

"Yes, well, I'm seriously considering it. I've been thinking that it couldn't be that bad!" Thelma says, sipping her cup of coffee.

"Hey, Thelma, I wasn't going to mention this, but...my mother has a practice and she's been very successful for over fifteen years. She deals with grief and more. Would you like her information, not to toot my mother's horn, but 'beep beep!'"

"Oh, she's that good, huh?"

"Yes, actually she is, she just got an award through the Social Services Division for making a huge impact on so many lives, and was in a write up in the New York Times!"

"Wow, I couldn't afford her if I wanted to."

"Well, if you decided that you want to have a visit, I can see what she is willing to do for you financially."

"Really? I couldn't ask her to do that," Thelma says.

"Thelma, really, it would work, because my momma always gives out three partial sessions a year to help out where she can. She says that it's important to give back! Here, take her card, and I will speak to her tonight. That's if it's something you want to consider?"

"Yes, that sounds good, and thank you very much!"

"Aww, you're welcome. After all, that's what friends are for."

"But wait, I thought you said your sister went to see a counselor. It wasn't your mother?" Thelma says looking confused.

"No, it wouldn't have been that effective with my mother, because my momma was grieving as well."

"I'll give her office a call. I really appreciate your friendship, Marie. Thanks again, chic."

"No problem, Chica!" Marie says, walking to the counter to greet a customer.

The next morning Thelma calls the counseling office to make an appointment. She hopes that it is something that can help her with the grief of losing her baby and her father. She gets an early Monday morning appointment with a Doctor Martin Phillips.

It has been a few months since she has seen or heard from Michael, and Thelma decides just to call Michael over to see how he is doing. She misses his friendship. Thelma dials his number. Michael's answering machine picks. "Hi, you have reached Michael. I'm sorry I missed your call. Please leave a message after the beep."

"Hey, Michael, it's Thelma. I haven't heard from you in a while I miss our talks. I hope all is well with you, it would be nice to hear from my old, but very good friend. Talk to you soon. Goodbye!"

Thelma says out loud to herself, "Wow, what's the deal? I guess he wants things this way, so if he doesn't call, I'm sure not calling him again! Let me go and see my girl Gloria, it's been a while, and we need to catch up on things."

# Chapter 23

# Regretful Heart

Thelma, Gloria, Chelsie, and Lydia meet up at a place called the Legacy to have drinks and to talk. Thelma arrives while the others are waiting. "Hey, ladies,"

"What's up, Thelma, long time no see," says Chelsie.

"Oh, hey, Chels, it has been a long time. Hi, Lydia."

"How are you, Thelma? I've called you a couple of times, but never no call backs, is this still your number?" Lydia leans towards Thelma and shows her a number in her phone.

"Yes, that's my number only if you switch the last two numbers around."

"Girl, that makes me feel better. I thought I had done something wrong to you because you sho wasn't answering or returning calls." Lydia laughs.

"Naw, Lydia, we're cool. So, Chels, you still working for that doctor's office?" Thelma turns and asks.

"And you know I am, I would be a fool to leave, after all he is HOT!"

"Girl, shut up," Gloria replied, sitting down at the table.

"Now I know you're not dating this one, too? Please say you're not! Because you know you love them older men!"

"Yep, I sure do. There ain't nothing wrong with getting your bills paid, and having the car of your dreams," replies Chelsie, while pulling out her phone checking it!

"Yea, you may be right about all of that, Chels, but it ain't nothing cool about dating a married man. And you know he is married!"

"Well, Gloria, everyone isn't perfect like you and have everything you have either, Little Miss 'I have everything already', and if I don't have it, my daddy will surely buy it for me."

"So sorry to bust your bubble, Miss Thang, but I work for mine. And I don't have to ask my daddy for anything because I can get it myself!" says Chelsie rolling her eyes at Gloria.

"Sure, Gloria."

"HEY, what is all of the arguing about? I come to see my girls and y'all want to argue! NOPE, it's not happening today," Thelma replies.

"I'm sorry, Thelma, but Gloria's always trying to call somebody out on how they live their life. She's been like this since we were younger, instead of concentrating on her business."

"And you can stop talking about me as if I'm not here. I only try and help my friends, not hurt them, but if you want to spend your life dating married men, and destroying families, then you go ahead, Miss Thang!"

Lydia and Thelma sit at the table shaking their heads.

"Well, thank you for your permission, Gloria. Now I can finally move on, chile, please!"

Chelsie turns to Thelma, starting a conversation with her, ignoring Gloria. "Anyways, Thelma, how have you really been doing, girl? You know, with you losing the baby and all."

"CHELSIE, FOR REAL?…What's wrong with you, how you just going to come out and ask my girl a question like that, with no remorse or anything? MAN, I swear." Gloria hits the table with her hand, upset with Chelsie and her actions.

"Dang, Gloria, you trippin' today. Thelma, did I say anything to offend you? You can be honest with me, because Gloria is acting like I said something really horrible!" Thelma stares at Chelsie.

"It's not what you said, it's how you said it, CHELSIE! Delivery is everything!"

"I believe I was talking to Thelma." Chelsie puts her hand in front of Gloria's face.

"PLEASE, both of you STOP! What's going on here, Gloria?" Thelma says, turning in Gloria's direction.

"T, I'm sorry, you know I didn't mean any harm, but, Chelsie, you know how to push my buttons, turn them and take them off and sew them back on again," Gloria replies out loud, shaking her head."

Chelsie looks at Gloria, and ignores her. "Yes, I'm sorry, too, Thelma. I was only asking you out of genuine concern, that's all. You know me, girl, I would never hurt you on purpose."

"And I know you were, Chelsie. It's cool!" Lydia's cell phone goes off, and she leaves the table.

Chelsie turns around to Gloria and confronts her after Lydia leaves. "So, since you're trying to make me out to be this horrible person, Gloria, are you going to tell your girl here about Lydia and Michael?"

Gloria looks at Chelsie with anger. "You're just messy aren't you?"

"What is she talking about, Gloria, what about Lydia and Michael?" Thelma says to Gloria.

Chelsie jumps in before Gloria can explain. "Oh, your girl, Lydia has been seeing your boy Michael." Chelsie snaps her finger. "Now, Boom!" replies Chelsie, looking at Gloria.

"Okay, that's it. Let me tell you something, Chelsie, you are the most messiest person I have ever met. You're so busy trying to get at me, when you're really hurting Thelma. Really, Chelsie? Really?"

Thelma interrupts them both. "Is this true, Gloria, and why haven't you told me?"

"It's not like that, T, not at all. Chelsie and I saw Michael downtown with Lydia one time, and it was nothing to where I felt I should notify you about. If I felt that way, you know I would have told you!"

Thelma sits there in silence.

"Girl, don't even trip. Men come a dime a dozen, you will find someone else, that's why I don't fool around with the young infants, I like me someone with stability!"

"I'm sorry, but if you don't be quiet, I'm going to have to leave. How are you going to talk about stability and you're dating a married man? And Michael is a very nice and respectable gentleman, who is perfect for Thelma," says Gloria to Chelsie.

Lydia returns back to the table. "I'm back, sorry I had to take that call. Oh yea, Thelma, Michael says hello." Everyone looks surprised by Lydia's comment.

"Oh really, well, tell him ain't nobody got time for his two-timing self!" Chelsie says, with anger in her voice.

"Umm, what are you talking about, Chelsie? Who are you referring to, Michael?" Lydia replies.

"Yes, I am."

"Why is he two-timing? What is she talking about y'all and why is everyone looking at me like I dun stole something or I stink?" Lydia says, looking around the table.

"I don't know, Lydia, you tell us!" Thelma says facing Lydia.

"Huh, what in the world is going on? I'm lost." Lydia, is looking at the girls very confused.

"Don't play games, Lydia. How you gonna come back from a conversation with Michael and tell Thelma, 'Oh, by the way, your ex says hello'?"

"First of all, Chels, I'm not stooping to your level, and second, Thelma, if you want to ask me something, I'll answer anything you want to know. I don't play games and certainly don't hurt friends!"

"No, it's okay, Lydia," Thelma says to Lydia, looking down at the menu.

"Alright then, I'll answer for you, the answer is, no, I'm not going out with Michael. It doesn't take me long to figure out anything. Michael and I are just friends, and besides, he only talks about you anyways. Thelma. You're my girl and I would never stab you in the back like that. It's not my style," Lydia says, reassuring Thelma on their friendship. "Feel better now, Chelsie? You starting all of that unnecessary drama wasn't worth it, was it?"

"Whatever y'all, I have somewhere else to go, all of this ganging-up-on-Chelsie-day is over, so I will see y'all when I see you." Chelsie gets up and leaves the table.

"Resist the devil and he will flee, that chile needs prayer!" says Gloria. "Yes, she does, Gloria. However, you two feed off of each other. I was thinking when is it going to ever stop. Remind me to never come around when you two are together in the future," says Thelma.

"Yea, you're right, and I do love my friend, but Chelsie is as ghetto as they come. You handled her well, Lydia, kudos to you," Gloria replies.

"All I care about is Thelma, and what she was thinking concerning Michael and our relationship. I'm surprised that crazy girl didn't bring up that you guys saw us that one time downtown, Gloria."

"Oh, she did."

"No way, Gloria."

"Way, Lydia." They all laugh together.

"Boy, that girl is a piece of work, isn't she?" Gloria says, drinking her ice tea. "Well, Thelma, I'm just glad were cool."

"Of course we are, Lydia. I wasn't going to get all bent out of shape over no man anyway."

"Yea, maybe not, but you seemed a little bothered when you thought that Lydia and Michael were together," Gloria says laughing.

"Not even, Gloria. I was cool and calm."

"Girl, you need to stop it and go on and give that man a call," says Lydia.

"Michael doesn't care about me, I tried to call him and I even left him a voice mail, and I haven't heard anything from him yet!"

"I'll give him a call for you." Gloria picks her cell phone up.

"No you won't, Gloria, it's cool. If he calls, he needs to call on his own."

"You miss him, don't you?" Lydia asks Thelma.

"Yes, I do. I really didn't know how much I cared about him until he stopped coming around. He was my Prince Charming!"

"Care about him? Chile, that is love in them eyes of yours," Gloria replies, teasing Thelma.

"Oh my God, Gloria, do you think I've fallen for him?"

"Chile, yes, Thelma, don't you feel it? Let me ask you this, would you rather have a life with him or without him?"

"Gloria, I don't want to live without him!"

"Well, there's your answer. Thelma, girl, you are in love with Michael!"

Thelma looks at her girlfriends and begins to wipe the tears from her eyes. "Oh my God, I am!"

"Awww, that is so sweet. Group hug!" Gloria puts her arm around both girls and hugs them. "I have to leave, I have to find Michael!"

"You don't have to find him. He's at home and he got your voice mail, too," Lydia says to Thelma, smiling and winking her eye at her.

"He did, Lydia?"

"Yes, T, I think you should go and talk to him, he really cares about you!"

After leaving her girlfriends, and having that really crazy day with Gloria and Chels arguing most of the visit, Thelma needed to reflect on some things before going to see Michael. *I love Michael, but do I love him just as a friend kind of love, or am I in love with him? The thing that I was scared of is happening. Wow! Michael is a man that makes me feel like everything is going to be alright, I really feel safe when I'm with him. I love how he makes me feel, and I can tell him just about anything. It's an amazing thing. Lord, please word my mouth and don't allow me to mess things up any more than it is.*

<><><>

Thelma calls Michael again, but no answer. "Michael, can you please pick up your phone? If you're there, I really need to speak with you. Michael! Okay, fine then, I'm on my way over!"

As Thelma drives over to Michael's place, she thinks about what she will say to him. It seems he is either angry with her or his feelings for her have changed. "How can I make it right?" she asks out loud to herself. "Oh Lord, I'm here and he is home. Welp, here goes everything."

As Thelma walks towards his door, her heart is beating so fast it feels like it will burst. The palms of her hands are sweaty and she's shaking. *Get it together, girl. What is wrong with you? All you have to do is tell him how you really feel, and it all will be okay.* Thelma knocks on the door and to her surprise, the door opens. There he stands, five-foot-ten inches tall, dimples and hazel eyes. Thelma can't stop smiling. Michael opens the door for her to enter.

"Hey," Thelma says, staring with the biggest grin ever on her face.

"Hello, Thelma, how are you?"

"I'm better now." Thelma walks into his apartment, and although he allowed her in, his vibe seemed very distant. Thelma knew then, she had work to do.

"Have a seat, would you like something to drink, water, soda?"

"Oh, no, I'm fine," Thelma answered.

"So what's up?" Michael says, drinking his soda.

"I would say that I was in the neighborhood, but that wouldn't be truthful."

"Well, what would be the truth?" Michael is speaking looking down at a hand game.

"The truth is, Michael. I wanted to see you and see how you have been, since someone won't answer my calls. Did you receive them?"

"What, your calls?"

"Yes, Michael, and can you please put down that game?"

"Yep."

"Yep what, Michael?"

"Yep, I got your two calls, Thelma!"

*Lord, he is trying me today. Okay, breathe, Thelma, because he is really going to work the stew out of you. Lord, help me!*

"Let's cut to the chase here, Thelma, because I have somewhere to go in a minute!"

"Okay, Michael, I'll cut to the chase, since you don't have time!"

"Oh, there she is. I was waiting for the real Thelma to pop out!" Michael says looking at his watch.

"You know what? I'm sorry, okay? I'm sorry I gave you the impression that I didn't want to be in a relationship with you. I'm sorry that I didn't think I wanted more. I'm sorry that I never told you that I loved you, Michael, because I do." Thelma grabs Michael's hand, trying to get him to understand her.

"I know you love me, doesn't the Bible teach us to love everyone?"

"MICHAEL, I see you're irritated with me. I don't just love you, Michael, I'm in love with you!"

There was pure silence. Thelma was waiting for him to respond with maybe, 'I love you too,' or this big reunited hug or something. Instead, he gets up and walks over to the window without saying a word.

"Michael, did you hear what I just said to you? I said that I'm in love with you."

"I heard you, Thelma, I'm just trying to figure out why now, why all of a sudden you come up with this revelation of love for me? Or excuse me, being in love with me. How are you sure? Because, Thelma, I'm not willing to allow myself to get hurt in this. I have shown you how I feel about you. From the moment I picked you up in the cab when you moved here. My heart told me then that you were the one for me. At that moment, I had never been more sure about anything in my entire life before. It just felt right. You feel right to me, Thelma. I know I love you and I know the reasons why I do. But can you say the same?" Michael is still standing in the window.

"Michael, I know that I love you because the moment I couldn't be with you, I felt lost. I know I love you because when I was at work, there wasn't a day that went by that I wasn't looking for you to walk through those doors. But when I really knew, I mean, really, really knew? Is when I thought I had lost you forever, and getting up for me wasn't the same. My heart can't take any more loss, Michael. Losing Daddy almost killed me. Losing my baby pretty much sent me into a depression. But losing you, caused my heart to not want to beat again! I haven't felt complete since you walked out my door! MICHAEL, I LOVE YOU. I want to be with you. You're the man for me...my soul mate...my everything!"

Michael is standing in the window looking out, and when he turns around, he has tears rolling down his face, and then he says the most surprising thing. "Cool."

"Cool? For real, Michael?"

"Just kidding, babe. Do you really mean what you said about me being your soul mate? Because, Thelma, you really hurt me."
"Those were never my intentions, I had just been through so much and didn't know if I was going or coming."

"I know, babe, that's why God sent me to you. He knew you needed me and that I sure needed you! Thelma, I promise if you will let me, I'll hold you up and never let you fall. I'll protect you, Thelma, and do my very best to bring happiness to your life!"

"Michael, I have to be honest, I'm a mess. Everything I touch I seem to mess up! So, I need you to understand that there are some hurts and bruises that have never been healed, not so much physical but..."

"I understand all of that, Thelma. Let's just take it one day at a time, okay?" Michael says smiling.

"I'd like that, Michael, and all I can promise is that I'll be honest and love you the best I can!"

"That's all I can ask for, babe!"

The rest of that evening, Michael and Thelma just spent that time together, laughing, sharing, and crying. All in all, it was a good day! *I'm so excited and scared at the same time. I know that Michael and I can make it, one thing that I always remember dad telling us kids,* "Slow it down, just take it one day at a time." *So, I guess that's what Michael and I will do. Thank you, Daddy, because I know you're up there working on my behalf.*

# Chapter 24

# The Truth Will Set You Free

It's Monday morning and Thelma took the day off from work. She was a nervous wreck last night, worried about how the session with the counselor would go. She really didn't want a male counselor. She was hoping for Marie's mother, who was booked up for months when she called to make the appointment.

Thelma arrives at the office for her first counseling session. "Good morning," she says to the receptionist.

"Good morning, may I help you?"

"Yes, I'm here to see Dr. Martin Phillips."

"Okay, let me see." The receptionist looks down at her clipboard. "Oh, you're Thelma McKinney. Sign your name right here. You will not be seeing Dr. Martin today, he called in sick; however you will see Dr. Markinson today. Have a seat and I'll call you in a minute."

"Okay. Thank you." Thelma sat in the office wanting to get up and leave. She is caught up in her thoughts as she looks around the waiting area. *I don't know these people and they don't know me. Who sits down and tell someone all of your business? I've been through some pretty embarrassing moments in my life and I'm not sure that I want to open up those old wounds.*

"Ms. McKinney, Dr. Markinson will see you now. Please come this way."

"Thank you." Thelma follows the receptionist into the office.

"Dr. Markinson, this is Thelma, Thelma McKinney."

"Well, good morning, Miss McKinney. Please have a seat."

Thelma sits in the chair across from the doctor and takes a quick look around the room. It seems kind of comfortable, but Thelma's problem is that she's not good with meeting new people and certainly not good about telling all of her business to one. *So, we will see, one thing I can say is Dr. Markinson is a very beautiful lady. She looks like she use to model or something.*

"So, you're Thelma? It's nice to meet you," Dr. Markinson replies.

"Nice to meet you as well," Thelma says, somewhat shyly.

"I like to start my sessions off with me saying a word and then my client saying a word that reminds them of the word I just said, if that makes sense." She smiles. "Will that be alright with you?"

"Yes, ma'am, that's fine."

"Okay, let's first lose the ma'am. I want you to feel comfortable with me, so Ms. M is fine with me, OK?"

"Yes, ma'am, I mean, yes, Ms. M."

"Perfect, so I'll go first. My first word is… family, what comes to your mind?"

"Home."

"Okay, second word is, life," says Dr. M.

"Struggle."
"Okay, good, Thelma, you're doing great. Third word is, mother."

"Hate!"

"Hmm, and fourth is, father?"

"Love."

Dr. M. is writing on a little note pad.

"Okay, thank you for participating in that exercise, you did wonderfully! The exercise that I did is a typical one to find where your thoughts connect. We will not do any more of them through our sessions. I am what you call a listening counselor, because I like to hear what's from your heart and help you connect with what is disconnected, fix what is broken, and find what is lost. Only if you feel comfortable enough to allow me into your world and get a glimpse of it. You see, Thelma, all of us have a present, past, and we definitely have a future. So, the key is finding closure to the past hurts, dealing with the present, and welcoming the promise of our future. Now, enough of me talking, can you tell me a little about yourself?"

"Yes, I am twenty years old. I will be twenty-one next month. I'd like to think that I'm a very compassionate person. I love spending time with my friends. I'm a hard worker." Thelma pauses and waits for Dr. M to say something.

"Okay, thanks, Thelma, for sharing. What is it about yourself that lets you know you're compassionate?"

"Because I care about others and how they feel and are doing?"

"So, do you sometimes place others feelings before your own?"
"I use too, but not so much anymore."

"Can you tell me why you decided that you needed counseling. Did something happen to bring you here? Now don't get me wrong, you don't have to go through anything to get counseling, but I'm assuming so because I am a grief counselor and so is my partner Dr. Martin. Do you feel up to sharing anything specific?"

"Um, not today, I'm really kind of tired. It's been a very long morning for me and I didn't get much sleep last night. Maybe next time?"

"Sure, Thelma, that's fine with me, so you said maybe next time. That indicates to me that you're open to coming back, correct?"

"Maybe, not to sound rude, but my friend Marie gave me her mother's card, and told me that her mom was a great counselor, so I wanted to see her and decide where I felt the most comfortable. But she was booked for months so I decided to make the appointment with Dr. Martin to check him out first. My best friend recommended him to me. I mean, you seem great but I just would like to see if Marie's mom would be a good fit before I commit to coming back here. She speaks very highly of her, and because she's my friend and coworker... well, yeah...I can't commit right now."

"No need to explain, I totally understand. It's good that you understand that there should be chemistry between you and whomever you see. It should be that way with all of our relationships in life," Dr. M. replies.

"Wow, thanks for understanding, and for the record, you are very easy to talk to."

"Why thank you, Thelma, I appreciate you saying that. You are easy to talk with as well!"

They talk a little bit more until the 45 minutes is up. "Your time is up and I have another client waiting, is there anything else you want to talk about before you go?" Dr. M. says, smiling, while going to her desk to sit down.

"No, I can't think of anything."

"Alright then, Miss Thelma, I hope to see you again. If we don't, please keep opening up to others. I have a feeling instead of you getting help, you'll end up helping, because you have a very special and endearing presence about yourself!"

"Thank you, Ms. M., that really means a lot!"

"Well, I just call it like I see it, Thelma. You take care of yourself!"

Thelma really feels bad because she told this counselor that she needs to check out another counselor to see to see if she would be a better fit. *How stupid. Who says that! Now it's too late. I've already put my foot in my mouth, because the truth of the matter is, I like Ms. M and would love to stay here and see how she can further help me out. But I'm sure it's too late, let me just leave. Sometimes talking too much sure can get you in a mess. Oh well!*

"Thank you, Ms. M., and it was nice meeting you."

"You, too, Thelma. Oh, and Thelma, I'll tell Marie that I met you today. She will be happy to know!" Thelma laughs, and so did Ms. M. She was Marie's mother after all.

"You mean to tell me?"

"Yes, hello, Thelma. Now, if you decide to come back, after today, we can no longer speak about Marie. Only about your sessions, okay?"

"Yes, ma'am, I totally understand!"

"Good, it truly has been a pleasure meeting you, Thelma. Let the receptionist know when you can come back and fill out the forms. Let her know I said to please make room for you within the next month?"

"Yes, Ms. M. That will be great!"

"Wonderful. When you get out there, please also fill out the forms for the recipient fund and the first few sessions will be on me. OK?"

"Oh, thank you so much, Dr. M. Thank you!"

"You're welcome! I look forward to helping you release what you have to release, both positively and negatively, Thelma." Dr. M. smiles.

One evening a few months later, Thelma sits and writes in her diary.

*Dear Diary,*

*I've been seeing Ms. M for a few months now. She is so easy to talk to and I feel like I am really getting better with every appointment. She gives me exercises and I work on them between sessions. Even though she is Marie's mom, it has never caused any problems.*

*We have been working through how I have experienced so much more than other girls my age. When you see my story written down, it seems like I should be in my 30s or 40s, but instead I just turned 21. I thought by now I would be in my Junior year of college and instead I am a mother living in New York City without my child. It is really hard to think about how my life could have been if Johnny never came home. If I had not gone to his house all those times. If I had not allowed myself to get too close.*

*It seems that everything is starting to come together in a way. Michael and I are doing pretty good. We decided to move really slow with our relationship, so we can make sure it will last. He has become my rock and someone that I've really grown to love! I never dreamed that I would start to understand some of the terrible things that I've endured, and I can't say that I completely understand it all...but I feel I have more clarity.*

*He and Ms. M have helped me to understand that my past does not dictate my future. Oh, and it doesn't matter how bad things may look, it's how we handle things is what counts. The only thing I haven't talked about in counseling is my biological mother, and I'm fine if I never speak of her again. The sad thing is, I know I can't have closure or move forward until I do. Not happy about talking about her, but I guess I will next session.*

Thelma thought it would be nice to give her mom a call, just to see how she was doing. It seems like every time she tries contacting her, she is always too busy or something. Thelma wasn't sure what was going on. She was supposed to be her child who was far away from home, but her mom hardly ever checks on her. The last time they had words, she gave Thelma the big spill on how she felt. She let her siblings down, and her daddy would be disappointed that Thelma chose to stay away from them. Thelma honestly didn't know what to make of her mom. One day she's Mommy Dearest and the next she's Church Mother of the Year. Even though Thelma was away, she stayed in touch with her brothers and little sister and they were fine. In fact, TiTi was planning on visiting for the summer. Thelma feels like everyone has moved on except her mom. Since she was meeting with the girls for dinner, she decided she would call Momma later.

When Thelma arrives at the restaurant, only Gloria was there. It was so nice to see her. With their busy work schedules, they hadn't been able to talk as much. So, Thelma was looking forward to catching up.

"Hey, girl! How are you, beautiful?" Thelma greets Gloria with a hug.

"Hey, T, I miss you so much, it's been too many days," Gloria says, returning Thelma's hug.

"I know, right?" Thelma chuckles, taking a seat in the booth across from Gloria.

"Gloria, give me the scoop. Michael told me about this new guy on your job. Who is he and when are you getting married?" Thelma says laughing.

"Now there you go. I'm not getting married to no one, although he is really the ideal guy."

"Wait, what? I'm your best friend and I have to find out from Michael about this?"

"Thelma, I'm not dating him. In fact, he's Michael's old friend and he happens to work at the firm next door to ours. We only had lunch together one time, chile!"

"LUNCH TOGETHER? You have got to be kidding me! Lunch? Gloria Williams.. and when did you start working for your dad again?!"

"I went back a few months ago. They said I needed a degree and I'm not done with school yet. I am only going part time while I work. I don't want my dad to be my ticket through life. But we will talk about that in a little bit – I want to share something with you after. And as far as lunch… we only had lunch and it wasn't even planned." Gloria shrugged, attempting to downplay the situation.

"Mmm hmm. Yea, right, tell me anything."

"Thelma, it's nothing at all. Trust me, he's just a nice coworker. But I'm not going to lie, he is nice to look at, tho. But it's nothing more than that!" Gloria said, leaning forward on the table. "Enough of me, how is counseling going for you? Really to me, you seem happier,"

"Honestly, I think I'm getting there, Gloria. I never thought I would feel this way. My counselor, Dr. M., is so nice and very easy to talk to; she understands me! She's even given me things like perfume and tickets for her daughter and me to attend the theater."

"Hmm, that's cool, but isn't that kind of unprofessional of her, crossing the barriers a little?" says Gloria, sipping her coffee.

"She has been contributing her services to me free of charge since I've been seeing her. That's nice of her, huh?"

"I guess, if that's what she does, I just find it kind of odd!" Gloria says, with doubt in her voice.

"The way I see it, there are still some good people in the world. And I'm just counting it as a blessing. Maybe God is finally moving on my behalf!"

"Yes, you're right. As long as you feel these sessions are helping you out, and things are getting better for you, that's all that matters to me!" Gloria replies, looking at her watch.

"I wonder what happened to Lydia?"

Gloria calls Lydia and learns she can't make it. "I'm starving. Let's order!"

"Yes, I'm a little hungry, too. Where is our waitress?"

"I got you!" Gloria calls the waitress over and then the girls spend a couple hours together catching up.

"So what's on your mind, T?" Gloria says.

"Remember I told you before Daddy died, I was having those dreams about him?"

"Yes, I do, the ones with him on that road?"

"Yes! That one."

"What about it, Thelma, you're not still having them are you?"

"I wasn't, but for the last two weeks they have returned. But this time he has some children with him, a little baby girl and an older female. I am across the road from them, and trying to get to them all, but cannot. It's funny, although I don't recognize the others, I feel as if I know them in the dream."

"Hmm, that's strange, now you say there was a baby, and she was a girl? Thelma, do you think that little baby girl is your baby Joy?"

Thelma wipes her tears away. "That's who I thought it was, too. Daddy seemed to be leading the older girl and carrying the baby in his arms. When Daddy turns and walks away, he always smiles at me. I keep calling his name, telling him to wait, but he tells me to go on without him!"

"Man, I'm sorry, boo, that has to be pretty confusing, and at the same time upsetting."

"It is very upsetting, Gloria, and I cannot for the life of me figure out who the older girl is, I just wish the dreams would stop all together!"

"Have you talked or shared it with your counselor, and if so, what did she say about it?

"I have told her and she thinks that I'm subconsciously thinking about my dad and baby. She doesn't have any explanation on who the older girl is. But listen....this is getting heavy. Let's change the subject. You wanted to tell me something...what's up?"

"Well, I got a job offer. All this time I have been studying law, I realized I didn't want to be a lawyer. I wanted to work with people and give back. Your Daddy always taught that to us as kids, remember? To give back to the community and help others become stronger, because that is what Jesus did."

"You already know what I'm going to say, Gloria. I am super happy for you if you want to do something else. So what's the offer?"

"Our firm has adopted this place called Hally's Peace. It's an organization that raises funds for children that need cosmetic surgery due to burns. That's where I have been the past few weeks. I was volunteering and I loved the atmosphere. So I applied as an Administrative Director and they offered me the job."

"That's great, but Gloria, are you sure that's what you want to do?"

"I have never in my life been so sure of anything on this earth, Thelma. I love the kids there, and the best part about it is, at the end of the day, I feel like I've made a difference in the lives of little children that suffers with something they didn't have any control over! And…I don't have to rush my education to take the position because they care more about passion and experience in the community than they care about the letters after your name. I will still finish but I can keep going part time."

"Oh, Gloria, you can see it in your eyes, the compassion. You go, girl."

"Thanks, Thelma, but there's one other part that you should know, and it's that the job I'm taking is located in Atlanta, Georgia."

Thelma is listening to her best friend for life, sit there and tell her that she's moving far away. Her heart sinks because she sees the light in Gloria's eyes. One thing about Gloria, she has always been one to give her whole heart in everything she does. And she never starts anything that she won't finish, that's one of the things Thelma admires about her. Thelma fights to hold back her tears, because the very thought of Gloria leaving is bittersweet.

"I'm really happy for you then, it sounds like you've already made up your mind."

"Thelma McKinney, how long have we been best friends? It's been over ten years, so I know you. I can hear it in your voice that you're really not thrilled, but it will be a life changing experience for me. I just feel like it's what I'm suppose to do. God spoke to my heart and said, 'Do it!' That's all I heard, and the urgency of that voice led me to believe that it was him!"

"Wow, Gloria, then who can argue with that? If you feel like you've heard God speak, then you probably did."

"No, T, there is no probably to it, it was him." As Thelma sat across the table looking at the joy on Gloria's face, she thought to herself, *Wow, Lord, it was prophesied over me years ago that I would hear your voice, and you're even speaking to Gloria now? Have you forgotten about me? It's like, what have I done wrong that was so bad I should lose everything that is important to me? Can I get a break?*

Tears began to run down Thelma's face, she could see in Gloria's eyes that she's worried.

"T, what's going on with you, how are you really feeling about all of this?"

"It's not you leaving that's making me feel kind of sad – although I'll miss you like crazy, girl, it's just that I feel as if I can't catch a break. It feels like I've been picked out to be picked on. Finding out that my mother who raised me isn't really my mom which is one lie, then I end up pregnant, had to deal with all of that drama. Then Daddy gets sick, the stress of that alone was almost too much. Forced to leave town because I didn't want to bring shame upon my family. I was immediately forced to grow up fast. Daddy passes away, I lose my baby, my biological mother tried to resurface, now you're leaving. I'm sincerely happy for you, I'm just going to miss you so much, girl. I'm just saying, Gloria. I need a break! I sometimes get the impression that God is not pleased with who I am or he's disappointed in what I've become!"

"Hey, now you know I'm with you on you needing a break, but the part about God being disappointed in who you've become? That's where you're on your own. You see, Thelma, you are not like me, and don't take what I'm about to tell you the wrong way. You are different then I. You see, I'm that person who has always been confused about who I am and what my purpose was in life. I never quite understood my purpose until now. See, Thelma, some people walk around pretending to have it together or to have clarity in their purpose, but in reality, don't have a clue! But see you, Thelma, you were born with that calling on you. I mean, when we were little you spoke with great clarity and understanding about God's word. When we were kids, we use to watch how we acted around you because we somehow felt that you had a direct contact with God. And whatever we did wrong, God would get us because you would inform him. I had so much respect for you then, and I respect you even more now. Remember that song you use to sing, 'I surrender all, I surrender all, all to thee my blessed Savior, I surrender all?'"

"Yes, I remember."

"Well, Thelma, maybe God's just waiting on you to let go of everything and surrender to him. I think he gets tired of us always trying to fix it, when he's standing there saying, 'Okay, I'm here, and when you're ready for me to fix it for you, I will, but until then, I'll just stand over here while you mess things up.' I'm guilty of everything I just mentioned, Thelma! All I'm trying to say is…maybe God is just trying to get your attention." Gloria takes a tissue out of her purse and wipes her eyes.

"Well, if that's the case, he's got it!"

"Yea, but does he have you completely, T? I'm serious, I remember when we were at that revival your dad had that one year, and that prophet called you up and said that the hand of God was upon you, and you would endure much. But you were called for God's purpose! Thelma, what you're going through wasn't meant to be your curse, it was a blessing!"

"Wow, Gloria, that's a lot, and I appreciate everything you've said, but…"

"I know, you're not ready for all of that. Am I right?" Gloria replied.

"Gloria, I can't even answer you, because I know everything you've said to me has some truth in it. I've heard those same words almost my whole life. I want to throw my hands up and just surrender, but…I want to understand first why God would choose me to get crucified the way I've been. I know God is love, but sometimes I've wondered! Daddy would roll over in his grave if he heard me say that, but it's just how I'm feeling. You never even told me, when you're moving away. So when are you leaving, Gloria?" Gloria sits quietly and looks with hesitation.

"Next Friday, T. Next Friday."

"What? Are you serious, you're leaving that fast?" Gloria and Thelma both looked at each other and the tears began to flow, because they knew that they were both going to miss each other so much.

"Thelma, this is going to be harder than I anticipated, but we've been apart before and we stayed close. We are best friends forever. I mean that! Being in different states won't change anything!"

"You're right, girl. I'm happy for you. But, you're always leaving somebody!" Gloria laughs.

"I love you, Gloria, and I am so proud of you. Never forget it."

"I won't forget it as long as you know that I feel the same! I love you, too, T!"

# Chapter 25

# Peace Be Still

After having lunch today and receiving the news about her girl, and some of the things she said, Thelma spent a lot of time thinking. She felt so confused and drained from everything. She felt the need to reevaluate her entire life. But what has really been bothering her was… she's been thinking about Estelle, her biological mother!

Thelma hated it, but some reason, she could not stop thinking about her. *How dare she even occupy any place in my mind, she doesn't deserve it! I go to counseling tomorrow and I think I'm ready to talk about this now. I want to bring it up and talk about it so I can move on. I need closure from this woman once and for all! Dr. M. says, we can never move on in the future, unless we deal with the here and now. So let's deal with it!*

Michael wants to come over before he heads to work, and Thelma wanted to see him because now he works nights as an RN at the hospital. He loves helping people. She teases him and tells him, "Don't be letting them sick patients get healed by you good looks and gorgeous eyes."

Michael arrives around 7:45 and says he was late because traffic was bad. There's some kind of conference going on and people from all over the country have been coming into town. When he comes in, his hands are behind his back. He pulls out a dozen of roses.

"Michael, they're beautiful! What's the occasion?"

"The occasion is that I love you, and I also heard that you've had a very rough day, is that true?"
"Yes, it is, and how did you know?"

"Gloria called me after you guys had lunch today."

"Well, yes, I'm going to keep it real with you. I had a terrible day, babe."

"Aww, I'm sorry, hun," Michael replies.

"It's okay, I feel better now that you're here."

"Thank you, babe, and I'm so sorry. So, Gloria told you, huh?"

"Yes, did you know?"

"I can't lie, yes, I did. Only because I saw her when she came back from volunteering. Maybe I should say I knew about the charity and her volunteering, but not about her moving away until yesterday!"

"Yea, I'm really excited and happy for her. I'm just going to miss her so much."

"I know you will, babe, but it will all work out for everyone, I promise!" Michael says.

"Well, I sure need something to turn around for me, I want to share something with you, Michael." I pull out the letter and hand it to Michael.

"What's this?"

"It's a letter, a letter from my biological mother."

"What do you mean, your biological mother. You're adopted?"

"Well, I found this letter a few years ago, and it was written by my biological mother. Her name is Estelle. I never knew her last name and I never wanted to know. So, all of my life, I have been living a lie. Probably still would have if I had not found it."

"Wow, Thelma, I don't know what to say. What did your dad have to say?"

"Oh, Daddy never really said much, but he never wanted me to get hurt. His plan was to tell me when I was old enough to understand. My momma had the nerve to get all upset at me, and mad at Daddy for never destroying the letter. But it did explain why my momma always treated me differently than my siblings. My momma would give me no breaks on anything. It was almost as if I was Cinderella: 'Thelma, do this, Thelma, do that.' I use to think she acted this way because I was the oldest. But my dad, he stood up for me most of the time, especially when there wasn't a reason for her to treat me badly or blame me for something. Don't get me wrong, I love my momma, and my life was okay growing up, but she could have treated me a whole lot better. I couldn't believe she kept the secret from me, too!"

"I'm sorry, babe, and I sure don't want to upset you any more than you are already but, all due respect to your pops, it really wasn't your mom's responsibility to tell you that important information. After all, he was the one responsible for most of what happened. Him and your real mom! It sounds like you're trying to blame your stepmom for everything and not your dad."

"Is that what it sounds like to you? Because I'm not really trying to do that at all. I love my momma. We may have not always seen eye to eye — well, we hardly ever did — but I love her!"

"I know you do, babe. I'm just saying to try and see her point of view. I'm guessing she may have never wanted you to find out. That had to be a difficult place for her to be in."

"Yes, you're right, I'm grateful that she loved me in her own way. But we're alright. I would love for us to be closer, but I know she loves me. I wanted you to know, Michael, and in counseling tomorrow I want to deal with this issue. I'm ready for closure now and I think it's time. I'm just tired, Michael. I feel like if I don't make a change in my life, I will lose it!"

"Baby, I'm so proud of you, and I think you're right, you need closure with this situation. We all need closure, its healthy! I see things turning around for you and when you're happy, I'm happy. You deserve the world, Thelma. I love you, girl."

"I love you, too. I don't know what I would have done if you weren't around. You are my guardian angel!"

Michael smiles. "My brother's wife is an evangelist and I've been meaning to introduce you two. Her name is Rhonda, and I think you would like her. I was going through some things years ago, and she ministered to me. She told me I was having a wilderness experience, long story short, it really helped me! Oh, wow. Look at the time, babe. I have to go, I'm so sorry!"

"It's okay, I'm heading to bed anyway, I'm exhausted. But I feel much better that we've talked."

"Well, good. You going in to work tomorrow?"

"No, I called in already, I just need to get myself together a little. Tomorrow is going to be a 'me' day. Go to work, hun, and I'll talk to you later, OK?"

"Yes, I'll call you later. Can I get a hug and kiss?"

"Of course!" After Michael left, Thelma headed off to bed. Totally drained.

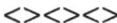

The next day, Thelma hardly slept for having a lot on her mind. She was thinking about everything Gloria shared with her and contemplating whether to share the letter with her counselor. Thelma arrives at the office and is greeted by the receptionist.

"Good morning, Ms. McKinney."

"Good morning."

"Dr. Markinson will be right out to get you." Dr. Markinson walks right out to receive Thelma.

"Good morning, Thelma."

"Oh, hello, Dr. M., how are you today?"

"I'm doing well, and you?" Dr. M. replies.

"I'm pretty tired, but I'm good!"

"Come on in and have a seat, and I have some coffee or tea over on the table, so help yourself."

"Thank you, Dr. M."

"So, Thelma, tell me why you're lacking sleep, are you alright? You seem pretty overwhelmed, if there's anything you would like to talk about, that's what I'm here for," Dr. M. says, drinking some tea.

"Yes, actually there is something that I feel I'm ready to talk about. It's my understanding that I have one more session with you, correct?"

"Yes, correct, but if you feel as if you need more time I can arrange that for you."

"Oh, no, Dr. M., you've already been too kind and I really appreciate your services. I thank you for everything."

"Everything that you've accomplished, Ms. Thelma, you did it not me. You have followed the program well, and I'm so proud of the progress you have made. So, thank you, for accepting my services. It's been a pleasure to have worked with you!"

"It's not goodbye, Dr. M. I'm sorry. why am I getting emotional about this? Wow, I'm just a mess about everything!"

Dr. M. smiles and puts her cup of coffee on the table. "Go ahead and share what it is you want me to know, Thelma."

"This subject is a very sensitive one for me, but here it goes. A few years ago, when I lived home with my family, I found a letter. This letter was written to me, letting me know that my mother who raised me as her own was not really my mother. Shoot, I don't want to cry about this anymore!"

"It's alright, Thelma. It's a very emotional subject, so finding this letter, exactly how did it make you feel?"

"I felt so angry."

"Okay, stay right there, why did you feel angry? Let's deal with the anger for a minute. Other than the obvious reason."

"I was angry because I felt that I had lived a lie my whole entire life, this woman that's raised me my whole life is not my biological mother. It explained why I've always felt that I was treated differently than the rest of my siblings. It was always my fault, or I had to do everything right, but my brothers and little sister could get away with murder."

"Oh, really? Well, that doesn't seem too fair. How did your father handle this?" Dr. M says.

"Daddy would do his best, to keep the peace. He did the best that he could to control the situation. So, I brought the letter so I can finally get closure from it all!"

"How is your relationship with your stepmom now?"

"I don't refer to her as my stepmom; she's my mom. We have our differences, but I loved her for loving another woman's child when my own sorry biological mother wouldn't even try."

"How do you know she didn't try? Sometimes life throws us several curve balls and obstacles, and some people don't know how to handle it."

"She shouldn't have had me then. Can I just give you this letter to burn in your fireplace over there?" Thelma said, pointing to the fireplace. "I was hoping to get some kind of closure today, but instead I'm getting angry all over again!"

"Thelma, just breathe. I know this is difficult, but it's going to be alright! Why don't you read me the letter. Do you feel up to doing that?" "Yes, I think I can. I'm sorry I'm a mess with all of this crying."

"It's natural for you to feel these emotions, you're doing just fine!" Thelma takes a deep breath.

"The letter reads: 'My dearest, Thelma, it is so hard for me to write this letter to you. There is so much I want to say, but I don't know how to say it. I am a woman with a lot of problems. Your dad and I didn't work out the way we planned, but it's so important that you know how much we both loved you. You are our love child! Your father promised me that one day — when the time is right — he will make sure that this letter finds you. I pray that it does. Always know that it was never your fault, I just could not raise you in my situation. Your dad, on the other hand, could. He is a wonderful man who even deserves better than me. This choice is hard, I'm sure I'll regret I did it every day of my life, but the mistakes and choices I've walked into, leaves me no other choice. There is one thing I'm sure of, and that is—'"

Dr. M. finishes the letter for Thelma without looking at it. "Is that you were not a mistake, you are and will always be what has given me a purpose to even feel like I belong. Baby, I love you, and I hope we will meet one day, and you will find it in your heart to forgive me when the time comes!" Dr. M. looks at Thelma, with tears coming down her face and says, "Thelma, I love you, honey, so much. I am your mother, Thelma?"

"What did you just say to me?" Thelma stands up out of her seat, and starts to back away from Dr. M.

Dr. M. is reaching towards Thelma with her hands out. "I know, honey, I'm so sorry. I just didn't want you to know in the beginning. I thought that it was God allowing us to develop a new and trusting relationship in his own way!"

"You're my mother? I don't believe this." Thelma has tears streaming down her face.

"Thelma, everything is going to be alright!"

"JUST STOP WITH THE LIES.....NO MORE LIES!"

"Thelma, wait! Please let me explain!"

"DON'T TOUCH ME, I have to get out of here!" Thelma runs out of the office, frantically, as the tears stream down her face. She leaves her jacket and purse behind. She gets in her car and reaches for her cell phone to call Gloria, and realizes that she left her phone in the office. "GOD, why are you punishing me, am I that bad of a person? Come on, please, Lord. Okay, I give up, ALRIGHT? I literally cannot take one more thing, it's way too much."

As Thelma sits in her car, Dr. Markinson comes toward her holding the purse and jacket in her hand. Thelma sees her coming and realizes she can't start her car without her keys, which happen to be in her purse.

"Thelma, Please! I just want to talk to you to properly explain everything."

"The only thing you can do for me, lady, is give me my purse and jacket and leave me alone. Please give me my things and just go, after all, you're great at leaving!"

"I deserve that, Thelma, and you're right."

Thelma is sitting in her car, holding her head rocking back and forth, crying out of control. "DON'T!...Don't try and use your reverse psychology on me, Doctor Markinson; that's if you're really who you say you are!"

"Thelma, I understand and I'm—"

"What, you're sorry? Well, thank you, that makes it all better now. Bottom line is, you tricked me into believing that you cared for me as your client, knowing all along you were planning this."

"No, honey, that's not the case at all. I never planned any of this, I didn't know you were coming to my office until the day you showed up. And when Marie mentioned you to me, I never had a clue. I tried to contact you by letter, and never heard back from you, so I figured you didn't want me to bother you anymore. The last thing I would ever want to do is hurt you more. I know this hurts, and I didn't want this to happen. Not this way!"

"Look, I'm tired, just tired, and I can't do this right now. Can I please have my things?"

"Yes, Yes, here are your things. Thelma, again, I'm so sorry, I'm—"

Thelma starts her car and takes off quickly, not wanting to hear anymore lies.

She never saw the truck coming the opposite direction. The driver tried to swerve but could not avoid her because of how quickly she took off. Upon impact, her car spins in fast motion and lands on the opposite side of the road hitting a large tree. Thelma is thrown into the front windshield, hitting her head, causing the glass to shatter.

"OH MY GOD," screams Dr. Markinson. "HELP! My baby is in that car!" Dr. Markinson is running across the road as several cars stop to help out. "Somebody call 911!" Dr. Markinson screams.

A lady getting out of her car says, "I've called. They are on their way."

By this time there is a lot of people running to Thelma's rescue. One man is making sure that her car is secure with no leaking fuel, and checks to see if he can get Thelma to respond.

Dr. Markinson is crying and screaming Thelma's name. "Ma'am, I need you to calm down, so I can make sure that this young lady is okay. Everybody move back!" a man says. "

THAT'S MY DAUGHTER IN THERE!"

"Ma'am, I understand that, but I still need for you to stay as calm as you can, she might be able to hear you and we don't want to frighten her any more than she is already."

"I understand," answers Dr. Markinson. The paramedics remove Thelma from her car, fastening a neck brace on for security. They place her in the ambulance where they continue to perform CPR on her. Dr. Markinson jumps in the ambulance with Thelma and they arrive at the Bellvue Medical Center.

While Dr. M waits, she calls Marie to see if there is a way to reach out to any of Thelma's friends. Marie works on it while Dr. M waits in the waiting room. Hours go by and the doctor comes out and walks up to her. "Hello, I'm Dr. Trevor, and you are?"

"I'm Estelle...Estelle Markinson."

"And your relationship to the patient?"

"I'm her counselor."

"Okay, is there anyone here that is her next of kin?" "

Well, right now I'm the only one here, how is she?"

"She has suffered some severe head injuries the x-ray shows that there is swelling on her brain, and in this case, by the brain being so complex it's really difficult to tell what's going on. However, her vitals are stable, but her blood pressure is highly elevated, so we're working to get that down."

"Oh my God, this is terrible, can I go in and see her now?"

"Yes, you can. I'll take you in right away. Do you have any other contacts for her immediate family?"

Dr. Matkinson looks down at the floor. "Yes, I'm working on getting them notified."

"Okay great. Given the circumstances, I think it's appropriate for you to see her since you rode over with her. Right this way." As Dr. M walks into the ICU, Thelma is lying there with several tubes coming from her. Dr. Markinson begins to break down and cry. She walks closer to her and takes her hand. "Thelma, honey… oh, honey, I'm so sorry. None of this would have happened if I hadn't allowed my own selfishness get in the way. By insisting on telling you who I was. I've caused you enough pain, and now this? Oh Lord, how could this happen? She is a good person with a kind heart, just trying to find herself. Lord, please this is my child, and if you would just spare her life for me, I'll give you all of the praise, honor and the glory. I will completely submit my life over to you. Lord, do it…give her a second chance to live her life and to be happy in it, even if it doesn't include me!" Still crying, Dr. Markinson lays across Thelma and continues to pray.

Marie, Dr. Markinson's daughter arrives at the hospital. The nurse comes in a notifies her that Marie is there, along with her is Michael, Gloria, Mr. Williams, and Granny. Dr. Markinson comes out of the room to talk to Marie.

"Mom, what happened? Is Thelma going to be okay?" Marie says with great concern.

"I don't know, honey, it's pretty touch and go right now, all we can do now is just pray."

Marie introduces her mother to Gloria and everyone else. "Mom, this is Gloria, Thelma's best friend; and Michael, her boyfriend; and this is Gloria's dad and grandmother."

"Hello, everyone. I am sorry we're meeting under these circumstances," says Dr. Markinson.

"I need to see her." Gloria begins to lose it, crying with tears streaming down her face. Michael grabs Gloria and hugs her. "It's going to be alright, Gloria." Michael says as he consoles his friend, tears begin to cover his face also.

"Where is the doctor?" Gloria asks.

"The doctor is with other patients, but the nurse is around the corner."

"Thank you, Dr. Markinson," Gloria says.

"Oh Gloria, have you contacted her family?" asked Dr. Markinson.

"Yes, I've contacted her family. Her mom, brother, and sister are on the next flight here."

"Oh, OK, that's good." Michael and Gloria walk over to the nurses' station to find out more information about Thelma. "Excuse me, nurse, I'm here for Thelma McKinney."

"And you are?" "I'm her best friend Gloria, and this is her boyfriend Michael. Can we please go in and see her?"

"Wait one moment, let me check out something first. We generally don't do this, but because her family is out of town, you'll be her next to kin as far as I'm concerned," the nurse says, smiling at the two of them. "Both of you can go in, she's in room 112. Let me buzz you two in, okay?"

"Thank you." Gloria and Michael are buzzed through the doors that lead to Thelma's room. As they turn the corner, Gloria sees Thelma and immediately starts to cry. Michael walks up to her and kisses her on the side of her lips. "Hey, baby, look at you, what are you trying to do, break up with me? If you didn't want to be with me any longer a phone call or letter would have worked. Oh, babe," Michael says, jokingly, but ends up breaking down crying, putting his face next to Thelma's face. "I love you so much. You're the best thing that's ever happened to me. Please wake up!"

Gloria looks at Thelma, touching her hand. "Hey, bestie, I love you, girl. I won't leave, Thelma, I'll stay here and keep the same job, just wake up for me. I can't make it without you. You have to wake up. We have so much to do. We have to grow old together, right?"

Michael and Gloria stay in the room with Thelma and pray. Meanwhile, in the waiting room, Marie is questioning her mother about what happened to Thelma. "Mom, what happened? Do you know what happened to Thelma?"

"Marie, her car got hit by a truck as she was leaving my office."

"Was it a drunk driver, mom?"

"I don't know, honey, all I know is I was there and she drove off and got hit…It all happened so fast!" Dr. Markinson gets upset and starts crying again.

"Mom, you're upset. I'm sorry. Are you okay?" "Yes, baby, it's just so upsetting. I felt so helpless at the accident. I just pray she will be alright!"

The next night, Thelma's mother and siblings arrive in New York. They enter the hospital to see Thelma. Gloria meets Mary McKinney, TiTi, and Word at the hospital door, and shows them where to go. Michael, Dr. Markinson and Marie are waiting in the Family Room. Mary McKinney, Thelma's mother, was frantic, telling Gloria to take her to Thelma.

"Where is she, Gloria?"

"She's in ICU. The doctor has been waiting on you to give you updates on Thelma's condition. He will be coming to meet with the family in the family room later today."

"Okay, I'm so worried about my baby, have you seen her?" Mary McKinney is crying and upset.

"Yes, I have, Aunt Mary."

"Is it bad, Gloria, just tell me?" Mary is looking at Gloria with anticipation in her eyes.

"It doesn't look to good, Aunty. I'm sorry." Gloria hugs Mary and leads her to the family room. They walk into the family room and immediately, Dr. Markinson knows who Mary is. She stands up and walks away towards the window to cover her face.

"Hi, everyone, this is Thelma's mother Mary, her sister Tonya, and brother Tim." Michael stands up and walks over to introduce himself, along with Marie. And then, Dr. Markinson turns around and walks over to Mary McKinney. "Hello, Mrs. McKinney, I'm Thelma's counselor, Dr. Markinson."

Mary McKinney looks at her and realizes exactly who she is. "Estelle Markinson?"

"Yes." Dr. Markinson stands there looking at Mary.

"Can I speak with you in the hallway, please."

"That would be great," says Dr. Markinson.

Mary McKinney and Dr. M. walk into the hallway. "What are you doing here? How did you find her?"

"Mrs. McKinney, I don't know what you're talking about, I'm confused."

"Well, let me help you understand. I know who you are, Estelle, and you have to go. GET OUT!"

"I'm sorry, I had no idea that you knew who I was."

"Why wouldn't I know who you are? My husband, Gregory and I were very close, and everything he felt I should know about my daughter, he shared it with me. Listen, Estelle, I'm not sure what you're doing here, and frankly, I'm not concerned, the only thing I'm concerned about is my daughter's recovery. So, right now, I'm asking you to leave because only family should be here!"

"I'm not sure I want to leave, I love Thelma, and no disrespect, I may have not been there for her, but I'm here now. And you know what, Mrs. McKinney? It's not the time for any arguing, and Thelma wouldn't want us to!"

"How do you know what my child wants? You know nothing about her, because you gave up that right a long time ago!" Mary says to her, getting angrier.

"I totally deserve that, and I thank you for raising her, but I cannot leave."

"Put it this way, if I see you around her room or any of us, I will have you removed and escorted out of here as quick as you can say Thelma's name! Do I make myself clear?"

Dr. Markinson walks away and tells her daughter Marie that she's leaving. The doctor comes in the family room and talks over Thelma's condition with the family! Meanwhile Thelma lies in her hospital bed helpless and still in the coma.

Thelma opens her eyes. "Where am I? I hear a voice."

"Thelma, give me your hand, just walk with me."

"I cannot explain the feeling that I'm having, but wherever I am, feels amazing!"

"That's because you're in an amazing place, Thelma."

"Is this place heaven?" As Thelma walks with this beautiful person, she looks a little further and there is a group of familiar faces in front of her. She can't make out the faces, but they all look familiar. She knew them, and felt as if she was home. Thelma wanted to see the person's face she was walking with, but the vision was too bright. But it was so beautiful. She wasn't frightened. At first, she wondered where her family was. She knew she had had a misunderstanding with Dr. M, but with how she was feeling at the moment, none of that mattered. All she knew was that she was happy and felt at peace. The colors around her were so vibrant and Thelma felt so much love. "I just know that my Daddy is here, can I see him?"

"No, not right now, I need to speak with you about your life."

"What about my life? I know it hasn't been that great, I've made some terrible mistakes that I wish I could change, but it's too late isn't it?"

"Thelma, my grace is sufficient and my mercy is everlasting. I love you with an everlasting love, a love that's greater than you or anyone can consume."

At that moment, Thelma knew who this person was. She began to cry and apologize for her actions, and mistakes she'd made in her life. "Jesus, I know your voice." She began right then and there worshipping him, and feeling so excited and happy.

"Thelma, I need you to forgive. You are called for my glory only, but those that don't forgive will not receive forgiveness from me or my Father!"

"If at all possible, Lord, can I stay with you? I don't want to go back there, I don't feel love there like the love that's here, I need to be with you."

"I am with you, always. Your life isn't just for you, Thelma. Your life is meant to help others get through their trials. If you live your life just to please yourself, then you do not bring glory to my Father! You have to forgive, Thelma. Letting go of the past is a new beginning for yourself. If you love me, then you will forgive!"

"But, Lord, it's too hard there. I can't go back, it hurts too bad. The burdens are too heavy for me to carry, and I've lost everyone I love."

"Well, let me carry your burdens, lay them down and leave them here. Your faith in me will outweigh any heavy burdens that you've ever carried, I am he who will supply all of your needs. You will do a great work for me! Always remember that. I will be with you, even to the ends of the world. You just follow what I'm going to say to you, then your life will not be in vain and the glory will be given back to my Father. You will be a light to a dying world!"

Thelma was so overwhelmed with joy and love. It all was exuding inside and outside of her, it's like, immediately, she was changed, but this time for the better.

"Thelma, when you go back, tell them about my love and my grace. Let them all know that I'm not an illusion of the mind, share with them about forgiveness. No one will grace my Father's presence unless they forgive. And finally, let them know about heaven, that I am preparing it here for them to return home to me, with no more pain, crying, dying or disappointments. Their trials will be worth it all, and I'm there for them, only if they will say yes to my will."

And then she said it, the words that have been down on the inside of her since she was a little girl, but the enemy for so long had been trying to steer her away from saying, "YES LORD!"

When she said it, she felt her spirit jump and began to rejoice. Thelma knew that after this experience, no matter what comes or what may be, everything was going to be alright!

He began to walk Thelma towards this bright light on a road, and in front of her stood her father. He was holding a beautiful little girl. She saw her father, and her baby girl Joy. "Daddy, oh, Daddy! Look at you, you're perfect."

"Yes, baby girl, I am, for we are all perfect here."

Thelma was able to embrace her father one more time, and see Joy one more time. The little baby girl looked into her eyes and she knew just who Thelma was. Thelma's time with them was short, but real. Thelma realized there is definitely a heaven, and if she had it her way, she would stay. As she walked away from her Dad, he called her name. "Thelma."

"Yes, Daddy?"

"Take this ribbon, and keep it with you until I see you again." Thelma looked down at her hand and it was a beautiful little gold ribbon out of her baby girl's hair. Thelma held it tightly.

"Thank you, Daddy. I love you."

"And I love you, baby girl. One day we will all be together again."

"Thelma, it's time. You must go back and began the work you're called to do." Thelma held on to his hands as long as she could, and then, like a vapor, she felt her body become one with her soul again!

<><><>

Several days later, Mary and Tonya are in her room. Tonya is standing there holding Thelma's hand and saying a prayer, asking God to wake her sister out of the coma and give life to her again. Word and his mother are sitting in the seats against the wall.

"Thelma, wake up, please, Sis, I can't bear it anymore. I love you so much, please wake up for me!" TiTi walks away and Word leaves the room for a minute to call their brother Mick.

Granny Shepard arrives a few hour later. "Hello, everyone."

"Hi," TiTi says to Granny.

"You must be Tonya?"

"Well, yes, ma'am, I am, and you are?"

"I'm Gloria's grandmother. You can call me Granny, just like my Thelma does. I just came up to pray over my sweetheart Thelma, and tell her 'Enough sleeping, it's time to get up, in Jesus' name!' Where is your momma?"

"She's in the hallway," TiTi replies.

"Go get her, baby!"

"Yes, ma'am." While Granny waits for TiTi to return, she brings a bottle of blessed oil out, and begins to anoint Thelma's head all the way down to her feet.

"Oh, what a beautiful sight, Mother Williams."

"Oh, Mary McKinney, you haven't changed a bit, darling. You're still just as pretty as ever!"

"Thanks, Mother Williams."

"You're welcome, baby. Now I have come here because the Lord spoke one word to me. He said, 'PRAY' and so that's what I come to do. It's time for Thelma to wake up now!"

"Yes, it is, Mother Williams. Yes, it is!" Mary McKinney has her purse in her hand and puts it down.

"Take my hand and take your daughter's hand as well," Granny says to Mary McKinney. She then she closes her eyes, bows her head, and begins to pray. "Father God, in the name of Jesus, we come to you right now speaking life into Thelma now. Lord, you have called her to do a work for your kingdom, and she is ready now. Lord, we just thank you for the miracle you have performed in her life, for sparing her for your glory only, Lord. So that you may get the honor, you may get the glory, and you will get the praise out of her life. Now Satan, the Lord rebukes you, Thelma's life does not belong to you. I rebuke that spirits of depression and oppression, and speak hope, peace, and joy in her life! Thank you, Jesus, for your healing power. In Jesus' name, Amen!"

Thelma's mother is crying and rejoicing and believing in the prayer that was just spoken over her daughter.

Granny kisses Thelma on the head. "Now, Thelma, it is time for you to wake up. No more sleeping, you have work to do, baby. Granny Williams is here, and I'm believing within a few days, you're going to wake up. And I rejoice in your new beginning, sweetheart!" Granny turns to Mary McKinney and TiTi and says, "It is done!"

"Thank you, Mother Williams."

"Oh, don't thank me, honey, you thank the Lord, for he is worthy to be praised!"

As Granny releases Thelma's hand and preparing to leave the room, TiTi notices a tear rolling down Thelma's face. "Momma, look! Thelma has a tear coming down her face. Look!"

"Oh my Lord, Praise God, my baby's healed. She's going to wake up."

With all of the commotion the nurse from the nurses' station comes into the room. "Is everything okay? I heard all of the commotion."

"Yes, ma'am, my Thelma is crying! There are tears coming down her face!" Mary McKinney says with joy.

The nurse walks over and checks Thelma's vital signs. "Well, her vitals are all stable, but sometimes the tears are a sign of a normal body function."

"I know you have your medical opinions, and I respect them, but God is healing my baby and she is going to wake up! Please take no offense, I'm just a believer that my God can do anything but fail!"

"No offense taken, I know how you feel. My daughter was in the same kind of accident two years ago and any kind of hope and prayers were appreciated when I was in your shoes. I'm really hoping the best for your daughter." The nurse starts to walk away, and Mary stops her.

"Excuse me, do you mind me asking you, how's your daughter?"

"My daughter, Cindy? She didn't make it!"

"Oh, I'm so sorry."

The nurse walks away, but looks back and says to Mary, "Thank you very much. I pray your outcome will be different."

Word returns back to the room. He walks over to Thelma and whispers in her ear. "Time to wake up, Thelma."

"Word, what did you say to her?" Mary McKinney asks. "Momma, God revealed to me that she's alright! He told me to pray and I did."

"Yes, baby, I believe that, I just believe in my heart that Thelma's going to wake up soon. We will all be alright, God's in control of it all!"

"Mom, I sure hope so, I've been hearing Thelma singing 'I Surrender All,' you know she used to always sing with that beautiful voice of hers. I really miss her, Momma. I just know God wouldn't bring us together all to say goodbye, would he?" TiTi says, feeling sad about Thelma.

"Baby, God is great and never makes any mistakes. His will is always perfect, Tonya. We just have to remember that life and death is in the power of our tongue, so we will speak life over her every day."

"Yes, we will, Momma, and as Daddy use to always preach, 'You shall live and not die!'" TiTi replies.

<>〈〉<>

The next morning, after more tests, the doctors call for a family meeting to update them on Thelma's condition. "Good morning, everyone. I won't hold you long, I just wanted to update you on Thelma's condition. There is not a lot of changes other than the swelling has gone down on the brain a great deal. This is always a good thing. There's a reaction in her pupils and her blood pressure is down a substantial amount. So, these are all good signs, but we are still watching her closely. She does seem to be dehydrated, so we're going to add more fluids today and tomorrow. Are there any questions?"

"Yes, I wanted to share that Thelma had tears come down her face yesterday. Isn't that a good sign?" asks Mary McKinney.

The doctor ponders. "Well, yes and no, I only say that because she could have been crying, or the body was just acting naturally, releasing tears. All I can say to you, Mrs. McKinney, is your daughter is a fighter! Let's meet again in a couple of days, if that's okay. In the meantime, we will monitor her and go from there."

"One more question, Doctor. Why isn't Thelma waking up? It seems to me if she is making great progress, why isn't she awake?"

"Good question and I understand your concerns. It's difficult to say whenever we're dealing with the brain. The brain is a very complex muscle, and it pretty much does what it decides to do. Some people may say that her brain is recuperating from such an extreme trauma, but truthfully, I can't say to you why. The best way I can put is that we will have to wait and see. I'm sorry I can't give you better answers."

"I understand. Well, we will just have to be patient until she fully recovers and wakes up!" says Mary.

"Good enough, I will see you soon, Mrs. McKinney, and the rest of you hang in there!"

"Thank you, Doctor," the family answers.

"Momma, I'm going to see Thelma," says TiTi. "Wait, baby, I'm coming with you. Word are you coming?"

Mary and TiTi hold hands and heads down to Thelma's room. Mary is praying, crying, and praising God in the hallways. As they approach the room, Mary slows down. "Momma are you going to be okay?" Titi asks.

"Yes, baby, I'll be down shortly. I just want to take a minute and pray."

Word and TiTi walk towards Thelma's room. As they approach, they see the doctor and nurses standing together on the outside of Thelma's door. They began to run towards the room in a panic. "Oh my God, what's wrong with my sister?" Word cries.

"Now, calm down, your sister is fine. In fact, we were just getting ready to page your family. It seems like Thelma is regaining consciousness. She's only a little alert, but she's waking up," says the doctor.

"Word, go get Momma!" TiTi yells with excitement. "I'm on my way!" TiTi goes in the room with Thelma.

"Thelma, Sis, can you hear me?"

"She may not hear you at this moment. It's important to know that we're still in the waiting stages. But talking to her is always good," the doctor explains.

"Thelma, it's Tonya. I love you so much. You shall live and not die, sis. Come on out of there, in Jesus' name!"

Thelma opens her eyes, just as Mary and Word walk in the room.

"Thelma, baby, you're awake! I'm so glad to see you back with us," Mary says, leaning over Thelma and crying.

Thelma sees her mom and begins to cry, trying to reach for her. "It's okay, baby, don't try and do too much, you just rest. Oh Glooory to God, Halleluiah. Lord, you are so worthy to be praised!" Mary goes into a praise, crying, and thanking God for waking Thelma up from the coma.

"Well, Mrs. McKinney, looks like those prayers of yours worked, and very fast I might add."

"Yes, Doctor, my God is good, and he will come through for us. For you, too!" Mary grabs the doctor's hand and pats it with her hand.

"Well, I certainly won't argue with that!"

# Chapter 26

# A Fresh Start

It is Sunday morning and Thelma is trying to pull the breathing tube out. Mary tells her to wait and pages the doctor in. Thelma becomes frustrated with waiting and tries again but the doctor interrupts her by walking in. He talks with Mary and agrees they can try to take the tube out after outlining the risks of doing so.

"Will it hurt while you take it out, Doctor?" TiTi asks.

"No, it doesn't cause much pain, only a little discomfort. It seems like it's extremely long, but it's actually not. It will only take just a moment. Her oxygen is at approximately ninety-nine percent, so I think she's doing well enough to come off of it now."

The Doctor prepares to remove the breathing tube, so that Thelma can talk and be more comfortable. "Alright, Miss Thelma, just relax." The Doctor grabs hold of the tube and pulls it out.

"There you go, and it's out!" Doc looks at the monitor to see where her oxygen level is. "And it looks good. Well, look at you, Thelma. Boy, you're a fighter. You are breathing almost one hundred percent on your own!"

"Thank you, Jesus," whispers Thelma. "I love you, Momma. Hey, TiTi." Thelma speaks to them with her raspy voice, and with the biggest smile ever.

"Oh, baby, we love you. How are you feeling?"

"I feel a little tired, but I feel so blessed, can I have a little water?" The nurse comes over and hands Thelma a small green mouth sponge to suck on, which allows her to intake fluids slowly.

"Oh, that's so much better. Mom, I have so much to share with you."

"I know, baby, but you have to rest."

"No, Momma, I have to tell you this," Thelma replies with urgency in her raspy voice.

"Doctor, will she be alright talking to me?" asked Mary.

"Sure, she will. But, Thelma, we are going to need you to rest some more after you speak to your mom, okay?"

"Yes, Doctor. Momma, I know that you will not believe what I'm going to tell you, none of you will." Thelma is so excited.

"Oh, baby, after God healed you the way he has, there's nothing I won't believe."

"Okay, here it goes. Mom, I have seen, walked, and talked with Jesus! I really did, and he is so beautiful, loving and kind. Oh Momma, I wish you could experience what I have, heaven is so real and there is so much love there. I did not want to come back," Thelma says, speaking in a low tone.

"Thelma, baby, slow down, so you're telling me that you actually died and saw Jesus?"

"I don't know what to call it, but I can say with a clear mind and understanding 'YES, I saw him!'"

"What did he look like, Thelma?" TiTi replied.

"Oh TiTi, his voice is so beautiful. I remembered trying to see his face, but the light from his face was so vibrant, I had to turn away. But somehow, it didn't stop his beauty from shining through." Thelma pauses with tears streaming down her face.

"Momma, I believe her. Thelma, it was real, wasn't it?" says TiTi.

"Yes, TiTi. Jesus, heaven, love, peace and happiness is all so real! We just have to live according to his plan and the perfect will he has for each and every one of our lives, and…" Thelma pauses from being so tired.

"Thelma, baby, we're not going anywhere, you can tell us about it later," replies Mary.

"No, Mom, everything will be just fine. I have to finish telling you this, the one message that he kept trying to get me to really bring back here with me was 'Forgive.' He kept saying 'In order to please his father, we have to forgive. For if we don't forgive, then the father will not be glorified!' So forgiving those that have hurt us, abused us… it doesn't matter, we have to forgive them!"

"Wow, baby, you really did talk to Jesus, I can tell that you're different. It's like you're a new person," Mary says, stroking Thelma's hair back off of her face.

"I am, Mom, and I will never be the same again, this experience changed me for the better. Momma…I forgive you, do you forgive me?"

"Thelma, yes, honey. I'm so happy for you, baby. God is so good. Your daddy would be so proud!"

"For some reason, I think he already knows!" Thelma says, and lays her head back down to rest.

A few days pass and Thelma has fully recovered from being in the coma. Her vital signs are great and they are going to try and get her up out of the bed and see how far she has made progress. The doctor comes into the room along with a physical therapist. "Well, today is the day, Miss McKinney. Are you ready?"

"Yes, I think I am."

"Good. We're going to take you just down the hall, and then circle around. It will be good for you to start moving around, we're going to get you out of here soon. We all are so proud of the progress you've made, you're doing just great!"

"Thank you, all glory to God. I'm just grateful!" Thelma replies to the physical therapist.

"Okay, so let's get your legs and turn them around towards the floor, very easy now."

"It hurts a little."

"It's going to take some time, Thelma, but we will take it slow. The main thing is that you're trying," replies the nurse.

While Thelma is going on her first trial walk with the nurses, she runs into her coworker Marie, who happens to be coming to see her. Marie heard the good news about Thelma and wanted to see her.

"Oh my God! Thelma, I'm so happy to see you."

"Hey, Marie, it's great to see you, too. It seems like forever."

"It really does. Can I walk with you?"

"Yea, sure you can. It won't be too far because I'm already feeling tired." Thelma and Marie laugh together.

"My mother will be so happy to see you, she was so worried about you. She really took your accident very hard. I mean, seriously, she really did," Marie says to Thelma.

Thelma is shocked to hear this about Doctor Markinson, but realizes Marie may not know the secret. "Oh, well, tell her I'm fine, and recovering well."

"I sure will! How are you doing, Thelma?" Marie asks, but Thelma's getting tired.

"I think I'm ready to head back to bed."

"Certainly, let's turn you around. Or do you need a wheelchair?" says the nurse.

"I think I can make it to the room." Thelma gets to her room and back in the bed.

"Wow, Thelma, you're a walking miracle, really you are. I was so worried about you. We all were. Everyone at work was wanting updates every day. You have tons of cards and flowers. I have them for you at home since you couldn't have them in the ICU. So how are you feeling?" Marie asks Thelma again.

"Oh, I'm fine. Actually, I'm doing great, and the doctor says the trauma I suffered lots of people don't make it. So I'm so very grateful to God for sparing my life." Thelma lifts her hands in a praise position, tears began to come down her face.

"Thelma, I have to tell you, I'm looking in your eyes and it may sound weird, but you look different. As if you are Thelma, but you're not. I don't know, I can't explain what I mean."

"It's okay, Marie, you don't have to explain yourself. I know just what you mean. That's because I am different. God has totally changed my life, Marie, and it's for the better."

Thelma was released from the hospital one week later. Michael was there to pick her up, get her home, and help her settle in. Upon arriving at Thelma's apartment, Michael turns to Thelma and hugs her very tightly. "Thelma, I knew I loved you from the first time I saw you, but now I know that the love I have for you is so real. Seeing you lying there in ICU, and just the thought of you leaving me tore me apart. Baby, you are the best thing that has ever happened to me, and I want to spend the rest of my life with you." Michael reaches in his pocket. "Thelma McKinney, will you marry me?"

"Michael, this ring is so beautiful. I don't know what to say. I love you, too, just as much as you love me. Words can't explain what you mean to me, you totally make my life complete."

"So can you see me and you together forever, me as your husband?" says Michael.

"Yes, I can, but right now, I have so much to do. Not saying never, just not now. I'm sorry."

"Wow, I didn't expect to hear this, I just knew you would say yes. I was not talking about getting married tomorrow, maybe be engaged for a few years."

"Yes, I know, and just because I said no right now, doesn't mean it's no forever! That's if you're willing to wait for me. There is so much I have to get straight before I make any commitments."

Michael was disappointed that Thelma didn't say yes to the engagement, but was glad that she was all better. "Thelma, I'll wait an eternity for you, and I mean that!"

"Eternity is a very long time."

"If that's what it takes for me to marry my very best friend? Then eternity, it is! You see, Thelma, what you fail to realize is, some people pray and wait almost a lifetime to have or find what we share, and I know that we are meant to be together. I love you so much, you think that your life is so turned around, but I haven't told you all that I've been through. You only know a small portion of it. I don't know what the future holds for me, but I do know that there is no future for me without you!"

Thelma looks at Michael with tears rolling down her cheeks. "You blow my mind every time, the truth is I didn't want to bring all of my baggage to you, I felt that you deserved much better than me. I know that you're a great and marvelous man, I don't feel like I deserve you. Michael, I do love you and I'm happy I've found you, and I would be honored if you would wait for me. But I don't want you to feel obligated, you know?"

"I know, whatever we have to face, as long as we do it together is all that counts for me."

"Me too."

Michael kisses Thelma's hand. "Let's get you in here, so you can rest some more."

"Frankly, I'm tired of resting," Thelma says.

Michael helps Thelma get out of his car, and into her apartment. Michael takes the key and opens the door. "SURPRISE!"

"Oh my goodness." Thelma is surprised by her friends and family, gathering to celebrate her coming home. Her mother and siblings, a few coworkers, Gloria, Granny, and Mr. Williams, and of course Michael. "Welcome home, Thelma."

"Wow, thanks, everybody. I'm so surprised, I do appreciate each and every one of you that's here, and if I haven't told any of you lately, know that I love you all. I'm so blessed to have you in my life!" Thelma wipes the tears from her face.

"We love you, too, T." Gloria walks over to Thelma and hugs her.

<><><>

For the past two weeks, Estelle has been calling Thelma and leaving messages. Thelma's mother, Mary McKinney and siblings are leaving to go back home the next day.

"Momma, can I spend the day with you? I want to talk things through."

"So, Thelma, I have to admit that you have made an okay life here, and you have some very nice friends."

"Thank you, Momma. I've learned from the best." Mary smiles.

"Momma, I want to say something to you and I just want you to hear me out first."

"Okay, baby!"

"Well, Momma, I know that we've had our ups, and God knows we have had our downs."

Mary shakes her head and agrees with Thelma. "Ain't that the truth," Mary says.

"But, Mom, I want to say thank you, thank you for accepting me, and loving me as if I was your own. It takes a certain kind of woman to raise another woman's child. You didn't have to, but you did. I also know that my attitude sometimes was horrible, too. Can you please find it in your heart to forgive me, Mom?"

"Thelma, baby, I already have. You have to understand that I've never thought of you like a stepdaughter. You have always been just my child. I've never loved you any less. I think it's time to share with you the true story on what happened." Mary McKinney sits next to Thelma grabbing her hands and looks her in her eyes. "I knew your father since high school, we were very good friends. Your biological mother, Estelle, also attended school with us. She was drop-dead gorgeous, and I couldn't stand it! You see, I had a crush on Gregory. But he never saw me in that way, he always had eyes for her. Estelle, well, let's just say, she lived a very fast life. A life that your grandparents would not approve of. But that never stopped your dad from pursuing her. I, on the other hand, was a church girl, and I felt that your father and I had a great friendship. I mean, we talked about everything, but Estelle won his heart! Well, one day after the ball game, I decided to wait for your father to come out of the locker room. My sisters had convinced me that 'Closed mouths don't get fed' in other words, I should go and express to your father how I felt! I waited, and when he walked out, I did it. I told your daddy that I had fallen for him, and I knew that one day he would belong to me."

"What did he say, Momma?"

"Oh, not much. He said, 'I appreciate your friendship, Mary,' then he kind of looked at me and smiled. Then he gave me a hug and that pat on the back, that no girl wants!" Mary McKinney laughs. "At the end of the hall waiting for him, was ole green eyes, Estelle Markinson. So, long story short, she won and I didn't. But it never stopped me from loving your father. Your dad ended up getting your mom pregnant with you, and he thought the right thing to do was to marry her. Although his parents did not approve of her, he loved her, but by then, your mom wanted to go out on the road and sing, and got herself tied up with Willie Brown."

"Who was Willie Brown, Momma?"

"Oh, chile. Willie Brown was a music artist and town producer that went around selling young girls a dream that if they are with him, he would get them signed to a major record company! Well, to say the least, your mom fell for that dream and ended up on drugs after you were born. It broke your father's heart, and to see his heart broken, broke mine!"

"Wow, Mom, that's true love, but if dad was in love with Estelle, how did you two fall in love?"

"I have to admit, I've always felt in the back of my mind that your daddy always loved her, even when he and I got together, but when he married me, by then that didn't even matter. I loved him so much! Estelle ended up in a very bad state in life, she got so heavy into drugs that, I was even sadden by it. Your Grandma and Poppa McKinney kept you until your dad and I got settled in

306

our first little home, and then we came and got you. When you were a baby, you didn't remind me as much of her until you got a little older. That's when you started looking more and more like her. Those beautiful eyes of yours would look at me, and sometimes it seemed as if she was looking at me through you! Silly as it sounds, but that's how real it felt! Listen, honey, yes, we've had our bad times, but we have also had some wonderful days, too. I am so very proud of you, baby. You went out and did what you thought was best at the time, and made a life here for yourself. Congratulations, baby girl!"

"Momma, I've waited for so long to hear those words. Just hearing that you are proud of me, fills my heart with so much joy. I've carried around hurt, and envy against you for so long, Momma. Thank you for the gift of love, right now, Mom, today. I feel so free and amazing, Momma."

"Thelma, I have to tell you something," Mary says smiling.

"Yes, Momma?"

"I saw Estelle at the hospital when I arrived, do you know who she is?"

"Yes, Momma, I found out the day of my accident. I was so angry, because I felt she tricked me into thinking she was my counselor just to meet me. I know in my heart she didn't, I was just so angry about it!"

"How do you feel bout her?"

"Truthfully, I don't know, Mom. I know she and I had wonderful chemistry, and I certainly see the resemblance of her in me. I just don't know how to feel, how does it make you feel, Momma, to know that I've met her?"

"Well, baby, I knew this day would come. In fact, I think it always scared me because I thought when it did happen, I would lose you forever!"

"Never in a million years would you lose me, Mom. How can a mother lose a daughter that loves and needs her so much?"

"Thelma, do you mean that?"

"Yes, Momma. I need you more now than ever!"

Mary was so overwhelmed with what she heard Thelma say, she grabbed Thelma and cried. "Thelma, I needed to hear that. Thank you!"

"You're welcome, Momma." Thelma smiles at Mary.

"Just know, Thelma, that I respect you as a young woman and whatever decision you make concerning this, I support you one hundred percent! Some choices that Estelle made, were maybe not the best ones, but she loved you. This I know for sure."

"Thank you, Momma!" Thelma hugs her mother tightly.

"My little girl has grown up to be a responsible young woman. Your daddy would be very proud."

<><><>

*Dear God, why won't you let me sleep at night? I toss and turn thinking about Estelle. Lord, I need your help, what should I do about this situation I'm in? I know you want me to forgive, and in my heart I've felt I have, but this situation with Estelle, I just don't know about! Please direct my path in the way that you would have me to go. All I can say is I totally submit to your will!*

Later on that day, Marie calls and seems very upset. Michael answers the phone. "Hello."

"Hi, Michael it's Marie."

"Oh, hey, Marie, how are you?"

"Umm, I'm okay. Is Thelma available, or is she resting?"

"She's resting a little, is everything okay, Marie? Because you seem a little upset!"

"Michael, I am, I'm just beside myself. I can't talk about it, but please ask Thelma if she feels up to calling me, will she?"

"Yes, sure, Marie. I hope you feel better."

"Thank you, Michael." Michael hangs up from talking to Marie.

Thelma wakes up later and goes into the family room looking for Michael. "Hello," Thelma says.

"Hey, love, are you feeling better?"

"Actually, I have a slight headache, but all in all I'm good."

"Great, that's what I like to hear. Oh, babe, the doctor's office called and said that you need to come in for check up on Tuesday morning at 9:30. I can get off from work to take you, if you like?"

"Michael, I can't ask you to do that, you've already altered your life around mine."

"Don't worry about it, that's what I'm here for, I love you, babe!"

"Awww, thank you, Michael."

Michael walks to the kitchen to get himself and Thelma a glass of Cranberry juice. "Oh, babe, you got a strange phone call from Marie from the coffee shop about an hour ago."

"Why would you say a strange call?"

"I say that because she seemed upset, very upset, and said she needed to talk to you. What's up, why was she acting like that?"

"To be honest, I don't know what it could be. Hmm... real strange."

"I'm going down to the shop today and see how everything is going anyway."

"Thelma, I really don't want you going anywhere before you have your follow up. I just feel like you should wait and make sure everything is alright with you."

"Michael, I'm fine, and I feel great. I'm tired of lying down and resting. My mom, Tonya, and Tim are leaving tonight. I'm sad to see them go. It was nice to have them here.

"Yes, you have a wonderful family, I think they like me, too!" Michael says cheesing.

"Like you? They love you," Thelma replies, smiling at him.

"I know." Michael smiles.

"You know, babe, Mom and I had a very pleasant conversation yesterday."

"Really?"

"So you're feeling much better now about everything concerning the differences you two had?"

"I actually do, it was amazing how Mom opened up and shared things about my biological mother, her and dad, and more! And for the first time, I felt like she really cared about me. I could truly feel her love and sincerity. It felt really good, anyways, I know Daddy would have been proud of us both!"

"Babe, I'm always happy to see you smile. It looks like things are turning around for you, you go, girl!"

"You're so silly," Thelma says, throwing the couch pillow at Michael.

"There's something I've been really meaning to run by you, just to see what you thought about it."

"Oh Lord, whenever someone tells me, 'there's something they need to tell me' my heart drops."

"It's nothing, babe. I just wanted to say that my Grandma is ill and my sister called me and said that I may need to come and see about her. Only for a couple weeks, we need to decide whether to place her in a nursing home or not. She's suffering with dementia and she wanders off now."

"I'm so sorry, Michael. It's always hard when a family member is ill. It hurts, especially when there's nothing you can do," Thelma replies.

"Yea, that seems to be the case. Now, if I go, I'll need to leave on Thursday."

"This Thursday?"

"Yes, I'm afraid so, babe. Since I'm the eldest, I need to be there to help with the decision making, I'm sorry to have to leave you. Hey, how about you come with me? Thelma, I would really love it if you would."

"Oh, honey, I would love to, but I don't know if I should leave town just yet."

"Yes, you're right, I guess!"

"How long will you be gone?"

"Maybe a month, no more than that."

"Wow, okay. I'm not going to lie, that's a long time. I'm going to miss you, boy."

"Girl, you have no idea how much I'm going to miss you!"

"We better get ready to go pick up your family," says Michael.

"Yes, it's getting late. Baby, let's take them to that new restaurant we went to last time," Thelma says.

"Oh, you mean, The Stream?"

"Yes, their food is so delicious." Thelma goes to get changed for dinner, while Michael sits on the couch.

Later on that day, Michael and Thelma go to pick up Thelma's family, to take them out to dinner before their departure to the airport going back to Arkansas. They are sitting at the restaurant and talking.

"So, Michael, it seems that you and my daughter have become very close. I've heard all of the wonderful support you have given her. Thank you for being a great friend to my precious daughter."

"You're welcome, Mrs. McKinney, but you don't have to thank me, it is my pleasure. Can I share something with you?" Michael replies.

"Sure you can."

"One day, I plan to marry your daughter. If it was left up to me it would be sooner than later!" Thelma looks at Michael, and with her eyes, she is saying, "Please don't say anymore."

"Thelma? You didn't tell me the nature of your relationship with Michael was this serious."

Thelma clears her throat. "Well, Momma, it never came up."

"No, we've talked about Michael plenty of times on the phone, and I don't remember you ever saying that you had a boyfriend!"

"Okay, Momma, well, I'll share my feelings with you now about him now then. Momma, I love Michael. Michael has been a lifeline for me. He has held me up when I was down, and when I felt like giving up, he was there to encourage me not to. You know how you would always say that Daddy was your best friend?"

"Yes, I do, honey, and he still is."

"That's how I feel about Michael, Mom. I'm so grateful that I came to New York, because the biggest blessing God had waiting for me was Michael. And all I have been through, it was worth it all because I feel that I've truly found my soul mate. Momma, why are you crying?"

"I'm crying because, I know just how you feel, your dad made me feel that exact same way! You are blessed to have found each other, always remember that God is first in your lives. Momma's so happy for you both, now I know that God sent you here. You have been blessed with wonderful friends, Thelma."

Thelma looks over at Michael. "Yes, I have."

"Please spare me, with the throw up conversation," Word says, rolling his eyes and laughing.

"Shut up, Word." Thelma hits her brother in the arms, smiling at him.

"Michael, whenever you and my daughter decide to take the next step, you have my blessing!"

"That really means a lot, Mrs. McKinney. And I can reassure you while you're gone, your daughter is in great hands."

"That's what I like to hear. Question?"

"Yes, ma'am?"

"Have you totally treated my daughter with the utmost respect? If you know what I mean?"

"Mom!" Thelma says.

"Calm down, Thelma, I've been waiting to ask him, and I think it's perfect timing!"

"Oh my gosh! I just want to slide under this table and just disappear."

"It's alright, Thelma. I can answer your mom's question." Thelma is sitting embarrassed with her hands over her face.

"To answer your question, Ms. McKinney, I love your daughter and I don't know any other way but to treat her with respect. Now if you're asking me if I've made any inappropriate advances on her, then no. We've talked about waiting until we're married. But although it hasn't happened, doesn't mean I haven't thought about it. But loving her makes me want to do everything right!"

"Michael, you said all of the right answers! I love it how you respect Thelma, it's all her dad and I could ever dream of for her – for any of our children. God Bless you, son!"

"Thank you, Mrs. McKinney."

# Chapter 27

# A Turn Around

The next day, Thelma goes to check on things at the coffee shop and say hello to everyone. She is still out on sick leave but they are happy to see her.

"Good morning, everyone."

"Thelma, we missed you," says Donavin and others.

"I've missed you, too, Donavin. How is everything here?"

"Girl, it has been terrible since you have been gone. The South store sent that manager named Evelyn to fill in for you. She is of the devil. Just mean for no reason."

"Aww, Donavin, I'm sorry, boo. All I know is I cannot wait to return back to work. I am bored out of my mind!"

"I bet you are, girl, I heard about what happened and I want you to know, I was praying for you!"

"Well, your prayers worked. I appreciate all of the cards, flowers and support you all gave me! Is Marie here?"

"Yes, she's on break. I think she's in the courtyard! Girl, that's what I've been waiting to tell you."

"What?" Thelma says.

"Girl, while you were gone, Michael was on his job as your boo, honey."

"What are you talking about, Donavin?"

"Honey, he came down here, making sure that your job was good. He kept us current on your condition by calling and everything. Making sure we all knew he was your man!"

"Donavin, you're a mess, boy. I'll be back. I need to speak with Marie."

"Yes, she should be outside, she hasn't been in a good mood lately!"

"I'll be right back." Thelma goes to the courtyard to see Marie. Marie is sitting with her back turned from the door. "Hey, lady."

"Thelma, what are you doing here? You're suppose to be on bed rest, and here you are coming out already?"

"Well, I had to check on my favorite people, at my favorite job!"

"That's sweet. Do you have any idea when you might return? We really miss you around here. You bring a certain peace to the atmosphere. Because that new girl, Shelly, is an airhead. I have to supervise her on just pouring water, and that fill-in manager they sent over here is a mess!"

Thelma laughs. "Girl, stop it. It cannot be that bad."

Marie nods her head rapidly. "It's that bad. And then last week, we had the health inspector drop in and give us a surprise visit."

"Uh oh, how did that go?"

"We had one citation, the thermometer wasn't working in the fridge, but other than that, we passed with flying colors!"

"Whew, halleluiah! That's cool and you were here?"

"Yes, I was! Thelma, I called you the other day because I had something to talk with you about!"

"Yes, I got your message. What is it, Marie? It sounds serious," Thelma says.

"I don't even know how to start with this."

"Just say it, Marie."

"Thelma, my mother told me everything. Thelma, you're my sister?" Thelma sits there in total shock not knowing what to say.

"Marie, I don't know what to say either. What all did Estelle say to you?"

"I know it all. I know that this situation was the reason you got into that car accident."

"Wow, so she felt compelled to share it all, huh? All I can tell you is I know as much as you do, and I really don't know how I should feel. So, I'm really sorry you've been sucked into this entire mess!"

"Sucked in? Despite how you feel about her, she is my mother, and I wasn't there when you were born or when any of this happened. Yes, I have to admit, when she told me I was so angry at her for not telling me anything about you. I'm still confused as to why she didn't. But to be truthful, I was happy to know that we're sisters. I admire you, and besides, we do favor one another!"

"Wow, Marie, it's a lot to take in at one time. However, I thank you for talking to me about it and sharing your thoughts with me. I really appreciate you for that!" Thelma takes a tissue and dabs the corner of her eyes

. "I didn't mean to make you cry, Thelma, are you okay?"

"Yes, I'll be fine. I'm just emotional about this situation and a little angry, trying to understand it all. Like why I wasn't good enough for her to keep, but she kept you? No offense to you, Marie."

"None taken, Thelma. I couldn't even imagine how you must feel!"

"Can I ask you a question, Marie?"

"Yes. Anything."

"I remember you saying that you had a younger sister, are there other siblings?"

"Yes, I have a brother as well. His name is Chris, but we call him 'Man'. He has Down syndrome, but he happens to be the coolest little brother I could ever have. I wouldn't trade him for the world! Look, Thelma, my mom apparently has made some mistakes, but I think you should hear her out. Because the look she has in her eyes when she talks about you… I know that she loves you, and she is very sorry. She kept repeating to me, 'I almost got my child killed.' I felt so bad! One thing that I didn't appreciate was your mother asking her to leave the hospital. I didn't think that was necessary. I was livid when I found out that's why Mom had to leave!"

"All due respect to you, Marie, although I didn't know about my mom asking your mother to leave, my mom had a right to feel the way she did. She's been through a lot as well! It was not comfortable, I'm sure, to see her there! So please don't pass judgment on her. I can see how it can make you a little upset, but at the same time, she should have left!"

"I think we got off to a pretty good start, Thelma, so I don't want this to turn ugly. You love your stepmother and I love my mom, so we will probably never see eye to eye on this discussion," Marie says.

"Okay, first, let me just make it clear, and then we probably should stop talking about this. My mother, Mrs. Mary McKinney, is my mother, whom I love very much. She has and will never be referred to as my 'stepmother'. Second of all, she did for me what Estelle chose not to, which was raise me to be a well-rounded, God-fearing, smart and caring young woman! And I love her, with all of my heart and soul!"

"I'm sorry, Thelma, I didn't mean to insult her or you. Will you forgive me?"

"Absolutely, we're just doing what's natural for any daughter to do, defend them! Look, Marie, I don't hate Estelle. I'm just confused and upset. Maybe with time, I might grow to understand!"

"So would you agree to meet with her and maybe talk?"

"I don't know about right now, Marie. But prayerfully, God will give us the right opportunity to talk things over!"

"So, if I can ask you, where do you and I stand? Because I would love to develop our own relationship as sisters!" Marie says, sitting next to Thelma.

"As far as we're concerned, I would love that also. I mean, just looking at you it's like looking in the mirror. You really do favor me, especially your eyes and cheekbones!"

"Yea, it's kind of cool. Thelma, can I have a hug? I'm truly sorry about everything you have been through and I'm grateful you're better!"

"Yes, of course. Give me my hug. We're cool, we're going to always be alright. God has blessed me with another little sister! And he has given me a second chance at life. So I want to make sure this second time around I do it right! So, with that said, I better go, I'm getting a little tired. Plus, Michael should be on his way to get me."

"Before you go, can I share with Mom that we talked, and maybe, just maybe in the future, you're willing to speak with her?" Thelma smiles at Marie.

"Yes, I guess so."

"Thank you, Thelma. I'm glad we had a chance to talk. I feel much better."

"Yea, I kind of do, too."

"I better get in there before I get in trouble; my lunch break has been over! Thelma, did you want to come back in the shop and wait for Michael?" Marie says.

"No, I'm going to sit here, and enjoy and smell the flowers. I never realized how beautiful this courtyard of flowers is. It's a great day to be alive!"

"Amen, Thelma! I'll see ya later!" Thelma sits there while waiting for Michael. She spends time talking with God and just smelling the flowers. Life's free gifts that she used to take for granted.

"Lord, I haven't said thank you this morning, so, 'Thank you'. I don't know what you're doing, but I'm going to have to trust you with this one, just give me strength to carry on in the way you desire for me to. Order my words and direct my steps. Be with me in all that I do! I totally submit to your will for my life, and pray I can make you proud."

Michael pulls up and parks his car besides Thelma on the street. "Hey, beautiful, are you ready to go?"

"Yes, I am, handsome." Thelma smiles while walking to Michael's car.

"So how was your visit at the shop today?"

"It was very interesting, Donavin is the same, of course. That boy is a mess."

"Yes, he is!" Michael says, laughing and shaking his head.

"I had a talk with Marie, and found out what she wanted when she called the house the other day."

"Is everything alright, because, babe, when I say she was upset, she was!"

"Yes, and with good reason. Estelle told her that she's my biological mother."

"No, she didn't. Are you serious?"

"Babe, I'm telling you the truth. I was in total shock, unprepared and all of the above. I'm just really finding out all of this myself. Then Marie comes into this completely innocent, but wanting answers. I was pretty ticked off at the nerve of Estelle, Dr. M., or whomever she is. Starting confusion between everybody else…her nerve. All because she and I are having problems."

"Now, Thelma, you know I'm in your corner one hundred percent, right?"

"Yes. The way you said RIGHT sounds like something else is coming, Michael."

"It is, I think right now everyone is hurting, confused and more."

"Yea, I get that, Michael, but—"

Michael cuts her off. "No, just let me finish, Thelma, because I've been thinking about this a lot since I found out about your situation!"

"And?" Thelma replies, getting mad.

"And I just think that something on this level will take time. And maybe Estelle had a good reason for her decisions!"

Thelma gets a little frustrated with Michael's view of her biological mother, and Michael senses it. "You know what, Michael? I've had enough of hearing about her feelings and how hard she must have had it."

"I get it, babe, and I really didn't mean to get you upset. I only want you happy, it seems like you've had nothing but heartache the last year. If I can have anything to do with you being happy in the future, I'll do everything in my power to make it happen! You accept my apology?"

"Michael, it's okay, I appreciate you. I just think I need some time to at least consume what Marie had to say."

"Babe It's cool. I understand. So what do you want to do now?"

"I just want to go home and lay down. I have a headache!"

# Chapter 28

# A Clearer View

Thelma is feeling very overwhelmed with everything she has endured. Trying to follow her promise to God, on trusting, loving, and forgiveness. She can't hold back her tears. She feels overwhelmed, confused, and hurt. Feeling like no one understands her.

"Dear God, I come to you as humble as I know how, asking you for clear direction. Lord, it seems like I haven't done anything lately, but pray and cry. I'm not going to lie, I'm hurting, and badly. You tell me to forgive, only to face another hard trial in my life! How am I supposed to forgive a woman who walked away from me, never tried to find me, until now, and now wants to be Mother of the Year? I'M TIRED! Tired of always having to be the bigger person, or the one to understand no matter how bad I'm hurting in the situation. When am I ever going to be happy? I'm grateful for all you've done for me, giving me a second chance and sparing my life, but...this is why I didn't want to come back here, it's too hard, Lord. The pain is too much to bear. So, I'm asking you, Lord, to please help me!"

Thelma's window was open as she was praying, and she always kept her Bible on the desk next to the window. Thelma witnessed something amazing happen as she was praying. It was like the pages themselves were being turned by unseen fingers, and suddenly, the pages stopped turning. However, the wind was still blowing, because the curtains in the room were still blowing in the breeze. Something on the inside of Thelma compelled her to get off of her knees, walk over to the Bible, and pick it up. As she looked down, there was a gold ribbon with a glittery design to it. And to her surprise, she remembered it was the ribbon that her dad had given her when she was in the coma. It can't be real. This can't be happening! Thelma looked and rubbed her fingers across the gold ribbon. It was the very ribbon that came out of her baby Joy's hair, that her dad gave me in heaven!

*Lord, is this a sign?* Thelma looked down at the Bible and it was like a light pointing to the scripture: Psalms 27:1. She began to read it. "The Lord is my light and my salvation, so whom shall I fear? The Lord is my fortress, protecting me from danger, so why should I tremble? When evil people come to devour me, when my enemies and foes attack me, they stumbled and fall. Though a mighty army surrounds me, my one thing I ask of thee, Lord, the thing I seek most, is to live in the house of the Lord all the days of my life, delighting in the Lord's perfections and meditating in his temple, for he will conceal me there. When troubles come; he will hold my head high above my enemies who surround me, at his sanctuary I will offer sacrifices with shouts of joy, singing and praising the Lord with music. Hear me as I pray, O Lord. Be with me. And my heart responds, 'Lord, I am coming.'"

Thelma realized that the Lord was reminding her that, even if she has trials, as long as she dwells in him, he will be with her. That he is her light and all she needs to do is follow him. "Thank you, Jesus, for loving me, the way you do. I know now that I can do this! I can do all things through Christ that strengthens me."

# Chapter 29

# *And Now I See*

Two days have passed and Gloria is getting things together to make the big move. She feels that she can move forward now that Thelma is much better. She picks Thelma up to go grab a bite to eat and catch up on everything that has happened. After arriving at the restaurant, the girls begin catching up.

"Gloria, it seems like forever since we've done this, huh?"

"Yes, it does. You know, Thelma, I have to tell you that your surviving that accident has been the best present God could have given me."

"Aww, girl, that's sweet."

"Thelma, I was so scared I was going to lose you." Gloria is tearing up, while she expresses to her best friend how she feels.

"Gloria, I'm sorry you all had to experience a scare like that. I can't even imagine."

"Did you know anything? I mean, you know they say the last thing that goes on people is their hearing. Could you hear any conversations, prayers, crying? Did you even know you were in a coma?" Gloria asks curiously.

"No, I can't say that I did. I don't really remember anything in that order, but what I can tell you is that I remember walking and talking with Jesus." Thelma smiles, while Gloria looks surprised.

"Wait, wait, wait one minute. What did you say?"

"You heard me right. Michael didn't tell you what I experienced?"

"Michael hasn't said anything to me about anything like that! What do you mean, you walked and talked with Jesus?" Gloria is in shock with her mouth open. She reaches for a glass of water.

"I know you probably don't believe me, but it's true."

"Why would you say that I don't believe you, Thelma? I don't think that you would say that, just to be saying it. So what happened?" Gloria moves in closer to Thelma.

"I really don't remember exactly when and what order or day it took place, but all I remember was I opened my eyes and seeing a really bright light. And then I heard the most beautiful voice you ever could hear in your life calling my name. I looked and there he stood. He had the most warmest presence, it was like Christmas when you are a child, times ten. I tried to look at his face, but his presence was too great, I had to turn away...but although I couldn't see him, I knew how beautiful he was. If that makes sense?"

"Yes, kind of, were you afraid?"

"No, that was the beauty of it. I wasn't afraid, it was the total opposite, I felt like it's where I belonged, Gloria. Put it this way... I love y'all, but I didn't want to come back at all! He said to me, that it wasn't my time, and that I had more work to be done. His main message to me was 'forgive'. He kept telling me that, none of us would make it into heaven unless we forgive, that if we don't forgive, then his father will not be glorified. Gloria, I know it's a lot to take in, but please...you have to believe me. It was as real as you and I are talking right now. Oh, how I love him. He was so kind and loving. The love I felt there was nothing like the word 'Love' that we all playfully throw around. His love for us, is so great it was almost too much to take in. All I know is now, after having that experience, I'm not afraid of death, because I know it will be the only way I'll get back to that beautiful place and to him!"

"Thelma, I've always wondered what it would be like, but Thelma, I'm afraid of dying."

"Oh no, Gloria, it's not like that at all. I wish I could give you a small glimpse of what I experienced. Heaven is real, it's so very real. And Jesus loves us so much; he only wants the best for us! And then, He took my hand, and there was, what seemed like a heavy fog appeared in front of me...I closed my eyes and when I opened them, my dad and baby Joy was standing in front of me."

"Thelma, the dream you had of your dad, and a young baby girl and that other young woman in your dream...must have been you. Remember, Thelma?"

"I had forgotten all about that, Gloria. Oh my goodness. You think I'm crazy, huh? You think I've lost it, right?"

"Thelma, the look in your eyes right now, the way I'm feeling just hearing what you shared this with me, I believe every word you're saying. I know it happened to you. I can feel it and see the joy, leaping from your spirit. It's so beautiful to watch and feel. And all I can say is WOW! What did your dad say to you? This might sound dumb, but...were you able to touch him? Remember when we were little, and in Bible study, they would teach about heaven and angels? I've always wondered would your hands go right through a spirit. That sounds silly, huh?" Gloria says, laughing with excitement.

"No, not at all, and yes, I was able to hug him, but not a really long time. I felt my father's arms around me, and it was really my baby Joy, too! I had forgotten all about this, but before I left them to come back here. Daddy took a little golden colored ribbon out of Joy's hair and placed it in my hands. That ribbon was like a transparent gold. And I had forgotten all about the ribbon, until last night. I was praying and asking God to help me with what to do about my biological mother, Estelle. My window was open and the wind began to blow. The pages in my Bible started to turn, but not from the wind…it was like fingers were turning each page until it landed on a specific page. The page was Psalms chapter 27:1 'The Lord is my light and my salvation…whom shall I fear?'"

"Girl, yes! You know I know that scripture. We better remember it, we use to have to quote that scripture along with John 3:16," says Gloria.

"Ain't that the truth! Mother Lester was no joke when it came to teaching us kids the Bible and us knowing the scriptures."

"Wow, Thelma, that's amazing."

"Wait, girl, I'm not through. When the scripture opened… the gold ribbon was in the Bible! The same ribbon my daddy placed in my hands was in the Bible."

"Thelma…"

"Yes, I have the ribbon, it's at home."

"Girl, this is waaay, too much!"

"I know it's a lot to take in all at one time, but Gloria...it was the best experience I could have ever had. It changed my life, and for the better. I will never be the same." For a moment, total silence grew at the table where Thelma and Gloria sat. The best friends that were once girls together realized, they were two grown women sharing an experience that only they could. No one knew Thelma better than Gloria, and vice versa!

"I'm feeling really good, Thelma. I'm so excited about us and our new beginning in life. For the first time in my life, I finally feel as if I belong, I'm happy with me."

"Yea, I kind of feel the same. It's like everything I've been through, it all led up to this moment and it was all for my good. The strange thing is...my counseling sessions with Estelle really helped me get here, as much as I hate to admit it. She really helped me to realize that being me is okay, and that life's curve balls don't always feel good, but sometimes those pains, hurts, obstacles...are for your own good."

Gloria looks at Thelma with a smile. And snaps her finger. "By George, I think she's got it! Thelma, I wish that you could see your face when you talk about her, you miss her don't you? Why are you crying?"

"I don't know, Gloria, it's like I meet this counselor and she helped me open up like I never thought I could. We actually became great friends, which is totally against the rules, but I felt a bond with her and she with me. Then when I found out who she really was, I felt betrayed. It felt like 'Oh, here's the catch.' It hurt me really bad, and I was so angry. I'm still a little, but in order to forgive her means I have to love her, and I do, Gloria. I do love her. I really wanted to punish her for a while, but my near death experience won't allow me to. It will all be in vain if I don't learn to move on!" Thelma is wiping her eyes.

"Thelma, is this really you talking? This is so amazing to me, just to see God's glory all over you and the change that has taken place. I want what you got, but I don't want to go where you have been. NOoo, chile!" Thelma and Gloria laughs.

"I know, I feel like pinching my own self, because it's so unreal. I have only chosen a few to share my experience with, I figured that others would think I'm crazy...but honestly, I don't care. I know what happened to me was real, but just letting my life shine is my lifetime goal!" "I think we need to go to church, what do you think, Thelma?"

"Church? I haven't been in a couple of years and I'm sad to say it, but it's true. Besides, I don't think there's no church or good preaching like Daddy's."

"You're right, your dad was one of a kind, however, Bishop Myer's church 'Church of Praise Church of God In Christ' services are off the hook!"

"Yes, I'll be willing to go. Wow, church? I will feel like the prodigal daughter coming home, I've messed up so much!"

"Yea, but you out of all people know that we can't mess up enough for God to remove his love for us! Thelma, I have to confess something to you."

"Oh Lord, your confessions make me nervous! Spit it out, Gloria."

"Well...your mother Estelle kind of contacted me a few days ago, and asked if I could try and convince you to speak with her."

"Are you serious?" Thelma says.

"Yes, very. I was shocked, and I asked her how did she even get my number."

"What did she say, because I'm curious how as well."

"She said, on your emergency contact form on your application for counseling services, my name was listed."

"Yes, I did put your name down."

"Man, I just wish she would leave me alone," Thelma says feeling frustrated.

"Maybe she will if you would go on ahead and hear her out. I mean, Thelma, it seems to me that you're ready!"

"How do you figure that?"

"Chile, you are a new person. Listening to how God has turned your life around and your testimony alone...you have to be changed. All I'm trying to say is, go on ahead and meet with her and show her you're alright, that you're not letting her past and how she handled everything, dictate your life! I think you'll be fine, I believe in you, girl. I'll go with you if it will make it better for you."

Thelma sits listening to Gloria, pondering the thought of meeting with Estelle. "I have to really think about this, but if I do...I would love for you to be there with me."

"Girl, you know I will. We have been there for each other since we were little, I'm not about to stop now! On a much lighter note, Granny wants you and Michael to come to dinner tonight, can you come?"

"Yea, I can. I think Michael has to work tonight, but I'll ask."

"Cool, I wanted to give you this before I moved away, but I can't wait." Gloria pulls a box out of a bag, and hands it to Thelma.

"What's this?" Thelma says, looking at the bag.

"Just open it." Thelma opens the bag.

"Oh my, Gloria... It's beautiful, It's you and I when we were little, how did you get it this small enough to fit into this locket?"

"The jewelers over on Martin Street did it for me, you like it?"

"Like it...I love it, oh thank you. Now you messing up my makeup having me crying!"

"I just want you to know how much I appreciate your friendship, I love you."

"I love you, too, and thanks for your lifelong friendship!"

# Chapter 30

# A Full Recovery

That night Thelma went over to Granny Williams' home and had dinner with, Gloria, Mr. Williams, and Granny, just like old times.

"This is wonderful, Granny. And you cooked my favorite meal, fried pork chops, greens and cornbread, and oooh, Granny, candied yams, too?"

"Yes, Gloria. I wanted to celebrate your new job offer, and my dear darling Thelma's full recovery, with God's healing power!" says Granny, while she's preparing the food on the dining room table.

"Yes, Thelma, we are so grateful for God's hand upon your life. You're like my own daughter, and I've never prayed so hard in my life!" says Mr. Williams, while sitting down at the dinner table.

"Wow, that means a lot to me, Mr. Williams. I love all of you, and I'm just so grateful to be here."

"Yes, honey, I knew God was going to raise you up, he told me to come and lay hands on you with prayer and anoint you from head to toe. And I did just that, took that blessed oil from my pocketbook and anointed you from the top of your head, to the very sole of your feet. And I said with authority 'Thelma, it's time for you to wake up now, in Jesus name! And not soon after I prayed for you, a tear rolled down your face. You know what, baby? I knew then it wouldn't be long before you were awake! I know that my God is a healer!" Granny began to cry and thank God for Thelma's healing, by clapping her hands and speaking in tongues.

Thelma looked around that table and was grateful for her family and friends that God placed in her life. Thelma became very emotional. "Granny, I never knew you were there and prayed for me."

"Oh, honey, you had so many people praying for you, the church held a shut-in every week from Monday through Thursday! Bishop said we would hold it until you woke up from that coma. We all believed and trusted in God that you would!"

"I'm at a loss for words, I feel like I need to personally thank everyone from your church for their prayers and sacrifices just for me!" Thelma says wiping her eyes.

"Well, you can, honey. You can come to church with me anytime you get good and ready."

"I just told her that earlier that we needed to come to church, Granny." Granny smiled.

"Then it's settled, I'll be looking forward to seeing you walk through those doors and soon, okay?"

"Yes, Granny. I promise!" Thelma said.

"Now let's eat. I've been on my feet all day preparing all of this food. I also made your favorite, Thelma, peach cobbler!"

"Yes, Lord, and thank you, Granny!"

Thelma is caught up in her thoughts… *It feels nice to sit down and eat a homecooked meal like Granny's. Every time Granny cooks like this, it reminds me of home, the way Momma would cook those Saturday night meals for the church family. Me, Word, and TiTi would have to clean up every Friday night because the saints would be over the next night. I miss how Daddy would bless the food and almost turn his prayer into a sermon, Mom would tell him to hurry, by patting his knee. Noisy Sister Knowles would always try and start up gossip about somebody and Deacon would change the subject just to shut her up. I can smell the chicken being cooked after church when Momma would sell dinners to raise money for the building fund. I even miss singing for my Dad, and how the church would go up in a praise – shouting and lifting their hands towards the heavens. And when I was little, and the Evangelist laid his hand upon my head, speaking of the things I would endure. I can still hear that song "Yes Lord." Even today, I believe I kept that "Yes" hidden in my soul. I would get that chill up my spine, and that overwhelming feeling of a praise being deep down in my spirit, even as a young girl. I knew my soul connected to that song, I guess it's important to cherish the times you're in, because we never know when they'll be over! But I know now not to take life, family and friends for granted. All of our lives are like a puzzle, and each piece of that puzzle represents an event or a trial, hurt, obstacle and more. It's necessary to experience them all, because we learn something from each piece of that puzzle. And like a puzzle, once it is complete, we can look over it and see how vital and important each piece played in the completion! And although the shapes were all different, they worked together to get the end result.*

She couldn't explain it, but Thelma went home the next day, she felt compelled to call Estelle. *I don't know how this will end up, but…I have to ask her to forgive me, and I have to forgive her!*

"Michael, I'm going to do it. I'm calling Ms. Estelle over to speak with her." Thelma jumps off of the couch, feeling determined.

"Babe, I think that's great, when are you going to call her, and why the mind change?"

"I've just been thinking a lot about my life and what God requires of me, of us all. And at the top of his list is forgiveness. So I need to speak with her."

"Wow, Thelma, I'm proud of you. Shocked, but proud!"

"Yes, I know you are, and to be honest, I'm surprising myself. But I'm ready to move forward, holding on to your past will not allow you to move forward with living in the present or future!"

Michael walks over to Thelma, hugging her with both arms around her waist. "I have to say, baby, you've been coming up with some impressive quotes. I may start calling you Dr. Thelma McKinney."

"Well, honestly, Dr. Estelle Markinson kind of helped me understand things in life a little more than I did. Although it was her job to do so, I could feel that her heart was in it the entire time!"

"I'm very happy for you, dear, and I hope that everything turns out just the way you want them to! So when are you going to call her?"

"I think I'm going to stop by her job around noon. I know she started doing half days on Mondays." "Did you want me to go with you?" asked Michael.

"No, babe, I think this one I have to do alone. Gloria offered, too. But I got this!" "Well, you go, girl," Michael says.

"Thank you, babe. Oh, babe, about that trip to see your grandmother, I would love to go with you, if the offer still stands."

"Of course it still stands, you'll really do that for me?"

"Weren't you there for me? Michael, I'll never forget what you have done for me, and the friendship you have demonstrated to me. I know I've said it a million times, but, thank you!"

"I'll always be here for you until I take my last breath on this earth, and I mean that from my heart, Thelma."

"Oh, believe me, I know you do. You're the best friend a girl could ever have," Thelma says, putting on her shoes.

"OK, enough of the mushy stuff. It's 10:55, you know her office is quite a distance away, are you sure you don't want me to drive you there, babe? I can wait in the car."

"Okay, yes, I think I want you to take me. I'm getting nervous already."

"Don't be, just be yourself and God will do the rest, right?"

"Yes... you couldn't have said it better. I'm ready!"

"We better head over there, just in case she leaves early or traffic is heavy." It felt like forever riding in that car. Thelma could literally hear her heart beating out of her chest. She didn't know if it was bad nerves or the anticipation of seeing her again. As Thelma looks outside of the window, she wonders exactly what she will say to her? The last time they had words, it didn't go to well. She was so angry with this woman when she found out she was her real mother. Sitting in sessions talking to her about her biological mother, revealing how it made her feel to know that she had left her. Then she lowers the boom! *Lord, please be with me through this, because I have no idea what's going to happen.*

Once they get close to her office, Thelma's heart is pounding even more. She looks to the side of the road before Michael turns into the parking lot, and it's where she had her accident. Thelma looks at this metal barrier ripped out of the ground from the impact of her car hitting it. She was told that she was hit by a four-wheeler truck and was knocked into oncoming traffic moving full speed and then lost control and was thrown into a tree. That's what they said caused her to lose consciousness which resulted in her being in a coma. Thelma has an overwhelming feeling of thankfulness. She was just glad to be alive. And then she was reminded that she had another chance at life when most people don't. She wanted to make things right.

"We're here, babe. I'll drop you off in front of the building and then I'll park the car and wait outside for you. Take your time and don't rush, I'll be right here waiting!"

"That was cute, Michael, but you're coming inside with me," Thelma says grabbing his hand.

"Oh, you're so spoiled. I'll be in as soon as I park. Go on in so you can see if she is here."

"She's here, there's her car. I'm heading in." Thelma walks into the front office, and is greeted by the receptionist that knows her from previous visits.

"Good morning, Thelma. It is so good to see you."

"It's great to see you as well, is Dr. M. in her office?"

"Yes, she is, but she is finishing up with another client. Did you have an appointment?"

"No, ma'am, I don't. Could you let her know I'm here and I'll wait."

"Sure, you seem like it's an emergency."

"It kind of is."

"Well, in that case, I'll be right back."

"Thank you!"

Michael walks in the office. "Hey, babe, have you seen her yet?"

"Um, no, her receptionist is letting her know that I'm here, so I'm just waiting. Come sit next to me." Thelma says, patting the empty seat next to her. "Why are you way over there?"

"Relax, girl, everything is going to be alright, you'll see."

The receptionist calls Thelma's name."Thelma, she will be ready for you in a moment, okay."

"Yes." Thelma sits there with Michael, feeling nervous. The clock says it's 12:25, and the little red hand on the clock is moving around slowly. *I wish I could get up and leave, but...it's too late now.*

"Hello, Thelma, will you join me in my office?"

"Yes, I'll be back, Michael. Please say a prayer." Thelma turns around to Michael and crosses her fingers.

"I got you, babe."

"Please have a seat. How are you feeling, Thelma? You look great!"

"Oh, I've been doing well and I feel pretty good. Every now and then I'll get a headache, but the doctor said that it's normal. Especially with a head injury! How have you've been, Dr. M.?"

"Well, Thelma, I have to be honest. I've been doing the best that I can under the circumstances, with your accident and what happened between us. It tore me apart, and I have never prayed so hard in my life, asking God to spare your life. I need you to know that I never stopped thinking about you, after giving you up. I wondered how you were, and wanted to know things like… what your favorite color was, your hobbies and did you love to sing like I did. Every year for your birthday, I used to send you a card with some money, up until you reached the age of five years old. Your father wrote me back and returned all of the letters I had sent to you, and he asked me never to contact you ever again! He felt you would be better off without me being in your life! So I felt that I've caused you enough pain, and since I never made any good choices for my own life, I didn't want to mess yours up!"

"I never knew you wrote me anything. I found out about you three years ago."

"You're kidding me? I knew they didn't want me around, but I knew for sure you knew about me."

"I don't know why my parents made that decision and I'm hurt that they did that. But right now I just have to respect their choice, and say they must have felt that it was the best decision at the time. However, I do thank you for your prayers, and I would like to apologize for my mother asking you to leave the hospital. I'm really sorry."

"No need to apologize, I understand her position. If I were in her shoes I probably would have done the same thing. Look, Thelma, I just want you to know that I love you and I'm sorry for every hurt, disappointment, and any confusion I have ever caused in your life. Please forgive me."

"Dr. M., I have already forgiven you, and I want to thank you for what you did for me."

"I'm not sure that I understand what you mean, what I've done for you?"

"Yes, you gave me the opportunity, despite what you were going through, to have a life that many kids don't get the opportunity to have. I'm grateful because my Dad and Mom provided for me the best atmosphere and upbringing they knew how. I was taught to love from my heart, and to put God first in everything I do! I have wonderful siblings, and I love my family. So, thank you. My mother told me the obstacles you were faced with and why you made the choices you did concerning me. I also want to say I appreciate the skills you have taught me from your professional counseling services. The tools you gave me really helped me to see life in another perspective! You taught me that if I can't see my own mistakes in life, then moving forward with anything is impossible. Also, that it's okay to let go of my past, but to never forget it, for my past is only a reminder of how far I've come!"

"Thelma, I don't know what to say."

"Just say that you forgive me for how I acted towards you. My personality isn't to lash out or say hurtful things to anyone, I was just so angry with everything."

Estelle Markinson smiles at Thelma and says, "I forgive you. You reacted as anyone else would have, being in your shoes. Wow. God is so good, he's answering everything I ask him for. Marie told me that you both talked, and I'm happy that you did."

"Yes, I'm glad we did as well. Marie is a very sweet person and she really loves you!" says Thelma.

"That's my girl. I hope you eventually get to know your other siblings, one day!"

"Yes, I would like that, too!" Thelma says, standing up from her seat.

"Is there anything else you would like to ask me before I go, Dr. M.?"

"Yes, if it's not too much to ask, can I please hug you, Thelma? It's all I ever wanted to do!"

Thelma did not expect to hear her ask that question, although she has forgiven her and has released most of her anger that she has towards her biological mother, it was a stretch for her to just fall into the loving arms of her long-lost mother. But at the same time, she's looking at the look on her face. It is a look of being hurt, regret and desperation. For some reason, Thelma felt sorry for her, and the hurt that she had endured. Thelma didn't want to add to her pain! "Yes, sure, Ms. M., you can give me a hug," says Thelma.

"In the future, can you call me Estelle?"

"I sure can, Estelle." Thelma walked over to her and put her arms out.

Estelle reached and grabbed her and held her tightly, whispering in her ear, "I love you, baby girl!"

And before Thelma knew it, the words "I love you, too!" came out of her mouth.

"You do?" Dr. M. asked.

"Yes, Estelle, I do."

Dr. M. began to cry, and thanked Thelma for giving her another chance. She told Thelma to let her know when she was ready for meals with the family and a deeper connection and Thelma agreed to keep her informed. Thelma walked away knowing she had done her part. She knew that it was only God that could have made this situation turn around, and she is grateful!

# Chapter 31

# Yes

A few weeks passed and things settled down. Michael is still in Thelma's corner and she has been thinking about him a lot. Since the accident, she has been reflecting over her life. Learning not to take things or people who are closest to her for granted. Life is short, you can be here one day and gone the next, if anyone knows this it's Thelma. She loves Michael and would never want to lose him. She doesn't know how she's made it this far without him in her life.

Thelma decides to make a special dinner for him, so that they can have some quality time. With so much going on, it seemed as if they had to check their schedules just to see each other. But even through all of her junk, Michael was still there. Thelma heads to Gloria's house to talk with her and Granny.

"Hey, Granny, has Gloria made it from work yet?"

"Yes, honey, she's here. You look better and better each time I see you."

"Oh, thank you, Granny. I'm just trying to keep up with you."

"Well, you can't do that, but maybe one day." Granny smiles.

"Oooh, Granny, no you didn't." Thelma starts laughing.

"So, what is the big secret you have to talk with me about, is everything okay?"

"Yes, Granny, I just need some wisdom from the queen of wisdom herself."
"I'll see what I can do."

"I'll be right back, Granny, let me go upstairs to get this girl."

Gloria comes downstairs.

"It's about time."

"Hush, chile, I was coming. What's going on with you and why you couldn't tell me over the phone?"

"Because what I have to say, couldn't be said on the phone. Can you just sit down next to Granny? I can't hold it any longer!"

"Oh, Lord, I'm scared. Thelma, what is it?"

"Well, Granny, Gloria... I think I'm going to ask Michael to marry me."

"WHAT?"

"Yes, you heard right, Gloria. Granny, did you hear what I said?"

"Yes, baby, I heard exactly what you said," Granny says looking stunned.

"Well, Granny?"

"What's wrong with him asking you, baby? That's what's wrong with you girls today, y'all can't wait for the men to make a move; you have to make it for them."

"Grandma, he did ask her first, and Thelma told him no!" Gloria replies.

"He did, and you said no?"

"Yes, Granny, and thanks a lot Gloria."

"What? I'm just speaking the truth, and you know what the Bible says."

"What does the Bible say, Gloria?"

"It says, that the truth will set you free, and make you free! Now that's the word," Gloria says, rocking side to side as if she was in church.

"Shut up, Gloria!" Thelma laughs. "Anyway, Granny, don't listen to her. I was scared when he asked me. I also had a lot going on in my life at that time."

"Girl...it wasn't that long ago." Gloria rolls her eyes. "You make it sound like he asked you last year."

"Look, all I'm saying is I feel like it's better timing now than it was then!"

"When did he ask you, honey?"

"It was a couple of weeks ago, Granny, but I just wasn't ready."

"I understand, honey. You do have more stress off of you, and time brings about a change!"

"Yes, it does, Granny!"

"Well, honey, let me ask you this, how do you know for sure that you love him? And be honest with me, because Granny can look in them eyes and see the truth!"

"How do I know I really love him?"

"Why are you tearing up, Thelma," Gloria asks.

"I'm tearing up because, this man is so amazing. And to answer your question, Granny. I know that I love him, because he's the first person that I think about when I wake up in the morning. And the last person that's on my mind, when I go to bed! He makes me feel like I can do anything and that he's my number one fan. And when he tells me he loves me, each and every time... my heart tells me, he's the one!"

Granny smiles at Thelma, and can tell Thelma means it. "Baby, the look in your eyes when you talk about that man; I can tell it's real love. Don't you let him get away, I think he's your angel sent to you straight from heaven!"

"Yes, ma'am I know, and your opinion means a lot to me. Gloria, what do you think?"

"Thelma, you're my best friend, more like a sister to me, and I've been telling you that he was, for the longest time haven't I?"

"Yes, you have."

"I am so happy for you, Thelma, and I know you two are meant for each other. I can tell the way he looks at you when you're together. Yes, you should ask him, only if I can be there!"

"No way."

"Well, you can't blame a girl for trying. All jokes aside, T, I couldn't be more happier for you, you go girl. You deserve to be happy!"

"Aww, thanks, y'all, group hug?" Thelma holds her arms out.

"You're so corny, Thelma."

"Oh, here's the ring." Thelma pulls out the ring, it's a wide, white gold ring with channel diamonds going down the middle of it.

"What, you got him a ring? When did you do this?"

"On last Thursday."

"You have been holding out on a sista, I see how you are!"

"Oh, stop it, I knew I was going to have this talk with you and Granny, and you know you're my BFF."

"Yea, you're right, so when are you popping the question? Man, that sounds weird saying this."

"I was thinking tonight. I'm cooking him a romantic dinner just us two and then asking him to marry me!"

"We are excited for you, aren't we, Gloria?" Granny says, hitting Gloria in the arm.

"Yes, we are, and you be sure to call or text me on what he said. Deal?"

"Girl, you know I'm going to act like I have to go use the restroom and then call you."

"No, you can call Gloria tomorrow!" Granny teases.

"Granny, you're right, Gloria can wait until tomorrow." Thelma teases Gloria.

"Lord, you're just torturing me," replies Gloria.

"I know I am, but you're my girl, I won't leave you in the dark. You'll know! Well, I better get going, I have an important night. Thanks, Granny, I love you!"

"Oh, sweetheart, I love you, too, and you know I'm already praying for you!"

"Yes, Granny, pray, pray!"

"And, Gloria, I will be in touch."

"Alright then, girl, make sure you call me as soon as you get time. You know I'm nosey, the suspense alone is going to kill me!"

Thelma walks away laughing. "Yea, I know, I will!"

Later that evening, Thelma cooks a romantic dinner for Michael and asks him to come over around 6:30. "Oh my Lord, it's almost 6:30! Lord, keep me near your cross," Thelma says just as she hears a knock on the door. "He's here!" Thelma takes a quick look around to make sure everything is perfect before heading to answer the door. "I'm coming. Hi, babe." Thelma says opening the door.

"Hello, how are you?"

"I'm well." Michael kisses Thelma on the cheek.

"These are for you."

"Michael, you always buy me the most beautiful flowers. Thank you!"

"Oh, flowers are a sign of endearment, and you mean a lot to me."

"You mean a lot to me, too."

"Man, it smells great in here, did Granny cook?"

"No, Granny didn't cook, I did." Thelma playfully hits Michael on the arm.

"Ouch, I was just kidding."

"As long as I slaved over this stove, nobody's taking this credit, not even Granny. But please don't tell her I said that." Thelma laughs.

"I'm telling." They both laugh.

"So what's the occasion?"

"Why does it have to be an occasion for me to cook dinner for my man!"

"Oh, your man, huh?" Michael says suspiciously, then breaks into a huge grin.

"Yes, that's what I said," says Thelma, reaching to take Michael's coat.

"I like the sound of that. This is fun, but you're different tonight. Calling me your man, you never say that. What's up?"

"Man, you're messing up everything, Michael!"

"I'm sorry, baby, but I can feel something has changed. What's going on?"

"Well, I wanted us to eat first, but since you keep prying. Michael..." Thelma takes both of his hands, and leads him over to the couch. She sits him down, and looks him in his eyes. "You know we have been through a lot together, and I want you to know that I don't ever want to lose you"

"And I've told you before, only death could take me away from you," Michael says, gazing into Thelma's eyes.

"I know you have, I love you with all of my heart, mind and soul. There isn't another man on this earth that could ever be half of the man you are to me."

"You're scaring me, Thelma. What is it?"

"Michael, will you marry me?" Michael sits there looking at Thelma, in total disbelief of what he has heard.

"Excuse me, what did you just ask me?"

"I said, Michael, will you marry me?"

Michael has tears rolling down his face, and places his hand over his heart, "Thelma, you mean you want me to be your husband? I can't believe what I'm hearing! YES, babe! I'll marry you. Come here!"

Michael grabs Thelma and holds here as tight as he can. "LORD, I THANK YOU! Thelma, you have made me the happiest man on earth. Wait a minute, are you sure that you want this?"

"Michael, yes, I'm sure! Give me your hand, I have a ring for you!"

"I can't believe this. I love it! Wait one moment." Michael wipes his eyes with a tissue, reaches down in his shirt, and pulls up a chain, and on the chain was the engagement ring he had bought for Thelma, earlier.

"What, you wore this around your neck, Michael."

"Yes, I did. I prayed that the right time would present itself, and I could ask you again. I wanted to always be prepared, but I never dreamed you would ask me. Can I put this ring on your pretty little finger, and ask you a question?"

"Yes!" Thelma says excitedly, her face wet with tears.

Michael kneels on one knee. "Thelma McKinney, will you marry me, will you be my wife until God calls one of us home?"

"Yes, Michael, I wouldn't have it any other way."

"Can we kiss on it?" says Michael, he leans in and pulls Thelma into his arms. Giving her a kiss that only a man that loves a woman could do.

"Michael, where engaged!" Thelma's eyes danced with happiness.

"Yes, baby, we are. Thelma, you have made me the happiest man alive, and I promise you from this day forward, the best is yet to come for you, baby. It was all worth the wait!"

"Hmm, I think I'll take you up on that."

"You can take it to the bank and cash it, baby, I can't believe it!"

"Michael, with all of this taking place I'm not trying to mess up the mood, but…just so you understand, I'm going to stay celibate until we get married. Nothing has changed. You mean so much to me, and I think our marriage deserves the very best, and waiting and doing it God's way is the best way. Why are you looking at me like that?"

"I'm looking at you for even saying that to me. Have I asked anymore from you the entire time we have been together? I'm not upset, but you're my queen as well. I've always respected you in that manner. Has it been hard for me not to try anything with you? Yes, it has, but you're well worth the wait! I'm in this marriage until we're so old if someone was to touch you or I, our limbs would just break off and turn into dust on their own." Michael and Thelma both laugh. "You get my point?"

"Yes, Michael, I do. You're so crazy. Okay, limbs falling off." Thelma is still laughing. "Dinner is served, Michael, my fiancé."

"Thank you, Thelma, my soon to be wife."

"Aww, I love the sound of that." Thelma sits down at the table across from Michael, staring at the clock.

"Uh, babe, go ahead and call your girl Gloria. You know she's pacing the floor with her nosey self!"

"Seriously, you won't mind if I do?" Thelma dials Gloria while she's talking to Michael.

"You're already calling, it don't matter what I say." Michael smiles and shakes his head.

"Hello, Gloria." Thelma screams into the phone, "GIRL, HE SAID YES!"

Before Gloria's departure on Tuesday, she and Thelma planned to go to Granny's church Sunday morning and the very thought of it makes Thelma nervous. She hadn't been to church in a very long time, trying to stay away from it since her Daddy's passing. She had convinced herself that no church would be like theirs. But the truth is, she has been running from God. She remembers her dad's words. Ain't no use in running, when God is watching you the entire time...it's not like he can't see you. Thelma would laugh when he'd say that, but it was a true statement, so she prepared to go.

*One thing I do know, when we go? I don't care where they all sit, I'm sitting waaay in the back of the church. I don't need nobody coming up to me rubbing my back if a tear falls, or the preacher looking at me while he preaches. I just want to go and get this over with!*

Michael picks Thelma up at her apartment, before heading to church. "Baby, you look nice all dressed up in your Sunday morning clothes." "Be quiet, Michael, you sound so country."

"Aww, is my baby still nervous about going to church?"

"I'm fine," Thelma states, but with a little attitude.

"Okie dokie, if you say so. You going up for prayer if they call a prayer line?" Michael says laughing.

"Okay, Michael, you got jokes. What if the Bishop calls you out? You won't be laughing then."

"You're right, I won't be laughing, but if I do, he won't see me."

"Why is that?"

"Because I'm going to be in the very back where you are!" says Michael.

"Granny, said to meet them there around 11:00," Thelma says. "Michael do you have the address?"

"Yep."

"Let's go!"

Thelma and Michael arrive at church and Gloria is outside waiting for them.

"Hey missionary," Gloria says to Thelma.

"Don't even start, Gloria."

"What? I'm just saying, you're all dressed up all you need on is a COGIC hat."

Thelma laughs at Gloria. "Don't you fool yourself, my Momma did teach me how to dress. Where's Granny?"

"Granny is inside already. She says to bring you so you can sit next to her."

"Umm, where is that?"

"Oh, on the front row. You know Granny serves on the Mother's Board," Gloria says cracking up.

"The devil is a liar, I'm not sitting on no one's front row!" Thelma says nervously.

"Girl, relax, we can sit further towards the back, let's just go in first. We're already late, and that music sounds good!"

"Yes, let's go and get a seat, IN THE BACK!" As they entered the church, Thelma observes that it is triple the size of her dad's church. There were so many people there. But she could feel the same energy that you feel when the spirit of the Lord is moving.

"Gloria, let's sit over here. It's not too far in the back or too close to the front."

"OK," Gloria replies.

As the girls are seated, they realize – due to their lateness – that they arrived right at offering time. This takes Thelma way back. The choir sings as church members walk around to place their offering in the offering plate. There are church women there, with their grand hats, and they are so beautiful. The Elders of the church were dressed up in their nice suits, and the choir is huge. There had to be at least a one hundred voice choir, and they sound like angels!

Thelma can smell the smell of chicken frying downstairs, because most churches sell dinners after service to raise money for a program or mission. Tears begin to form in Thelma's eyes because this was a familiar atmosphere for her. She looks at the Bishop and he's sitting in his chair waiting for his time to bring forth the word of God. Just like her daddy would!

"Baby, are you all right? You look upset," Michaels says, putting his arm around Thelma.

"It's just a lot of memories for me." Michael holds her hand, and starts to rub it for moral support, and then a woman walks up to the mic. The choir stands up, and the music begins to play a tune so familiar to Thelma. They began to sing, "I feel like going on I feel like going on though trials they may come on every hand, oh I feel like feel like going on..." Thelma began to cry. She was unable to stop the flow of tears.

The Pastor walks up to the microphone and says, "Saints, God is leading me in another direction. The spirit of the Lord is in this place and it's telling me there is someone here that has been feeling like giving up, but you have literally heard the voice of the Lord. He told you to forgive, let everything go, and give it to him. You know the way, from a young child, God has called you from your mother's womb. If you are here, please come forth so I can pray over you. Don't ignore the voice of the Lord. He is here to meet you!"

Thelma began to weep. She knew he was talking to her.

"Thelma, do you want me to go up for prayer with you?" Thelma heard Gloria's voice, but could not respond.

The Bishop continued, "My child, you can no longer run or hide from God. He has been watching you the entire time, and he loves you. You should be tired of running, it's not like God can't see you!" *Those were my Daddy's words exactly,* Thelma thought.

Right then and there, Thelma didn't care if Gloria or Michael came with her, she found her way up to that altar, with her hands lifted, crying "Yes Lord, Yes Lord!" She could hear the Bishop's voice hovering over her, with his hand on her forehead. "Daughter, the hand of God is upon you and he's been waiting on you. You already know this. You have been chosen from your mother's womb to bring healing to God's people through a ministry of song. Today is your day!"

It was almost too much for Thelma to bear, and then, the woman leading the choir began to sing the song she used to sing for her Daddy before he began to preach, *"I surrender all, I surrender all, all to thee, my blessed Savior, I surrender all…"* Thelma thought she was changed before, but the feeling that came over her was of complete surrender. And then something happened, she began to speak in tongues. She tried to suppress it, but it just came rolling out of her mouth like water. No more straddling the fence, she heard her heart tell God 'YES!', her soul leapt for joy. Granny was right there for her, she saw Michael and he was on the altar crying, and she didn't know where Gloria ended up. All she knew is that she was back home again. Her soul had found its way back to God. It didn't matter what she had been through, God met her there that Sunday, and totally changed her life. And that praise that she was searching for, she didn't have to find it, it found her!

Two month later, Thelma sat in her home writing in her diary.

*Dear Diary,*

*Two months have passed and things seem to have turned around for me. I am really enjoying my engagement life with Michael. We set a date for our nuptials for July 18th, one year from now. Michael is excited about his new job. He works with at-risk youth full-time at the Justice Center; he loves his job. Finding Michael is a prime example to me that no matter how hard or bad things get if you wait on God, he will provide for you and give you the desires of your heart!*

*Gloria is all settled at her job, too. She, of course, will be my maid of honor in our wedding.*

*I was able to go home and visit my mom and help her out at Dad's church for a few weeks. I was also able to attend TiTi's graduation. I'm so proud of my little sister. And you guessed it, Word is very involved in the church and is doing really well in school! Mick has reenlisted in the military and still calls home to make sure everyone is okay.*

*Momma decided to temporarily allow Deacon Ramsey's brother, Pastor Dwight Ramsey, to be the acting pastor for the church. Like Daddy would say "The Lord's work must go on." Although I'm convinced that there still isn't a better pastor or man than my father, the honorable Pastor Greg McKinney, I have to admit that my new church comes real close.*

*As for my biological mother, Estelle, we are taking it slow. I do, however, spend a lot of time with my little brother Chris. We call him "Man". He has Down syndrome, but is one of the coolest kids I know. I just love him. Of course, Marie and I are doing well.*

*I have now joined the Church of Praise COGIC. Granny was thrilled, and I love it there. It's funny, now that I've joined and the Bishop has heard me sing. I sing a lot of solos for him. Go figure right? Although I've endured enough pain for a lifetime, I've CRIED and PRAYED, God has turned things around, and now I PRAISE him for all he has done.*

*I wouldn't trade the people that God has allowed to grace my life. I love me, and the woman God has called me to be. I look in the mirror and I like who I see. So, I guess if I had a message for anyone, it would be, "Don't give up, it may get hard, and yes, you will cry endless tears, but…if you will trust GOD, and keep the faith, it will all work out for you in, THE END!*

# About the Author

Kimberly Robinson Green is a woman with a vision dedicated to making a difference; her love for people is very inspiring! She is the Owner and Director of the Christina's Preschool Academy and the founder of Women with A Vision (WWAV), an organization for women that was created to inspire and motivate others! Kimberly is married to her husband of 25 years, David Green Sr., and she is the mother of three sons, all of whom have inspired her to move forward in her visions and dreams. Kimberly's mentor and inspiration is her mother, Mrs. Christine Robinson, an entrepreneur, businesswoman and visionary of many projects. Grateful to have a mother with so many attributes and qualities, Kimberly has patterned herself after her. She found her love for writing approximately four years ago and has written her debut novel, *Her Cry ~ Her Prayer ~ Her Praise*, and an inspirational book entitled *Encouraged to Finish*, which was released in late 2015.

Connect with Kimberly:

KimberlyRobinsonGreen@gmail.com
www.kimberlyrobinsongreen.com
facebook.com/KimberlyRobinsonGreen
twitter.com/kimberlyprtlnd